THE

FIRE

TOWER

A novel by
MICHAEL LINDLEY
Sage River Press

THE FIRE TOWER

Book #6 in the Amazon #1 bestselling *"Hanna Walsh and Alex Frank Low Country Suspense Thriller"* series.

Hanna and Alex begin to settle into their new life together on Pawley's Island, but a mysterious death and the return of a ruthless rival sends them off on a perilous journey to bring him to justice again and find out how and why Ally Combes died at *THE FIRE TOWER*.

Hanna and Alex risked their lives to put mob boss, Xander Lacroix, behind bars. When they learn of his early release from prison, and one of his henchmen starts a relentless campaign of harassment and revenge, they both find themselves again on the precipice of chaos and danger.

The alarming death of a local woman in Alex's hometown of Dugganville leads to a surprising chain of events that quickly escalates into a deadly struggle with the dark forces of crime and corruption in the Low Country of South Carolina.

THE FIRE TOWER is the latest release in the fan-favorite and Amazon Charts #1 bestselling *"Hanna and Alex"* mystery series.

A novel by

MICHAEL LINDLEY

Sage River Press

The *"Troubled Waters"* Suspense Thrillers by

MICHAEL LINDLEY

The *"Charlevoix Summer"* Series

THE EMMALEE AFFAIRS
THE SUMMER TOWN

The *"Coulter Family Saga"* Series

BEND TO THE TEMPEST

The *"Hanna Walsh and Alex Frank Low Country Mystery and Suspense"* Series

LIES WE NEVER SEE
A FOLLOWING SEA
DEATH ON THE NEW MOON
THE SISTER TAKEN
THE HARBOR STORMS
THE FIRE TOWER

DEDICATION

A quick note of thanks to the many readers, publishing partners, book retailers and fellow authors who have been so supportive in the pursuit of these stories.

"The boundaries which divide Life from Death are at best shadowy and vague. Who shall say where the one ends, and where the other begins?"

– Edgar Allan Poe

Table of Contents

Chapter One 1

Chapter Two 6

Chapter Three 16

Chapter Four 21

Chapter Five 26

Chapter Six 31

Chapter Seven 35

Chapter Eight 39

Chapter Nine 43

Chapter Ten 48

Chapter Eleven 59

Chapter Twelve 67

Chapter Thirteen 71

Chapter Fourteen 75

Chapter Fifteen 80

Chapter Sixteen 84

Chapter Seventeen 92

Chapter Eighteen 98

Chapter Nineteen 102

Chapter Twenty 108

Chapter Twenty-one 112

Chapter Twenty-two 117

Chapter Twenty-three 122

Chapter Twenty-four 128

Chapter Twenty-five 132

Chapter Twenty-six 138

Chapter Twenty-seven 147

Chapter Twenty-eight 150

Chapter Twenty-nine 156

Chapter Thirty 161

Chapter Thirty-one 167

Chapter Thirty-two 172

Chapter Thirty-three 178

Chapter Thirty-four 182

Chapter Thirty-five 188

Chapter Thirty-six 195

Chapter Thirty-seven 201

Chapter Thirty-eight 205

Chapter Thirty-nine 210

Chapter Forty 212

Chapter Forty-one 216

Chapter Forty-two 220

Chapter Forty-three 223

Chapter Forty-four 230

Chapter Forty-five 241

Chapter Forty-six 246

Chapter Forty-seven 255

Chapter Forty-eight 262

Chapter Forty-nine 267

A Note From Michael Lindley 271

Other Novels by Author Michael Lindley 272

About the Author 281

CHAPTER ONE

The breeze through the open windows to the ocean freshened and pushed the light cotton drapes about in a slow rhythm. The wind carried the scents of the salt air and late beach fires, and a chill from one of October's first cool nights. A flock of gulls screeched as they flew over the marshes behind Pawleys Island.

Hanna Walsh felt a wisp of hair blow across her face, and she opened her eyes to the coming dawn. The bedroom in the old beach house was cast in muted shadows in the early morning light, a soft glow of orange coming through the windows from the sun coming up just below low clouds across the far horizon to the east.

Her skin was tanned from the long season of sun, the wrinkles at the corners of her hazel eyes more pronounced. Clusters of freckles patterned her bare shoulders. Her sandy brown hair, cut to shoulder length, laid in random swirls around her face.

She shivered and pulled the sheet and blanket up around her, burrowing down deep into the pillows. Beside her, she saw the face of her husband, Alex Frank, his eyes closed, his breathing slow and easy in heavy slumber. His short-cropped black hair was fringed with gray at the edges, and even in his brows more recently. She always got lost in the warm and kind expression of his face, even asleep, but she cringed seeing the crooked bend of his nose, so badly injured not long ago.

As the reality of the morning and a new day began forming in her mind, Hanna studied the face of her new husband and thoughts of the past weeks since their marriage began playing out in her head.

The wedding had been a small but grand gathering here at the beach house, attended by close family and friends. She thought about the kiss they shared as the ceremony came to an end that day. It was the one moment that came back to her most often. The kiss had come with a reassurance that she had found her place with a man she truly loved, who loved her deeply as well, and how fortunate they were to have found each other.

They had spent their wedding night here at the beach house after all the guests had finally left late that evening. Even her son, Jonathan, and his girlfriend had stayed at a nearby friend's house to give them the night alone. Their lovemaking was not new as they had been together for some time, but it was different somehow, she thought, as the morning washed all around her. They had become husband and wife, and had made a commitment to spend the rest of their lives together. It was almost like a fresh beginning to a whole new life for both of them, particularly after all the trauma and fear they had recently been through.

The thought of her son brought her back to the reality of another new day. Jonathan had left rehab for his pain med addiction two weeks earlier. He was back in Chapel Hill with Elizabeth, both returning to law school. She spoke to him every night and he seemed to be doing well, recharged and committed to overcoming his demons and the terrible dependency he suffered.

Alex stirred beside her and turned away, still deep in sleep. His bare back was tanned and speckled with small moles, his muscles tight beneath. They had traveled to Key West for their honeymoon and chartered a sailboat for the week, making their way up and down the Keys in a careless journey of exploration and fun, pressing all thoughts of how close both of them had come to painful deaths in the aftermath of the terror attack that had targeted their city of Charleston and several others across the country.

The thought of Alex and the near deadly injuries he had suffered at the hands of Bassam Al Zahrani's men made her shiver again in the cool morning air. Images of his battered face and body still haunted her. His recovery had been slow and painful. His left hand was still nearly useless following the devastating wound he had endured.

The scar across the side of her forehead was a constant reminder of how close she had also come to a fatal end. She touched it now, no longer painful, but a constant reminder of how fortunate she was to be alive and to be here with this man in this house, a glorious morning breaking outside.

She reached over and stroked his hair, letting her hand linger there as she thought of trying to fall back to sleep. She knew it was a Monday though, and they both had work days ahead. She turned and looked at the old alarm clock on her nightstand. It was just past 6 am.

She rubbed the sleep from her eyes and stretched her arms up behind her, trying to be careful not to wake Alex. A relentless sinking feeling came back to her as she stressed again over her decision to close her free legal clinic in Charleston. After the incident where her beloved friend and assistant, Molly, and one of her clients had been killed in a brutal attack, and the assassin's bullet had almost ended her own life, she knew she would never be able to return to the old house and the offices there. The place had been put up for sale and was now being converted back into a residence by the young couple who had purchased it.

After closing out or referring all the cases that were active at the clinic, Hanna had left Charleston behind and moved up to the beach house here at Pawleys Island. She had returned to work at the small law firm just off the island where she worked full time now.

As Alex lay beside her, she thought about his own career calamities. Already on suspension from the FBI for his reckless attempt to take down the gangster, Xander Lacroix, his employment had been terminated following his unauthorized actions in tracking down the terror cell that threatened the city. Though he had been instrumental in helping to thwart the attack, his behavior and insubordination were deemed unacceptable to the Bureau, and his dream job had been taken from him.

Alex had tried to hide his disappointment, but she knew he was deeply troubled about his short tenure with the Bureau. He had worked in law enforcement for so many years and built a strong record of accomplishment. It had been enough to help him secure his new position in Washington, but in the end, his relentless style had put him at odds with his bosses and his position was terminated.

During their long cruise in the Keys they had talked about both their careers. Hanna had made the decision to close the clinic and move here to the island. Alex had decided he wanted to stay in law enforcement. On their return, he met with his old friend, Sheriff Pepper Stokes, and asked for a job here at the County Sheriff's Department. Stokes had enthusiastically taken Alex on, and this would be his first day of work. The new job would also allow Alex to live here at the beach with her. He had not renewed the lease on his apartment in Charleston and moved into the beach house after their honeymoon.

Hanna heard a soft moan from her new husband as he rolled on his back and covered his eyes from the early morning light.

"What time is it?" he said, softly, sleep still shrouding his voice.

"Time to go to work," she said, leaning over and kissing him on the cheek.

He turned to face her, and she saw his wonderful smile. Their eyes met.

"Good morning, Mrs. Frank," he said, reaching for her and pulling her close.

She felt the soft comfort of their two bare bodies together and snuggled in closer in the cool of the morning.

"Good morning, Deputy Frank," she whispered in his ear.

She felt him pull back and their eyes met again.

"It is a workday, isn't it?" he said.

"You look great in your new uniform," she teased.

"Been a long time since I was a street cop in Charleston and had to put a uniform on every day."

"I'm really happy for you," she said. "I'm glad Pepper had a position open for you."

"Not sure all his team are as excited as you are."

"Why is that?"

"Pepper had to fire one of his long-time deputies."

"What happened?"

"Not sure, exactly, but there was some corruption uncovered in the department, and this guy was one of the bad actors. Guess he has several friends still working who aren't really happy with Pepper's decision."

"So, a little excitement on your first day of work," she said, pulling him close again and kissing him on the ear."

She felt him lift up and look at the alarm clock.

"Don't have to be in til eight," he said.

"Yes, I know," she replied.

She felt him burrow his face into the crook of her neck. "I love you," he whispered.

"I love you, too."

CHAPTER TWO

Alex parked behind the Charleston County Sheriff's Department offices outside Dugganville and reached for his hat and bag. The new uniform felt stiff and uncomfortable. *Have to get used to this,* he thought as he placed the "Smokey Bear" hat on his head and got out of the car. Several department cruisers were parked nearby as the morning shift was just beginning.

The day was still cool even as the sun was climbing above the palms and live oak trees. He walked through the back door and down a narrow hall. He came up to an open door and leaned in.

"Morning, Sheriff," he said as he saw Pepper Stokes on the phone behind his desk. Alex held his hand up in apology as Stokes finished the call and put the receiver back.

"Morning, Deputy," Stokes said, a look of concern masking his usual friendly face.

"What's up?" Alex asked.

"Got a DOA down in Dugganville," Stokes replied. "One of our guys was just checking back with me. Young woman, don't have the name yet."

Alex's senses flared as he considered the death of someone in his old hometown, still the home of his father, Skipper Frank, the old shrimper and his second wife, Ella. "What happened?"

"Still trying to sort it out," Stokes said. "Why don't you put your stuff down and we'll run down there. Got a desk for you around the corner."

"Okay, give me a minute."

Alex walked into the large room where there were over a dozen desks, a few occupied this morning by other uniformed deputies. One nodded and gestured to an empty desk beside his as he talked on the phone. Another man, facing Alex's new desk, made eye contact and glared back with an angry scowl.

Alex had expected this after Pepper warned him of bad blood in the department after the recent firing of a popular deputy. He placed his bag on the desk that held a few personal items he thought would be good additions to his workspace; a framed picture of him and Hanna in Key West after their wedding, another of Hanna and her son on the beach out at Pawleys Island, a third taken at the wedding of him and Hanna standing with his father and stepmother. There were also a few personal files that he placed in a drawer.

He arranged the pictures on a low cabinet behind him and turned to look out across the deputy's room. The angry man was still glaring back at him. Alex stood and walked over, holding out his hand. "Alex Frank," he said, offering to shake.

The deputy kept his hands on the desk in front of him and said, "We don't give a damn about all your fancy background, FBI and all."

Alex started to protest, but the deputy with a name badge that read *Gallagher*, pressed on. "You earn your stripes here, just like the rest of us, understand?"

"Loud and clear... *Gallagher*," he replied, looking down at the name badge, trying to control his anger at the man's harsh disposition. "Nice to meet you, too."

Alex turned and walked back to his desk. The other deputy who had pointed out his desk smiled back, shaking his head at his colleague's bad behavior.

Sheriff Stokes came around the corner and said, "Alex, let's go."

Alex rode in the seat beside his new boss as they pulled into his old hometown of Dugganville, South Carolina. As usual, thoughts and memories rushed back as so much of his early life had been spent here.

Heavy brush and forest on the drive in from Highway 17 was now broken by the occasional old commercial building, an auto garage, a well drilling company, then closer to town, more small houses tucked back in the trees. They turned at the main road into the village and Alex saw the familiar old church he and his brother used to attend with their mother before she died, then the short two blocks of businesses, including *Andrew's Diner* where he often met his father for a quick meal when he was near Dugganville.

They drove through the little town, just coming alive for another day, a few trucks and cars parked and pulling up to the storefronts and small office buildings. Through town, they passed the park and the white gazebo up on the slight incline from the river. His father's house was another couple blocks up ahead. His shrimp boat, the *Maggie Mae*, was tied up at the dock across the street.

Alex looked to the side as Stokes turned the cruiser into a narrow drive to the park and pulled into a shaded spot. He saw another department cruiser parked nearby and two deputies gathered beside an ambulance pulled up across the lot at the base of a tall fire observation tower. It had been a landmark in the town for years but abandoned from active use for as long as Alex could remember. The tower rose high above the tree line, twelve flights of stairs leading up to a small, glassed-in observation room with a narrow wooden deck and iron rail all around.

Alex got out with Stokes and started over to where the other deputies were standing. The sounds of crows cackling in the trees above them broke the calm of the morning. Mist rolled in from the river, low across the park.

The two deputies stood aside as Alex followed Stokes up to them. Two paramedics knelt beside the body of a woman lying on her stomach, her arms and legs askew at odd angles, her face staring lifelessly to the side. She was a younger woman, likely near thirty. Alex didn't recognize her, and he was relieved that it wasn't someone he knew in this small town, which is what he was expecting. She was dressed in a denim skirt, faded and cut ragged along the bottom, and a bright red sleeveless t-shirt. One foot had a brown leather sandal, the other bare with the matching sandal lying close by. Her hair was bleached an unnatural shade of blonde, pulled up in a bun on top of her head, streaks of her real brown hair showing all around.

"What have we got here?" Alex heard Stokes ask.

"Local girl," one of the deputies answered, staring now at Alex with the same angry expression he had experienced back at the department. "Just found her purse over there," the man said, offering it up to Stokes along with the woman's driver's license. "Her name is Ally Combes."

Stokes said, "What do we think happened?"

The deputy, whose name tag read Oliver, replied, "Homeless guy over there," Oliver gestured to a shabby old man sitting on a bench by the parking lot, "found her lying here this morning when he woke up on the bench there. He walked down to the diner and had them call it in. Claims not to know the woman or anything about what happened. He was sleeping off a drunk from last night. Empty bottle of cheap wine over there seems to support his story."

The dead woman was lying just a few feet out from the base of the tower, just beyond an old wire fence. Alex looked up at the looming structure, rusting now in disuse. White clouds broke the deep blue of the morning sky and drifted above through the break in the trees.

He and a few friends used to sneak up to the top of the tower to drink beer when they were in high school. He also remembered a few make-out sessions with his ex-wife, Adrienne, up there. The structure was fenced off with warning signs to Keep Out, but it was easy enough to climb the low fence to get in.

"Think she was a jumper?" Stokes asked.

Alex looked back down at the woman's body and thought how sad that a life could end this way.

"Not sure, boss," the other deputy said. "Still checking things out."

"You been up top yet?" Alex asked, and both deputies stared back like he had no right to even open his mouth. They didn't reply.

Stokes repeated the question.

"Not yet, boss," Oliver said. "Been questioning the old man over there and starting to set up a perimeter for the crime scene.

Alex watched Stokes kneel beside one of the paramedics taking a closer look at the body. "No sign of other trauma, besides the fall?" he asked.

One of the paramedics said, "Nothing yet, Sheriff."

Alex looked at the woman's lifeless arms, tanned and fit. Her right hand was palm down and the fingers were dug into the dirt as if she was gripping the ground, perhaps a final reflexive action before she died. The other hand was clenched in a fist. He leaned closer to look.

"Mind if I take a look at this hand?" he asked.

Stokes replied, "Not until we get the crime tech team out here and get some photos."

"It looks like she's holding something," Alex said.

"Oliver, make sure they check that out," Stokes ordered.

"Will do, Sheriff."

As Alex stood up, Stokes said, "Come on."

He followed the old sheriff over to the gate to the fence. A park attendant had been by earlier to unlock the gate. He followed Stokes through and then up the crisscrossing flights of stairs. Stokes had to stop twice to catch his breath. Alex didn't mind the breaks either.

When they reached the top, they came out onto a narrow walkway that extended all the way around the small observation room. The tower had been used for decades by the Forest Service to look for fires out across the vast expanse of woods around Dugganville. The iron railing affixed to the platform was low, and Alex held on to steady himself, not particularly fond of heights.

Somehow, he had managed when it came to beer and girls, he thought, then pushed the memories aside. He followed Stokes all around the deck. The vast panorama of wooded flatlands to the west and marshes leading out to the ocean to the east with the wide river snaking through spread out before them. It was a breathtaking view, and Alex thought back to earlier times in his life when he had marveled at the sights.

They completed the circle and Alex looked down, holding tight to the rail, goosebumps prickling his skin. He saw the paramedics and deputies still huddled around the dead woman.

"Whaddya think?" he heard Stokes ask and looked over at the old sheriff.

"Long fall," was his first reaction, pushing back from the rail and looking through a small door into the observation room. There was an old wood desk and chair against one wall. The chair was knocked over. There were a few empty beer bottles on the floor. "Need to process these bottles," he continued, "but looks like they've been here a while."

Alex went over and looked more closely at the desk. The top was faded and scratched. *Oak, probably,* he thought. There were several stains. Most looked old and faded. One seemed more recent, even damp. He pointed it out to Stokes."

"I'll have the team get a sample," the sheriff said.

Alex took a pen from his pocket and slid it through the handle on the top drawer to pull it open, not wanting to leave any fingerprints. He and Stokes peered in. There was some old paperwork, a ledger perhaps of observation notes. He used the pen to push the papers aside. There was an open matchbook, some paperclips and a few pennies. He pushed the drawer closed with his fist and used the pen again to open the single lower drawer on the right. It was empty. He pushed it closed.

"You don't know the woman?" Stokes asked.

Alex shook his head. "I *do* know the Combes. Wonder if she's married to one of my old friends."

"Who's that?"

"Boyne Combes. Family owns the hardware here in town."

Stokes said, "Right, I know the parents."

Alex watched Stokes looking out over the long view to the ocean, then down to the dead woman far below.

Stokes turned and said, "Why don't you head over there. You know them."

"Sure," Alex responded, then followed his new boss a bit unsteadily over to the steps back down.

Alex pushed through the doors of the hardware store and was immediately greeted by a familiar face. His friend's mother, Irene Combes, was behind the checkout counter helping a customer. She looked up in surprise at the sight of Alex in his new deputy's uniform.

"Why, Alex Frank!" the old woman said. "Look at you."

"Hello, Mrs. Combes."

"You go to work for Pepper?" she asked.

"First day."

"Well, welcome back! Good to have you around again."

"Thanks, ma'am," Alex said, tipping his hat, the feel of it still unnatural and uncomfortable. "Is Boyne around?"

The woman's face grew concerned as she finished with her customer, who walked out the door. Alex walked over to the counter.

"He in some kinda trouble?" she asked.

"No, just need a word."

"Saw him headed out to exchange a propane tank. You can walk through the back there," she said, pointing to the back of the store. "Seems your old man and Ella are getting along okay," she continued.

Alex smiled back. "Who'd have thought?"

"Damn strangest pair. Never thought I'd see those two together."

"A match made in heaven," Alex said sarcastically.

"Heard you got married again," she said.

"Sure did! Great gal from Charleston. We live at her place up here on Pawleys Island now. Where'd you hear?"

"Your ex is in here all the time. Seems to have all the news of the world."

Alex cringed at the thought of his ex-wife. He'd heard from his father she'd stayed on in Dugganville with her son after the latest breakup with her second husband down in Ft. Lauderdale.

"I better go find Boyne," Alex said and stepped away. "Nice to see you, Mrs. Combes."

"You, too, son," he heard her say as he walked away, a nervous feeling in his gut about the news he was about to deliver to the woman's son. *Maybe the girl's unrelated*, he thought as he walked back through the store.

He found Combes in the back alley finishing up with a tank refill for one of his customers standing there. Alex moved closer as the customer walked away with the tank.

"Hey, Boyne." He watched as the man turned and a smile crossed his face.

"Damn, Alex Frank. What the hell you doin' in that get-up?"

Alex walked up and shook his old friend's hand. They had been good friends in high school and played football together. "How you been, man?"

A strange look crossed his friend's face. "Just okay, I guess."

"Why's that?

The man hesitated, then said, "It's my wife. We've been having some issues. She didn't come home last night."

Alex felt his heart sink into his gut. "When's the last time you saw her?"

"She went out after dinner..." he paused. "We've been havin' this thing."

"What thing?"

"Rather not get into it," Combes said, a look of embarrassment across his face.

Alex moved closer and took off his hat, then took a deep breath. "Sorry, Boyne. Is her name Ally?"

The man nodded back. "What's wrong, what happened?"

"I'm sorry, man," Alex began. "We just found her over at the park... at the base of the old fire tower."

"What the hell!"

"I'm sorry... she's dead, Boyne." He watched his friend's legs buckle and he reached over to steady him. "Looks like she might have jumped from the tower."

"What!"

Alex watched the shocked face of the man. "I'm really sorry."

"There's no way!" Combes said, tears welling up in his eyes.

"Someplace we can go talk?" Alex asked.

When Alex returned to the park, Pepper Stokes was getting ready to leave. A crime scene unit was processing the body and the area around the tower.

"You find the husband?" the old sheriff asked.

Alex nodded. "An old friend. He's really devastated."

"He seemed surprised?"

"Totally," Alex replied. "Said they got into a bit of an argument over dinner. She went out and never came back."

"He didn't go looking for her?"

"Thought she was staying over with a friend. Guess she's done that a few times. I told him you'd want to see him down at the office later today."

"Right," Stokes said. "Really looks like a jumper here, Alex. No sign of any struggle or anything else at this point."

"What about the hand?" Alex asked, referring to the woman's clenched fist he had seen earlier.

"It was a condom."

"Really? Alex thought for a moment, then replied, "Why in hell would she have that up there, particularly if this is a suicide?"

"I'm having Oliver head over to chat with the husband again. We'll see what else he knows."

Alex looked over his shoulder through the gathering of crime scene technicians at what he could see of the now deceased Ally Combes. He shook his head, a deep sadness coming over him at such a tragic end of life.

CHAPTER THREE

Brenda Dellahousaye walked along the ocean shore, her white linen pants rolled up to her shins, her bare feet splashing in the cool water as she made her way south away from her house. The big home loomed high above the dunes looking east across the Atlantic Ocean. A few lights still sparkled inside. A long row of cushioned beach chairs with blue umbrellas covering them stretched along the beach in front of the house.

She had a phone to her ear and a mug of coffee in her other hand. She was a striking woman in her early 50's, the widow and ex-wife of now deceased Remy Dellahousaye with whom she had shared the house until their divorce some years ago when he left her for a younger woman. Both were dead now at the hands of her rival, Xander Lacroix.

In a way, Brenda had always thought Lacroix had done her a favor. But, when he also moved quickly to take over the vast Dellahousaye crime syndicate, it was a personal affront and, more importantly, a financial crisis for her own future and the well-being of her two daughters, Ida and Ophelia.

"He's really getting out?" she said into the phone, then listened for a moment to the response from a man who had once been one of Remy's senior people, now working with her to regain the family's interests.

"How is that possible?" she shouted. "He had nearly a life sentence." She listened as the man explained that Xander Lacroix's vast army of attorneys had finally found a sympathetic, or otherwise well-compensated, judge who reversed the conviction on appeal.

"He'll be back on the street tomorrow!" She was flabbergasted. Just when they were ready to pull the trigger on a complex series of moves to take out Lacroix and his men from all aspects of the Dellahousaye empire, Lacroix would be out and an even more grave threat to successfully execute the plan.

"I want to know when and where," she demanded. "Don't we have someone who can take care of this?" she asked, thinking the easiest solution would be to have Lacroix taken out. She nodded as the man suggested a solution. "Let me know as soon as possible."

She ended the call and took a long sip from the coffee that was quickly cooling in the morning chill. She stood and looked out over the ocean, resting calm in the early morning, the sun's glare a bright streak of yellow across the deep blue of the water. Two young boys on jet skis broke the stillness as they raced by to the north about a quarter-mile offshore.

She pressed several buttons on her phone and waited as the line rang.

"Hello, Brenda!" came the response, the smooth flowing southern accent of former Senator Jordan Hayes.

"Jordan, we have a problem."

"What, *no good morning Jordan, how is your day going?*"

"Cut the crap, Jordan! We have a serious problem."

"And what would that be?"

"Somebody paid off a judge. Lacroix is going to walk... tomorrow!"

"What!"

"You need to get on this!" she said, turning and walking briskly back toward the house. "I pay you too much..."

"Brenda, please!" Hayes protested.

"Just take care of this... or I will!" She pressed *End* on the call without waiting for his response.

As Brenda walked by the pool and back across the long verandah along the front of her house, she noticed people moving about in her kitchen through the wall of sliders. When she walked in, she saw one of her twin daughters, Ophelia, staring into the open door of a large refrigerator across the back wall of the massive kitchen. She was dressed in an oversized gray t-shirt that said *College of Charleston* on the front, one of the many schools she had managed to get kicked out of. Her medium-length brown hair was a tangled mess.

Her latest boyfriend, some musician she'd met while staying at her apartment in New York City, sat at one of the bar stools at the big center island, his head low over a cup of steaming coffee. His morning attire consisted of plaid boxer shorts and cowboy boots. His bare arms and torso left little room for skin to show through the maze of tattoos.

Brenda grimaced when she saw the *grimy freeloader*, as she described him to her friends. His name was Streak, and he was the lead singer for some grunge band that had something near a hit once many years ago. They occasionally played as opening acts for touring bands that actually could attract a crowd. Mostly, he lived off the generosity of friends or girlfriends he could latch onto.

She and her daughter had been through numerous *serious* discussions about the future of this relationship. Ophelia had always been the *wild child* of her two twin daughters. The other, Ida, had recently finished college at Clemson and was now in grad school up in Boston. *At least one of my girls has a head on her shoulders*, she thought, as she walked across the kitchen, trying to ignore the boyfriend.

O, as she was often called, showed up three days ago at the beach with Streak, saying both needed a little time away from the city to *decompress*. They had been nothing but drunk and stoned since they'd arrived. The past night, Brenda had to pound on the door to her daughter's room when their raucous love making became incessantly loud and annoying.

O heard her coming up and turned, closing the door to the refrigerator. Morning, Momma."

"Thought you'd be sleeping til noon after all that nonsense last night," Brenda said.

"Sorry, we just need to blow off a little steam."

"And a little weed," Streak snickered, burying his face in his coffee cup.

Brenda ignored the comment. "Don't you have to get back to your job in the city?"

"I quit," came the curt reply.

Brenda had been able to convince a friend in Manhattan to give Ophelia a job as a hostess at one of the nicer restaurants in the city. It was nowhere near enough money to pay for O's lavish apartment off Park Avenue and her many other vices, which were funded primarily by her mother. The family's trust was doling out money in small increments to both daughters, but Ophelia was constantly complaining about how strapped for cash she was.

"I went to a lot of trouble to get you that job," Brenda said, trying to remain calm as she refilled her coffee cup from a carafe on the counter."

"I wanted to shoot myself every night I had to go in there," O protested, "sucking up to all those rich bastards."

"I don't have time right now to get into this," Brenda said, moving away from the stench of cigarette and pot smoke on Streak.

"We're going back on tour," Streak said. "O's coming with us."

Brenda walked out of the kitchen shaking her head, not responding.

CHAPTER FOUR

Hanna refilled her coffee cup and walked through the door out onto the deck overlooking the beach and vast ocean beyond. The morning's chill was easing as the sun continued up above the bank of clouds to the east. The water reflected the deep blue of the early sky, nearly calm on a breathless new day.

She'd put on a robe after showering and had put off dressing for work until she'd had breakfast with Alex and seen him off. She looked down the beach in both directions, and a lone fisherman far to the south was the only person she could see. She let the aroma of the coffee calm her as she took another drink, then placed it on the wood rail.

Taking a deep breath, she closed her eyes and allowed herself the guilty pleasure of being *thankful*, if even just for a moment. Her new life with Alex Frank was a warm and loving safe harbor from all the pain and chaos that had riddled her past few years. Her son was on a path to recovery that gave her great relief after how close she had come to losing him. Her career had taken a turn she would not have chosen, but she tried to convince herself it was for the best.

When she opened her eyes, she was startled to see someone standing down at the shoreline. It appeared to be a young woman. She had long flowing red hair and wore a sleeveless white dress that hung loosely and dragged in the sand.

She was looking out over the water, her back to the beach house. *Where did she come from? A moment ago, no one was there!*

Hanna held her hand up to shield her eyes from the sun.

"Good morning!" she yelled out.

The woman, over a hundred yards away across the smooth sand of the Pawleys Island beach, didn't respond or even acknowledge she had heard Hanna's greeting.

Her curiosity piqued, Hanna grabbed her coffee cup and started down the stairs to the beach. The sand was cool on her bare feet. The beach fire from the past night still glowed red with hot coals in the stone fire pit surrounded by old white Adirondack chairs.

She walked through the line of low dunes patterned with sea oats and beach grass and then on down to the flat beach to the water. She was halfway to the woman when she called out again, "Good morning!"

This time the woman turned, her red hair blowing across her face. When she reached to pull her hair aside, Hanna stopped in surprise, a familiar face staring back at her, a broad smile across the woman's face. It was a face she marveled at every day in an old black and white family photo on the wall up in the beach house. It was a face she had seen in person on two occasions... *but did I really see her?*

It was the face of her distant great-grandmother, Amanda Paltierre Atwell. The Paltierres had owned this house and the nearby plantation, *Tanglewood*, back before and after the Civil War. Amanda had shared a common journey of betrayal and great danger as Hanna discovered when she found her grandmother's journal in the attic of the house behind her.

"Amanda?" Hanna said softly as she took a tentative step forward.

The woman's eyes shone bright, and she smiled again before whispering, "I'm so happy for you, dear."

Hanna heard the words but couldn't bring herself to believe this was really happening. Twice before, she'd had similar encounters with Amanda, but no one else had ever seen her.

The loud roar of a chainsaw starting up behind her caused her to flinch and turn quickly. She saw her neighbor to the north walking around his house to a tree that must have needed trimming.

When she looked back, her grandmother was gone, the beach empty in both directions far down to the lone fisherman.

Hanna sat down in the black leather chair behind her desk at the law firm. It was a nicely appointed space compared to her sparsely furnished office downtown in Charleston. They could barely pay the light bill at the free legal clinic, let alone afford decent furniture. There was a window behind her that looked out over the marshes toward the ocean. She settled down into the comfortable chair and reached for her laptop to check her schedule for the coming day.

On the short drive over from the beach house, she was still trying to sort out what she had actually seen down at the beach. The image and voice of Amanda were as clear as if Hanna had been standing there with her 150 years earlier.

The legend of ghosts on Pawleys Island was often talked and written about. Hanna had shared her encounters with Amanda with Alex and others, and all had reassured her that yes, the spirit of Amanda was with her, and she should feel blessed to have these moments.

She did feel blessed.

The harsh ring of the office phone interrupted the pleasant thought. It was the office receptionist letting her know her first appointment of the day had arrived. *Ah, back to reality!*

Two hours later, Hanna looked discreetly at her wristwatch. It was a little past eleven. She had been listening to opposing counsel for a bank in a bankruptcy case drone on about one financial impropriety after another her own client was now trying to deal with. The fact the man had arrived at the appointment in his cream-colored Bentley convertible did little to help his cause. Hanna was hoping at best to keep him out of jail. Keeping the Bentley was probably out of the question.

The other attorney concluded his tirade of accusations.

Hanna stood and said, "I think we have all we need from you at this point, counselor. Your intent seems very clear. My office is checking with the court on a date for the preliminary hearing. We will be back in touch. Thank you." She picked up her files and papers and nodded for her client to leave with her.

Back in her office, Hanna scolded the man for the ostentatious show of wealth with the car outside. He owned one of the larger beachfront estates on the island and had apparently made his money in turning failing companies around. Now he was faced with trying to turn his own future around. It occurred to Hanna the man didn't seem particularly worried about losing his house, his cars and who knows how much else. He probably has a stash of cash in Switzerland or the Bahamas, she thought as he shook her hand to leave.

She had just sat back down when her phone rang. It was the front desk and she picked up the receiver. The receptionist said, "I have a call for you from a Mrs. Holloway. Can you take it now?"

Hanna shook her head in disgust. She hadn't seen Grace Holloway, her ex-best friend, for months since she'd tried to convince her to join in some scheme to recover money both their deceased husbands had supposedly squirreled away in the Cayman Islands. She thought about her client who had just left. *What is it about these South Carolina men and secret bank accounts offshore!*

The last thing she wanted to do was talk to Grace, but she knew the woman would not give up. "Put her through."

She tried to block the memories of the woman's betrayal, her affair with her husband, her complicity in his death.

"Hanna?"

"I have one minute. What is it?"

"No, *how are you, dear?*"

"Grace!"

"Okay, okay. I have a bit of a problem."

"You are a problem!"

"Hanna, please!"

"No! How many times have I told you I want nothing to do with you or your schemes?"

"I've been arrested," Grace said, cutting in.

"For what this time?"

"I'm still down in the Caymans trying to get access to Phillip's accounts... my accounts!"

"Grace, I told you... "

"I know, Hanna, but please listen. I had an attorney down here with me making the appropriate contacts, filing all the paperwork. Suddenly, he skips out and the cops are at my door and lock me up."

"Good!"

"Hanna! They've arrested me on some trumped-up fraud charges."

"I hope the food is terrible! Goodbye!"

Hanna hung up the phone, her temper simmering, yet a trickle of satisfaction crept in as she savored the abrupt ending to the call.

CHAPTER FIVE

Alex got out of the car when Sheriff Pepper Stokes pulled to a stop in the parking lot behind the department offices. The late morning sun was hot, and steam rose off the pavement along the shadows as the morning's dew slipped away.

Stokes looked over the top of the car. "Got a pile of paperwork you need to get turned in."

"Right," Alex replied, coming around the side of the car.

"And I want you to write up your thoughts on this Dugganville jumper."

"You think that's what happened?"

"Until we find otherwise," Stokes said.

Alex turned back toward his own car. "Need to grab my lunch cooler. Be right in." As he got close, he saw that his driver's side front tire was flat. He knelt down to take a closer look and noticed a slash in the sidewall.

His anger flared as he thought about the gruff reception he'd received when he first came in this morning. He decided to put the spare tire on later and walked quickly back to the office door. As he got closer, he noticed the video camera covering the back parking lot set high off the roof's edge. Looking back, he realized the camera view probably wouldn't get his car in the picture.

Inside, he walked down the hall to the deputy's desks and straight over to Deputy Gallagher, who was on his phone. He felt his fists clenched as he got near, and the familiar pain in his healing left hand sent a jolt up his arm.

Gallagher looked up and his expression didn't change as he continued his phone conversation.

Alex looked down at his desk and saw a Phillips-head screwdriver and hammer lying beside a pile of papers. He reached down for the screwdriver as his new colleague ended his call.

"You doing a little home improvement?" Alex asked, slamming the tool back down on the desk.

Gallagher's expression remained calm as he looked back up at Alex. "Desk drawer here wouldn't work. Why the hell do you care?"

"Desk drawer, right!" Alex fumed.

"Get out of my face, rookie!" Gallagher said, standing in a defiant posture.

Alex reached out and put his right index finger on the man's chest. "If this is how you want to play this, fine! Watch your damn back!"

"That sounds like a threat, rookie," the man said, placing both hands on his hips.

"You're damn right it is!" Alex said. "We've got a job to do, and this nonsense needs to stop."

"No idea what you're talkin' about," Gallagher said, smiling now.

"Right." Alex turned and walked back to his own desk, his face flushed in anger. He sat down and looked over again at Gallagher, who had picked up his office phone and was looking away in conversation.

Hell of a first day! Alex thought.

Hanna's caller ID came up on his phone and Alex pressed the screen to take her call, not putting it on speaker mode. He'd been working through all the new hire forms that Stokes needed.

"Hello," he said, "how is my beautiful wife's day going?"

"I love Mondays," she replied, the sarcasm in her voice thinly disguised.

"Mine's been great. Dead body up in Dugganville... some serious attitude issues here at the office."

"Who died?" Hanna asked.

"Not sure if you've met my old friend, Boyne Combes. His family has owned the hardware in town for years. He's running it now since his old man passed away a few years back. His wife was found at the bottom of the old fire tower down at the park this morning."

"Oh, that's terrible. What happened?"

"Not sure yet. Could be suicide. Could be foul play. She definitely fell or got pushed from the tower."

"Did you know her?"

"No, I've been away a long time. Boyne's really shook up as you can imagine, but they did have a fight about something last night. She went out and never came back."

"What's with the attitude issues?" Hanna asked.

"I told you Pepper had to let a guy go. Some of his pals aren't real happy I took his job."

"What are they, twelve years old?"

"I need to find out from Pepper what the hell's been going on around here," he said.

Hanna told him about Grace's arrest in the Caymans."

"Good!" he said. "That should keep her out of our hair for a while."

"We can only hope."

"Don't tell me she wanted you to help get her out."

"I didn't let it get that far," Hanna said. "Hey, I wanted to take you to dinner tonight. It's our two-month anniversary."

"Two months!"

"Don't sound so surprised."

"That might be a new record for me after my last marriage," he said, smiling as he watched Pepper Stokes come into the room.

"Let's not go there," Hanna snapped. "Last thing I want to do is think about your ex."

"Would love to go to dinner," he said as the sheriff came up. "Should be home around six. See you then."

He ended the call and stood as Stokes stopped across the desk.

"Heard about your tire," the old sheriff said.

"We need to talk," Alex replied. You had lunch yet?"

There was an old wood picnic table in the shade of a looming live oak tree behind the building. Alex sat across from his new boss, both opening the cellophane on sandwiches in front of them. "I need to know what went down with this guy you had to fire," Alex said.

Stokes took a bite from his sandwich, chewed for a moment before he swallowed and replied. "Man's name was Ingalls, one of my longest-term deputies."

"What the hell happened?"

Stokes leaned forward and put his chin in his right palm, scrunching up his weathered face. "Suspected for a while, the man was on the pad with the Lacroix bunch. They're still runnin' drugs up here, even after we took down your old friend, Beau Richards and his boy."

"And Lacroix's outfit is involved again?"

"Yeah, bad bunch," Stokes said. "They didn't miss a beat when the Dellahousayes were taken out. We've had two homicides in the last year linked to these assholes. They clear out any dead wood and threats real fast."

"And your man was involved?"

Stokes sat back. "Finally got enough on him to get his ass fired. The Feds are looking at him for the murders and other drug-related charges."

"What about his buddies inside," Alex asked, thinking about his run-in with Deputy Gallagher.

Stokes hesitated for a moment, then said, "I'm afraid we still have some bad apples in there. Just don't have enough to move on them yet. May need your help."

"Wish you'd told me about this before I took the damn job," Alex said, pushing his sandwich aside as his appetite waned.

"You havin' second thoughts?" Stokes asked.

Alex let the question sink in for a moment. He'd dealt with this kind of nonsense in the Charleston PD and was not inclined to run from another round of corruption. "You let me know what I can do," he finally said.

CHAPTER SIX

Jordan Hayes finished putting out on the 18th hole at the Ocean Course on Kiawah Island, south of Charleston. He had been a member for many years and often brought clients and friends out for a day of golf. Today, he was hosting the governor of South Carolina and two big donors to the man's upcoming campaign.

He shook hands with his guests as they walked off the green. He saw his assistant, Miles, standing by the golf carts and motioned for the man to join him away from the group. Hayes excused himself from the governor's party and walked over toward the clubhouse.

Speaking softly, Miles said, "We checked out the judge on the Lacroix case. He's dirty as hell, but our man doesn't believe there's enough solid evidence to call him out on it."

"You've got to be kidding me!" Hayes fumed. "One of the biggest gangsters in the country gets a free pass years before his sentence is up, and we can't touch this judge?"

Miles shook his head. "Lacroix walks later this afternoon."

Hayes turned and watched the governor and the two donors walking into the clubhouse for drinks and lunch. "You're absolutely certain there are no other strings to be pulled here?"

"No sir."

"Okay," Hayes said, his mind sorting through the necessary next steps. "I'll need to talk with Brenda Dellahousaye. Reach out and see if she's available for a call in about an hour. Text me. I'll be inside."

"If I may, sir, I would strongly encourage you to distance yourself from all of this," Miles began. "I don't have to tell you the repercussions from your past association with the Dellahousayes."

"Yes, I lost my damn Senate seat!" Hayes said, looking back now with an icy stare. He thought for a moment about his man's arguably good advice. "Look, I don't have to remind you how much Mrs. Dellahousaye is paying us."

"I understand, but..."

"No, we're not walking away from this," Hayes cut in. "It's not just the money. I can't trust the woman not to blow the whistle on past transactions that would be devastating if they were leaked."

Miles nodded. "I'll set up the call." He looked at his watch. "Will two o'clock work?"

"Yes," Hayes said, starting off to join his guests. "Text me to confirm."

At 2:05 p.m., Hayes was riding in the backseat of his long Mercedes sedan. His assistant sat on the seat beside him. His long-time driver and security man, Sharpe, was at the wheel. Miles dialed a number into Hayes' phone and then handed it to him as the call rang through.

"Hello, Senator," came the clearly impatient response from Brenda Dellahousaye.

"Brenda..."

She cut him off. "I already know that Lacroix will be on the street by four o'clock today. Why do I even pay you?"

"Brenda, please...," Hayes began, looking over at Miles, shaking his head.

"No, you listen to me, Jordan! You need to get someone to move on this judge."

"Brenda, there is not enough..."

"You're not listening to me!"

Hayes could tell she was furious and decided to just let her vent.

"I know it's too late to stop Lacroix from getting released this afternoon, but it's not too late to expose this judge and get them both back behind bars."

"Alright, give me some time on this," Hayes said.

"You had plenty of time and you came up with nothing! Not acceptable!"

She hung up before he could respond.

Hayes was furious. He was not used to being spoken to in such a manner. He turned to Miles. "I don't care what it costs, turn this judge upside down and find something we can use against him."

"Yes sir!"

Brenda Dellahousaye slammed her cell down on the desk in her spacious office in the beach house looking out over the Atlantic Ocean. The fact that her husband and his second wife had been brutally murdered in this house several years ago had not kept her from taking possession and moving back in. She had originally purchased and decorated the house years ago before her marriage to Remy fell on the rocks. In the divorce settlement, she had taken the New York penthouse, Remy got the beach house. It was hers again now, and she was committed to never letting anyone take it from her again.

She thought about her discussion with the Senator. She knew she had been too harsh on Hayes, but she also knew the man had considerable power and influence. Getting some dirt on this corrupt judge should not be an issue.

She did have a back-up plan.

Reaching for her phone, she placed another call. Carmen Broussard had been one of her husband's top lieutenants in the crime family organization. He was also leading her efforts to take back their interests from Xander Lacroix.

Broussard answered the call. "Yes ma'am."

"Lacroix will walk at four o'clock," Brenda said. "I'm sure security will be tight."

"Our man is ready," Broussard replied.

She thought for a moment. If Lacroix was taken out, her move on the syndicate would likely be easier. But, it could also spark a bloody war that she had little appetite for. Her resolve returned. "And you're sure we can also get to both of Lacroix's top guys?"

"Absolutely."

She looked out the window, the vast expanse of the ocean sparkling in the afternoon sun. She thought again about Jordan Hayes and the likelihood of him coming up with anything to put Lacroix back in prison, and even if he did, Lacroix and his men would still be formidable opponents. "Okay, make it happen."

CHAPTER SEVEN

Xander Lacroix walked down the hall past the warden's suite of offices. The new suit he'd just put on felt odd after wearing a prison uniform for so long. It had taken more time than he had hoped, but the judge finally came through with the commutation of his sentence. It had cost him $1 million, but a small price to pay in his mind to get out of this hellhole and back out running his business in person and living his life. His first stop would be his girlfriend's house for a long overdue reunion.

He was accompanied by two prison guards as he walked toward the exit door. His men would be waiting with a car. He had warned them to be armed and ready for any eventuality. He had many enemies. Some had tried to get him in prison, and he had survived two attempts on his life. He also knew that his old boss's ex-wife was making moves to take back Remy Dellahousaye's empire.

He knew he would have to deal with Brenda Dellahousaye soon and severely. He had worked too hard to wrest away control of Remy's business. He wasn't going to let anyone take that away, particularly now that he was out and free.

He stood waiting for the guards to unlock the next door and thought about other scores he needed to settle. One was personal, and he was waiting until he could deal with it in that fashion. The Charleston cop, Alex Frank, was the one most responsible for his incarceration. Since his first day in prison, he had been thinking about how best to deal with the troublesome cop, and his bitch wife, for that matter, he thought.

He had heard they were recently married. *What a shame it will be such a short marriage*, he thought, reveling in the revenge he had planned.

His sources had also uncovered the fact that the daughter of the man he had ordered killed, the murder that had landed him in prison, had actually survived his efforts to take her out as well. The woman was squirreled away in Witness Protection. He knew exactly where she was and would deal with that issue soon, as well.

He followed the guards into a small vestibule with an office to the right behind a glass opening. He stepped up and signed several papers, then took a brown envelope that contained his wallet, a watch and ring. He placed the wallet in the pocket of his suit pants and put the jewelry on his right hand. He felt one of the guard's hands on his arm, pulling him toward a door to his left.

As the other guard opened the door, the bright light of the afternoon blinded him for a moment, and he held his arm up to cover his face. The fresh air washed over him, and he breathed in the glorious taste of *freedom*!

The guards led him across a small parking lot with cars owned by the prison employees. At the end of the lot near the exit, he saw a long black Lincoln SUV with two of his men waiting beside the open back door. He watched the smiles spread across their faces as he approached. The guards stopped and let him proceed.

One guard behind him said, "Hope to see you back here again soon."

Lacroix held up his middle finger in response as he continued on without looking back.

Both of his men embraced him in tight man hugs.

"Welcome back, boss," the man named Cal Drummond said. He had been with Lacroix for years and was his top lieutenant. He had been running the businesses in Lacroix's absence since his incarceration.

Lacroix stepped back. "Good to see you boys," he said. He looked up at the blue Carolina sky and took in a deep breath again. He started toward the door to the car when the quiet of the afternoon was interrupted by the sharp crack of a rifle firing. He felt a hot rush of wind sweep by the side of his head. He turned to see the face of his second man, Hernandez, erupt in a plume of blood. The man fell back against the car as the crack of a second rifle shot exploded somewhere behind them.

Lacroix was already crouching low when the second blast exploded the SUV's front passenger window. He looked over and saw the guards ducking behind another car, one reaching for his radio. He turned and saw Hernandez slumping down along the side of the big black SUV and then limply to the ground, likely already dead.

"What the hell! was his first thought as he knelt beside the car. Drummond moved quickly down to shield him from any further fire. They both waited a moment, expecting another shot. When none came, Drummond pushed Lacroix up into the back seat and then ran around the front of the SUV to the driver's side, leaving the prone body of their associate on the ground.

Lacroix tried to catch his breath, pulling the door closed and leaning low across the back seat, expecting another round to come in at any time. He heard Drummond slam his door closed and start the engine. The big SUV lurched forward, tires squealing.

Lacroix cautiously pulled himself up and looked back through the rear window as they sped out of the parking lot and into the street. He saw Hernandez lying dead in a pool of blood leaking out around his head. He saw the two prison guards, one running now back to the exit door, the other yelling into his radio.

"You okay, boss?" he heard Drummond ask from up front.

"Just get us the hell out of here!" Lacroix yelled back, his heart pounding in his chest. His next conscious thought was the face of Brenda Dellahousaye. *She is a dead woman!*

CHAPTER EIGHT

Hanna walked out into the lobby of the law firm to meet her next appointment. It was the mother of her now-deceased office assistant, Molly. Hanna had become friends with Molly's mother and father years before the tragic incident that took her daughter's life. Her name was Beulah. She was a fifty-something widow who lived in Charleston. She was small and stooped and sat with her hands in her lap as Hanna approached.

Beulah had worked hard at a local department store and her husband in a small landscaping business to help put her daughter through college, then paralegal school.

As Hanna looked at the woman's face, images of the day the gunman had burst into her Charleston offices came back to her. She pressed her eyes tightly shut and stopped for a moment to calm herself and chase the horrific scenes away. When she opened her eyes, Hanna saw Beulah standing and coming toward her.

They both hugged each other. Hanna stood back. Molly's mother's hair was even grayer than the last time she'd seen her. Her face was ashen and drawn, all the joy gone in her once happy face since her daughter's murder. Hanna felt another terrible rush of guilt as she stared back.

"Hanna, thank you so much for seeing me," Beulah said.

"Of course, dear," Hanna said, reaching for her hand. "How are you doing?"

As soon as she said the words, Hanna knew what a ridiculous question it was. Beulah didn't reply. "Can I get you something to drink?" she asked.

"Coffee, please."

"Let's go back to my office." Hanna led the way and stopped in the kitchen to get the drink. Coming into the office, the wide panorama of the marshes behind Pawleys Island greeted them beyond the windows. She sat beside her guest on a couch against the far wall.

Beulah sipped at her coffee, then said, "I really do appreciate you taking time to see me. I know how busy you must be."

"It's not a problem."

"I know we've talked about this," Beulah began, "but I'm really struggling with what's happened to the man who killed Molly."

Hanna winced again at the thought of the shooter and how close he had come to killing her as well. She took a deep breath. "What we do know is all the men who were part of this terror cell were killed the morning of their attempted attack."

Beulah sat forward, a look of desperation on her face. "I know you've told me that, Hanna, but we don't know for sure if the man who shot Molly was even there."

Hanna had suffered through many sleepless hours with the same concern. The man who had burst into her office had not been directly linked to the terror cell, nor had he been identified as one of the dead terrorists after the FBI takedown.

From the few frantic moments, she had seen him before one of his bullets had struck her across the side of her forehead and she had fallen to the floor, consciousness fading, she recalled only the fleeting images of a thin man, dark-complexioned with a ball cap pulled low and mirrored sunglasses. Alex had been able to get photos of all the men killed in the FBI assault, but there was no clear indication any of them were the man who killed Molly. The thought this man might still be alive and out there somewhere continued to haunt her.

"There was one other man, Hanna, as you know."

She was referring to the captured terrorist who the FBI had finally coerced into revealing the imminent plans of the terror cell he had led here in Charleston. "He was in custody at the time of the attack on my office, Beulah, as I've told you," Hanna said, trying to be kind.

"Yes, but he must know something, don't you think?"

Hanna had asked Alex this same question on several occasions. Since his release from the Bureau, he had no access to really determine the fate of the man. Alex had heard through other sources that the surviving terrorist was now being held in Guantanamo Bay in Cuba, away from lawyers and journalists.

Even more frustrating, the leader of the entire operation, which had caused considerable damage and chaos across the country, the rich Saudi businessman, Bassam Al Zahrani, had been released at the request of the King of Saudi Arabia. Some deal had apparently been cut between governments and the United States had determined it was in their best interests to let the man go back to his home country and safe haven of the royal family. Hanna sensed there would never be a full accounting or public explanation of the deal that was struck.

Alex had also tried hard to get the Bureau to go after ex-Senator Jordan Hayes, who had obviously been working closely with the Saudi terror cell leader. The crafty politician and now lobbyist and his connections and leverage in Washington were apparently strong enough to head off any further investigation.

She looked back at Molly's mother, her heart heavy for the woman. "I'm sorry, Beulah, there's no way we can get access to this man. I just don't think there's anything more Alex or I can do at this point." The woman looked back with pleading eyes, then Hanna saw her face sink in final resignation. "I really am so sorry, dear."

Hanna stood with her and pulled her into her arms. They stood there together for some time, both letting the tears come again.

CHAPTER NINE

Brenda Dellahousaye threw her cell phone hard against the far wall and watched it shatter the glass in a framed painting, then fall to the floor. She turned in exasperation and looked out the window behind her desk in the big beach house. The broad panorama of the blue Atlantic Ocean greeted her icy stare.

She had just been informed by her man, Carmen Broussard, that the attempted hit on Xander Lacroix had failed. The man had escaped. Only one of his bodyguards had been killed by the long-distance sniper rifle of their paid assassin. She had been assured by Broussard that this shooter was one of the best in the world. *Apparently not!*

Her mind was racing with the implications and threats of the failed attempt at taking out her rival. Lacroix would know she was one of the most likely people wanting him dead and out of the way. *How quickly will he come back after me?* she thought, desperate now in knowing she had ignited an inferno of violence and revenge.

There was a knock on the open door behind her. She heard the voice of her daughter, Ophelia.

"Is everything okay? What broke?"

"Not now!" Brenda screamed, turning to face her daughter. The girl was barely dressed in a black bikini, her hair dripping from an afternoon in the massive pool in front of the house.

"What's going on?" Ophelia demanded.

Brenda took a deep breath, trying to calm herself. Plans for defending herself and her family or launching another attack were racing through her thoughts. She pressed her right palm against her forehead, squeezing her eyes shut hard. A moment of clarity edged into her brain. "We need to leave town, now!"

"What are you talking about! Streak and I just got here."

"I don't have time to argue with you, O! Get packed and get out of here now. I'm leaving, too."

"Mother..."

"Just do it!"

An hour later, Brenda watched through a front window of the big beach house as her daughter sped away with her ridiculous excuse for a boyfriend. She turned to go back to her bedroom where she was finishing packing. Broussard would be arriving in a few minutes to take her to the private terminal where her plane was waiting to depart for California, then on to Hawaii the next day.

As she pressed down on the last pile of clothes and belongings in a third suitcase on a stand in her massive closet, she kept thinking about what her next move would be to take down Xander Lacroix. She had several moves underway across the vast business network her deceased husband, Remy, had left behind. All of that would play itself out, as well as a list of others she had in reserve. But now, she had played a card that would inflame the situation to a tipping point. She had known there was a risk in moving so quickly to have Lacroix taken out but had made the calculated decision it was the best course of action.

She continued to fume about the failed assassination attempt and the ineptitude of the killer Broussard had hired. She would have to deal with that later, she thought.

She heard the back door to the garage open and footsteps coming into the house. She looked at her watch. Broussard would have to drive quickly to get her to the plane for the planned departure time. She heard the door to her bedroom suite open.

"Carmen, there are two bags out there you can have taken out to the car," she yelled out through the closet door. "I'll be right out."

There was no response, which surprised her.

She turned and felt a chill of fear rush through her body.

Two men, dressed all in black with black masks hiding their faces, came through the closet door and stood facing her. One held a semi-automatic rifle pointing directly at her face. The other had a handgun in a holster but held a long knife in his right hand.

Brenda instinctively started backing up. She ran into a wall of hanging clothes and stopped, holding up both hands in defense. "Please... no!"

The man with the knife came forward, now only a few feet away from her. He twirled the knife in his hand in a practiced move that sent another chill through her soul.

"Please, we can work this out..."

She pressed into the hangers of dresses until her back reached the wall. She looked desperately for any means of escape. The man now stood directly in front of her blocking all other views. His left arm reached out in a lightning-quick blur and grabbed her by the hair, pulling her back out into the middle of the room.

"Noooo!!!" she screamed as he pulled her hard and then lifted her head up to face him.

In a low, gravelly voice, the man hissed, "Mr. L knows you were behind the hit this afternoon. We're here to send a message. It's a very clear message. It's the last message you will ever hear, actually..."

Brenda pulled violently away, trying to break free, but the other man came up behind her and grabbed her in a vice grip around her shoulders with his arms. "Let me talk to him! We can work this out!"

As her frightened screams left her lips, she knew they were such empty and ridiculous promises that her attackers would not be persuaded. A sudden calm came over her, and she felt her whole body go limp as she accepted the fact that she was going to die.

The man in front of her moved close, his face only inches from hers. Then she saw the knife come up and felt it touch the skin beside her right eye. Her fear was surprisingly gone now. She was thinking only of her daughters, Ida and Ophelia, and what a blessing it was that they were away and safe and had their whole lives ahead. Resigned in the fact she had only moments to live, she took a deep breath and let the sobering realization wash over her.

She looked into the dark eyes of the man facing her through his black mask. She saw they were brown, and the whites of his eyes were patterned with red veins. She closed her eyes when he spoke again.

"Mr. L made it very clear that you would not see the end of this day, but also, that it would be a very painful day. Am I making myself clear?"

Brenda heard the words, but her mind was far away. She kept her eyes closed and forced herself to remember better times, earlier times with her daughters, with her husband, Remy, when they were still in love. *It had been a good life... until it wasn't.*

Her distant recollections were suddenly interrupted with the deafening crack of a gunshot, then two more in fast succession. She flinched, thinking they were intended for her. She fell back as the man behind her loosened his grip around her.

When she opened her eyes, she saw the assailant in front of her falling away to the side, the left half of his hooded head now red with blood. She fell over onto the floor, then looked back and saw the other killer falling back into her clothes, two holes in his chest spurting blood.

When she looked back at the door to her bedroom, her man Carmen Broussard was standing there, a silhouette against the light from behind. Both of his arms were pointed out into the closet with a black handgun, smoke trickling from the barrel.

As she lay there, trembling and trying to absorb the chaos and carnage all around her, she heard Broussard say, "Mrs. D, we need to go... now!"

Chapter Ten

Alex finished all the administrative work for his new job and began looking through some of the case files that had been left for him to review. Most were routine domestic issues, accident investigations, civil complaints. He was more than a little disappointed in the realization that his career had veered into the calamities of neighbors and spouses fighting and drunk drivers trying to kill themselves, instead of the work he had been introduced to in his short stint with the FBI.

He sat back in his chair, the stiffness of his new uniform slowly beginning to soften. The other deputies in the office had already left for the day. He had no further exchanges with Gallagher but was determined to start helping his new boss, Pepper Stokes, root out the rest of the corruption in the department.

He pushed the files aside and thought again about the new case from this morning, the death of Ally Combes over in Dugganville. The image of her body lying lifeless at the base of the fire tower was a grim reminder of her tragic end. He thought again about his conversation with the woman's husband, his old friend, Boyne Combes. He had seemed genuinely devastated at the news of his wife's death, and yet, as Alex had seen from many homicide cases during his career with the Charleston PD, it was easy to misread the emotions and reactions of people associated with a crime, particularly a murder.

Something about the whole situation continued to gnaw at him. Boyne and Ally had quarreled the night before her death. She had left their home and not come back. When Alex went to see him at the hardware to inform him of his wife's death, he openly admitted they were having issues. He also said he thought she had gone to stay with a friend overnight, something she may have done previously.

Questions came to him. *How many times had she left him to stay at someone else's home, and why did she feel compelled to leave? What were the issues the Combes were dealing with?*

He pushed his chair back and stood to leave. He reached for his hat on the desk and gathered his keys and phone. He saw Sheriff Stokes coming down the hall and then up to his desk.

"Well," Stokes began, a concerned look across his face, "you made it through the first day with this bunch."

"Not a real friendly reception."

"This ain't Welcome Wagon, Alex," the old sheriff teased.

"Come on, Pepper," Alex said in exasperation. "I've been through this before. I just need to know what we're really up against. If more of these guys on your payroll are taking some on the side from the Lacroix gang, you got some serious stuff to deal with still."

Stokes looked around the empty room and then back at Alex. "The main reason I brought you in, son... I could find a lot of guys who would be content to run speed radar traps and roust drunks, but I need someone here I can trust to find out what the hell's really going down here with Lacroix's gang. I also think we've got a real case with this Combes woman up in Dugganville."

"You told me you thought she was a jumper," Alex said.

"Spent a little time up at the diner there in town this afternoon," Stokes said. "Got an earful about the troubles your friend has been having with his dead wife."

"What kind of troubles?"

"Well, to start, Boyne has a serious gambling problem. Seems he's deep into some badass bookies who don't take *no* for an answer when it comes to paying up past losses. I went over to the bank. I know the manager. Boyne Combes is about to lose the hardware store his old man left him. Can't pay the loans he keeps extending."

Alex shook his head, trying to think through the new information. "So, what did you learn about Boyne and his wife? What's been going on there?"

"Word is, she's gettin' some on the side and Boyne found out about it."

"With who?"

"The few folks I talked to at the diner didn't know," the old sheriff said.

"It's a small town, Pepper. Hard to keep secrets."

"Don't I know!"

Alex was aware that Stokes was notorious for the roster of women he'd been running with over the years, some married. Even Skipper Frank's new wife, Ella, was hooked up with him before she married Alex's father.

Pepper Stokes had always been an enigma to Alex. He was a kind-hearted, community-minded man, involved in volunteering and supporting many non-profit organizations in the county. He was a tough and highly competent law officer who had built a heralded career with the Sheriff's Department.

And yet, there was another side to the man Alex could never understand. After his wife had died only ten years after their marriage from a sudden brain aneurysm, he seemed to go off the rails when it came to personal relationships in his life. He never had another serious girlfriend after a long period of mourning his wife's passing. It almost seemed like he was determined not to get too close to anyone again after the pain of his loss. As a result, there was a long history of tumultuous affairs and jilted women in his wake.

Alex thought again about the new revelations in the Combes case. Ally Combes having an affair would certainly account for some of the early facts discovered. Boyne had quarreled with her the night before she was found dead. She had left for the evening to stay with "friends" and had reportedly done so on many occasions.

He knew several sources in Dugganville who might have more on all of this. "Boss, let me stop by and talk to a couple of people on my way home tonight," Alex said, standing from his desk and gathering a few items to take with him. "I'll let you know if I learn anything."

He drove past the familiar storefronts in the little village of Dugganville, including Boyne Combes' hardware, then turned along the riverfront, boats of all sizes and shapes floating motionlessly in the calm current. Many of the boats were large shrimp boats like his father's. The park came up on his left, where the old fire tower loomed high above the trees. The yellow crime scene tape still surrounded the area where Ally Combes' body had been found earlier in the day, though Alex was quite sure the local kids had already contaminated any other evidence that might be found there.

Up ahead, he saw the sign out on the street in front of *Gilly's Bar*. He pulled his truck into the lot and found a space along the back row, one of only a few left, another busy night at *Gilly's*. As he got out, there was loud music blaring inside, a country song that he heard all the time on the radio... *"my wife left town with my best friend, and I miss him!"* Loud voices and laughter also echoed from inside. He wasn't surprised to see his father's old, rusted truck parked in his usual spot.

He left his new deputy's hat on the seat beside him and got out to go inside. As he walked up the steps to the front door, memories of too many late nights here started coming back to him, particularly the night a paid killer had tried to take him out right here in the parking lot. The bullet wound in his shoulder still caused him chronic pain.

The familiar smells and sounds of *Gilly's Bar* greeted him as he walked in, a combination of stale beer, kitchen grease and a cacophony of loud music and voices. The sight of his uniform caused many heads to turn and stare as he walked through the crowd. He saw his father up at the bar, his back turned, deep in conversation with the owner, Gilly, and several of his friends seated to each side. The man next to Skipper Frank elbowed him and nodded in Alex's direction. The Skipper turned and a broad smile crossed his face when he saw his son coming up.

"Well, look at you!" the old man said.

"Hey, Pop."

"Haven't seen you look this sharp since you first came home in your new Army uniform."

Gilly and the others greeted Alex and got in a few quick jabs about his new job and the uniform.

Alex leaned close to his father, "You got a minute, Pop?"

"Sure, sure. Gilly, top off this beer mug for me," Skipper said to the bar owner as he pushed his chair back.

They walked out on a back deck that was empty this early in the evening. The sounds of the bar softened as they closed the door behind them. The October sun was already falling low behind the trees across the river.

"How's your first day on the job, kid?"

Alex thought for a moment about the chaotic series of events that greeted him at his new place of employment. "Have to say it was exciting."

"How's that?"

"You hear about Ally Combes?" Alex asked.

Skipper Frank leaned back against the wooden rail of the deck. "Damn! Just found out from one of the boys. What the hell happened?"

"Not sure, yet," Alex replied. "I wanted to ask you about Ally and Boyne. I know you've been close to the Combes family for years."

"What about 'em?"

"We've heard they were having problems, marital problems."

"No secret, Ally was running around on the side."

"With who?" Alex asked.

"All I hear, some bad dude out of Charleston. Young Boyne's been trying to keep a good face on, but people are talking. You think Boyne pushed her off that tower?"

"Like I said, not sure yet," Alex said.

"What the hell would they be doin' up there, anyway?"

"Really good question. Who would know more about this Charleston guy?"

Skipper thought for a few moments, then replied, "Old Gilly hears more than anybody in town."

"He was already next on my list."

"He usually takes a break for dinner around seven before the big night rush comes in."

"Thanks, Pop. How are you and Ella doing?"

The old shrimper took off his dirty ball cap and rubbed at what was left of his scruffy gray hair. "That woman is a blessing and a curse, I swear. Most times, she loves me like I'm the last man on earth, then out of nowhere, I can't do anything right. Just this morning, we got into a big tussle about something I'd done."

"Something?"

"Well... I might have forgotten to pay the taxes on the house last year. Got a nastygram from the township office in the mail yesterday threatening to put a lien on our damn house."

"You forgot to pay the taxes!"

"I'll get around to it. Don't start..."

"What else you been forgetting?" Alex asked, worried again about his father's fading memory.

"Like I said, don't start!"

Alex could hear the anger rising in his father's voice and knew there was no point in pursuing it anymore for now.

"By the way," Skipper said, "your ex is back in Florida. The husband down there decided to take her back. Crazy bastard!"

Alex hadn't heard anything from or about his ex-wife, Adrienne, since the anniversary party she'd thrown for Skipper and Alex and was grateful he hadn't.

"Good to hear, Pop. The further away, the better." He paused for a moment, thinking again about his father's tax situation. "Don't get all crazy on me, but you need some help with money?"

The Skipper didn't take the offer well at all. "I got plenty of money! Just forgot about the damn tax bill. Stop worrying about it. Swear you're getting worse than my crazy wife!"

"Okay, fine," Alex said, impatiently, knowing this wouldn't be the last time he had this conversation with his old man about his fading mental condition. He looked at his watch and saw it was about time for Gilly to take his break. "How about you and Ella come out to the island this weekend for a barbecue."

"Great idea!" the Skipper said. "How 'bout some ribs? Haven't had a good rack of ribs in a long time."

"You got it. Saturday night," Alex replied, starting back toward the door. "You let me know if you hear anything else about the Combes."

"Sure thing," the old shrimper said. "You got time for a cold one after you talk to Gilly?"

"No, I need to get back to Pawleys and dinner with Hanna."

Gilly took Alex back to his office and closed the door to give them some privacy and relief from the noise out front. The little room was off the kitchen and cluttered with stacks of paperwork, packages of food, a few empty beer bottles. The walls were adorned with a dozen pictures of Gilly with various "famous" people who had visited the bar. Alex recognized a Hall of Fame pitcher from the Braves.

"How you been, son?" Gilly asked as both men sat across from each other at the desk.

"New job, Gilly," Alex replied. "I'll be around more now that I'm working for Pepper."

"Heard about your release from the Bureau. Sorry to hear about that. We all really appreciate what you did to take down those assholes trying to blow up that ship out in the harbor."

Alex winced at the comment, the recollections of his run-in with the terror cell down at the waterfront still a haunting memory. "Thanks, Gilly. Wasn't meant to be a G-Man, I guess. Probably for the best. I can be back here closer to home and my new wife."

"You did well with that one," Gilly said. "That Hanna is a real keeper."

"I count my blessings every day. Listen, Gilly, you heard about Ally Combes this morning."

"I did. Damn shame. Any idea what happened?"

"No, we're still early in the investigation. No clear sign yet of what went down. Thought you might have heard something about the issues she and Boyne have been having."

The old barkeep leaned back in his chair and rubbed his hands back through his long gray hair. "I hear a lot out there, Alex, as you can imagine," he said, nodding toward the door to the bar. "Most is total bullshit."

"What about the Combes?"

"No secret Boyne's wife has been cheatin' on him. Half the town seems to know."

"Who was she seeing?" Alex asked, leaning forward, his elbows on the desk.

"Seen the guy in here a couple times. One night, Boyne was here, too, and I thought we were gonna have a scrape on our hands."

"So, Boyne knows who the guy is?"

"No question."

"Who is this guy?"

"I'm told he works for the Lacroix outfit.... used to work for Remy Dellahousaye. People seem to think he's runnin' the drug operation up around these parts for old Xander."

"You got a name?" Alex asked. The mention of Xander Lacroix sent a chill through him as he thought about past run-ins with the man.

"Name's Lando, or something like that. Lando Tern. Heard the other night he's staying out at the old Dellahousaye fish camp."

Alex really flinched now as he thought back to the night he and Pepper Stokes had their last run-in with the Dellahousaye's at his father's camp out on the marsh south of town. "Any reason someone would want Ally Combes dead, Gilly?"

"Hate to say it, Alex, but Boyne Combes seems to be the only one with any real motive in this damn thing."

Alex nodded, sharing the same obvious conclusion.

"You know," Gilly went on, "I've spent a little time with Boyne and his wife in the past few years when they've come in for dinner or some drinks. She always seemed like a nice quiet type. Really surprised me when I started hearing about her screwing around with this mobbed-up guy."

"How bad is the drug running getting up here?" Alex asked. "Thought we dealt with that a couple years ago when we took down Asa Dellahousaye and the Richards."

"Didn't take Remy and his boys, and now Lacroix, very long to get it all up and going again," Gilly said. "So many bays and back channels to run product into around here, and major highways close by to distribute."

"Any other locals involved?"

"Don't know for sure, but I hear things, right?"

"Like what?"

"You know Boyne Combes has been having trouble keeping the hardware going. His old man must be rollin' in his grave."

"You think Boyne's messed up with these drug guys?"

"You hear things, Alex. Again, most of it is bullshit."

"Okay, thanks Gilly."

"Sure. I'll let you know if anything else comes up."

"Thanks," Alex said as he stood to leave.

"Probably shouldn't say anything," Gilly said. "Your old man's starting to slip some."

"How's that?" Alex asked, even though he knew where this was headed.

"Used to think he was just drunk when he couldn't remember this from that. It's worse now. I'm sure you've seen it."

"Yeah, it's been coming on for a couple of years," Alex replied.

"Me and the boys get worried about him out there on the salt. Doesn't take much for things to go south quick out there and you gotta have your full faculties."

"I know, Gilly. I've been talking to the Skipper about it for some time."

"He's got a good mate with him out there, but not sure how much longer the old coot can run the *Maggie Mae*."

"It's gonna be a tough call," Alex said, his heart heavy at the thought of his father fading.

"No doubt, son. I try to keep an eye on him when he's in here."

"Problem is, he's in here way too much."

"I know," Gilly replied.

"You might try sending him home early now and then," Alex said as they opened the door to the noisy bar.

"You don't think I try every night?" Gilly responded, his voice rising to be heard.

Alex just nodded back and patted his old friend on the shoulder.

CHAPTER ELEVEN

Hanna paid for the groceries with her debit card and waited for the woman to give her the receipt. The small store just off the island was her regular stop on the way home to pick up something for dinner. She rarely shopped for more than one night, not wanting to think any further ahead than one day at a time.

With the grocery bag in one hand, she searched through her purse with the other trying to find her keys as she walked across the parking lot to her late model Honda sedan. When she got to the car, she put the bag on the roof and dug deeper into her purse. She was just pulling the keys out when she heard a voice from behind.

"Hey pretty lady. You need some help?"

The voice was low and smooth, and it startled her as she turned. The man was just a few feet away and walking closer, a broad smile on his face. He was a tall, lanky man dressed in a flowered shirt and jeans. His hair was long and dark, brushed back wet from his face. The scent of a strong cologne cut the air between them. Hanna looked down and saw pointed black cowboy boots sticking out from the tight jeans.

Hanna's senses went on full alert. She quickly looked around to see if anyone else was near, but the lot was empty. She hurried to open her door, but the man came up close and put his hand over her shoulder on the roof of the car. She turned quickly and tried to slip away.

"Hey, no need to panic," the man said in a slow and easy drawl. "Just wanted to help you with your bags here."

"I don't need any help," Hanna said firmly, backing away to the rear of the car, looking around again for any sign of assistance. He took the bag of groceries off the roof.

"You want these in the trunk?"

"Just leave them alone!" Hanna said, her voice rising as she tried to calm the rush of fear running through her.

The man smiled again and put the bag back. "You look like you could use a drink. Been a long day?"

"My husband's waiting for me." She held up her left hand so he could clearly see her wedding ring.

"Look, just thought I might offer a pretty lady a drink," the man said. "Sorry, no offense. Name's Lando if you change your mind. Usually grab a cocktail after work at the bar down the street there. You live nearby?"

Hanna moved toward him now, her anger taking over the fear. "It's none of your damn business where I live! Get the hell out of my way."

He didn't seem surprised at her outburst and just kept smiling as he stepped away from the car door. "Don't have a name?" he asked.

"Just leave me alone!"

"Okay, okay," he said, his hands raised in mock apology.

She watched him back away and then turn, walking away and then getting into a long white Cadillac sedan. He pulled out of the parking spot, rolled down his window, and smiled again as he drove past, giving her a small wave.

Alex had changed out of his uniform and felt much more comfortable in a pair of old khaki shorts and a Pawleys Island t-shirt. He stood at the sink with Hanna, preparing dinner. When she shared the encounter at the grocery store parking lot with him, he was immediately concerned about how dangerous the situation may have been. When she repeated the name *Lando* he got her full attention.

"He said his name was Lando?"

"Yes, and he wanted mine, and he wanted to know where I lived!"

"He didn't follow you, did he?"

"No, I waited til he drove away. He said he was going to a bar down the street. Must be the Shamrock... only bar nearby in that direction."

Alex walked quickly to the counter where he'd dropped his car keys.

"Where are you going?" Hanna asked in surprise.

"Where do you think?"

"Alex, please, no!" she pleaded. "I took care of it. He won't be a problem. I shouldn't have said anything.

"This guy is probably the same one who's been seeing Ally Combes, the woman who died in Dugganville last night."

"What? How do you know?"

"I was down at *Gilly's* before coming home trying to get some more information on what's been going on with Boyne and Ally Combes. This guy, Lando, has been having a pretty open affair with the dead woman." He saw the concern in Hanna's face. "I just want to have a word with the guy."

"Let me come with you. I can point him out for you," she insisted.

"No, please, I want you to stay here. This guy is tied up with the Dellahousaye and Lacroix mob guys and I don't want you anywhere near that again."

"Okay," she said tentatively and then gave him a description of the man.

"I'll be back."

Alex pulled into the gravel lot at the *Shamrock Bar*, just south of Dugganville on Highway 17. It was close to dark, and the neon signs of beer names shined in the small windows across the front of the old place, white paint peeling and a metal roof rusted and sagging. There were more motorcycles than cars in the lot. The place had a reputation for attracting bikers and pool sharks. He imagined he'd be called here frequently in the future in his new job with the Sheriff's Department.

He reached into the glove box of his truck and pulled out a holstered 45 caliber revolver, his own personal handgun. As he got out of the car, he clipped the holster to his belt on the back of his shorts under the shirt.

His heart was beating fast as he climbed the steps to the low porch and then pushed the door open to go in. It took a few moments for his eyes to adjust and see anything other than dim lights behind the bar illuminating the many bottles of liquor. A Cajun song was playing on a jukebox in the far corner. Two men with leather biker vests were playing pool at one of two tables to the right.

As his eyes adjusted, he saw several tables with customers and one man sitting alone at the bar talking to a female bartender. When he saw the flowered shirt, he headed immediately toward the bar. There was a pounding in his ears and his fists were clenched tight at his sides.

He pulled a barstool out of the way and moved in close to the man, his left elbow on the bar. "You Lando Tern?" Alex asked.

Alex watched as Tern took a long sip from his bottle of beer, then turned slowly to face him. "Who the hell wants to know."

"The husband of the woman you tried to hustle at the grocery store down the street, asshole!"

Tern just stared back, expressionless, then an easy smile spread across his face. "Look man, I didn't know she was married. I don't want no trouble."

Alex willed himself to keep from slamming his one good hand through the man's teeth.

"Understand you know a woman named Ally Combes over in Dugganville," Alex said.

"Combes? Never heard of her."

"I'm told you've been spending a lot of time with her. She's married, too, or was."

"Was married?" Tern replied, seemingly puzzled.

"She died last night."

"Sorry for the man's loss. What, are you a cop?"

Alex looked around the bar, trying to calm himself.

"You a cop, man?" Tern pressed.

Alex didn't reply as he looked back.

"Have to say, you're a lucky man. Your wife's a fine-looking woman," Tern said.

Alex had enough of the man's smug bullshit and grabbed him by the shirt. "I find you anywhere near my wife again..."

Before he could finish, Alex saw the roundhouse punch coming and ducked as Tern spun, pushing the bar stool back with his hip. He heard the bartender yelling something. Tern's fist caught him with a glancing blow across the side of the head and he staggered back for a step before he came back up, pushing the man hard up against the bar. He heard a groan and a gasp of air.

He sensed a black veil of fury descending over him, all the past months and years of trauma and heartbreak and thoughts of this guy as a threat to Hanna was more than he could contain. He grabbed Tern by the neck with his left hand wounded in the beatings he took from Baz Al Zahrani's terror squad. A jolt of pain shot up his arm, but he didn't let go. He coiled back and let a punch fly with his good right hand, and in a lightning flash, it

The Fire Tower

caught Tern square in the nose. He heard bone and cartilage breaking and a scream of pain.

Tern slumped and then fell to the floor, one hand over his nose, the other trying to break his fall. Blood flowed out through his fingers and began dripping on the floor around him as he fell. He hit the floor hard and cried out again.

"Dammit, man! Stop!"

From behind, Alex heard the bartender yelling for help and that she was calling the police. Another man in the bar rushed over and grabbed Alex from behind, pulling him away. In his fury, Alex spun and was about to swing again, but the man held his hands up in defense.

"You got no beef with me, mister."

Alex's heart was pounding in his chest. His breath was coming in labored gasps. He looked back and Tern was lying on his side, trying to stop the bleeding from his nose. His left leg was twitching and the blood pooled next to his face.

Alex walked to the bar and grabbed a towel, then threw it down on the floor next to Tern. He looked around the room and everyone was staring back at him. Some had their cellphones out taking videos.

The woman tending bar came around from behind and got between Alex and the other customer who had pulled him away. "The cops are coming. You need to settle down," she said. She was a short and stocky woman with dyed blue hair and countless gold rings in her nose, lips and ears. Tattoos laced down both arms and up her neck.

"I am the cops," Alex said, pulling out his badge.

"What the hell!" the woman said.

Alex looked over as Lando Tern struggled to his feet, still holding his nose. "You broke my damn nose, man!"

The bartender reached for the towel on the floor and started helping Tern. Alex staggered back a few steps and then sat down on one of the bar stools. His head was still spinning as the fury slowly began to fade. He thought about Hanna and how strong she had been in facing down this asshole. He didn't want to think how badly it could have all ended. Images of Ally Combes lying dead beneath the tower made it that much more alarming.

He pulled his cellphone from his back pocket to call his boss, Pepper Stokes. He had a prime suspect in the death they were investigating. He'd also just gotten into a fight with the same guy for coming on to his wife. *Great start on my first day on the job,* he thought.

He tried the sheriff's cell and got voicemail, then his office and home numbers, leaving messages for Stokes on each call. He looked up when he heard, "What's going on here?" He turned and saw Deputy Gallagher from his new department, the man he had tangled with earlier in the day.

He came up to Alex and, with a surprised look, said, "Well look here. Deputy Frank bustin' heads on his first day on the job."

"What took you so long, Gallagher?" Alex said.

"Heard the 911 dispatcher. I was just down the road. You always go around breakin' guy's faces?"

Alex tried to regain his composure, still breathing hard. "This guy's a suspect in the Combes death over in Dugganville. He took a swing at me, and I laid him out."

Tern yelled out, his voice muffled by the hand still over his nose. "He's just pissed cause I hit on his wife!"

"That true, Frank?" Gallagher asked. Another deputy came in and stood beside Gallagher, a man Alex hadn't met yet. He had his hand on his gun.

Alex didn't answer the question.

The man who had pulled Alex away from the fight came around and said, "I saw the whole thing, officers." He pointed at Tern. "That guy threw the first punch."

Tern yelled out again. "That asshole threatened to kill me if I came near his wife again. I was just protecting myself."

Gallagher moved into the center of the crowd. "Okay, I've heard enough here." He turned to the deputy who came in after him. "Get this guy cleaned up and bring him down to the department. Frank, you and me are going in to talk this through with Sheriff Stokes. I got my own cruiser. I'll meet you down there."

Alex shook his head, trying to sort through how this had all gone south so quickly. It hadn't taken Tern long to push his buttons and push him over the edge. He watched as the other deputy led Tern over toward the restroom, holding the towel to his face.

"Come on, Frank, let's go."

CHAPTER TWELVE

"You did what?" Hanna listened on her cell as Alex explained again how he had confronted the man who had harassed her in the parking lot earlier.

"And you broke his nose!" she finally replied.

"I was only protecting myself. He tried to take my head off," Alex said in protest.

Hanna stood from the seat at the kitchen island and walked out onto the back deck overlooking the ocean. The sun was just down now beyond the marshes to the west behind the house. A soft glow of pink filtered the clouds drifting high above as the day faded. She walked to the rail, breathing deep, trying to compose herself.

"How much trouble are you in?" she asked.

"I'll take care of it. Pepper's coming down to hear me out on this and talk to this guy about Ally Combes."

"You really think he's a killer?" Hanna asked, a bit light-headed thinking about her close encounter with the guy.

"We're going to find out. Look, I'm pulling into the department. I've gotta go."

"Call me on your way home," she said, turning and leaning back against the rail, looking up at the old beach house. "And don't hit anybody else tonight, promise?" she said, trying to clear the air between them.

"Promise." He clicked off.

She turned again and looked out over the beach and the ocean beyond. The night sky continued to darken, and the first stars sparkled far off above the horizon. A big tanker lit up with a hundred small lights drifted by far offshore.

To the left, she noticed a woman walking slowly along the shore break, kicking water with each step. She thought again about her few moments with the ghost of Amanda Paltierre. She felt a warm rush of peace and comfort in knowing the spirit of her distant grandmother was here with her. *Is she my guardian angel?* Hanna thought, and then smiled at the thought. *Someone or something has certainly been watching over me these past crazy years!*

Alex walked down the hall following Gallagher to Sheriff Stokes' office. A few doors before they got there, Gallagher stopped and turned. "You have any idea how much shit you stepped in tonight?"

Alex stopped in surprise. "What's that supposed to mean?"

"That guy you popped is heavily mobbed-up," Gallagher said, a wry smile spread across his face. "I've heard about your past run-ins with the Dellahousayes and Xander Lacroix. You got a death wish, man?"

Alex pushed past without reply. He walked into Stokes' office. The sheriff looked up with a furious expression. "Close the damn door!"

"Pepper, look..." Alex began.

"Sit down!"

He took a seat across the desk. He couldn't remember ever seeing Stokes angrier.

"Let me hear your side of this before I decide whether I'm going to fire you on your first day on the job."

"I stopped by to see Gilly over in Dugganville on the way home tonight," Alex began slowly, trying to contain his anger and frustration. "He confirmed that Ally Combes has been having an affair with this guy, Lando Tern, we just brought in."

"And who the hell is this guy?" Stokes asked, pushing back from his desk and kicking one leg up on the corner.

"Gilly thinks he's heading up the drug ring for Lacroix around here."

"We'll see about that. Now why the hell did you try to knock his head off?"

"I got a tip he was down at the Shamrock."

"Where'd you hear that?" Stokes pressed.

Alex hesitated, then said, "I got home tonight, and Hanna was upset about this guy who came on to her in the parking lot over at the grocery store. She finally was able to brush him off, but he said he was going down to the Shamrock if she wanted to have a drink with him. I went down there to find him and check out the Combes connection."

"And what did you learn before you smashed his nose in?"

"Claims he doesn't know Ally Combes, but his answers were sketchy, boss."

"And then you tried to put his lights out?"

"Look, Pepper, I'm sorry," Alex said, leaning in. "He kept pushing me on Hanna, and when I told him to back off, he took a swing at me. I just reacted and threw back."

"Gallagher has a different version of the story," Stokes said.

"Of course he does!" Alex said, standing and pushing his chair back. "Get him in here and we'll clear this up."

"Sit down, Alex!"

He pulled his chair back and sat down. "Pepper, this guy is dirty on too many levels. Let's get in there and dial it up on him."

"Seems you already did that."

"Come on, Pepper!"

Stokes scratched at his gray stubble of a beard, then said, "I want you on the sidelines with this guy. I'll take it from here. Stay away from him. Is that clear?"

Alex hesitated. "You need me on this Combes investigation, Pepper. I grew up with these people."

"I just want you nowhere near this Tern guy."

"Okay."

Stokes stood to end the meeting. "Go home. Be with your wife. Cool off, dammit! And let me again be very clear, this department doesn't go around bustin' heads to get our job done. This won't happen again! Are we good on that?"

"Yes sir."

CHAPTER THIRTEEN

Xander Lacroix had zero patience for failure and incompetence. There were no second chances in his business.

"Who hired these idiots!" he fumed, staring down his top man, Cal Drummond.

"I went to our usual source," Drummond replied, his right hand shaking visibly at his side.

"And now Brenda Dellahousaye is still on the right side of the dirt and probably has somebody coming back after me as we speak."

"We're trying to find her, boss."

"You're trying?" Lacroix hissed, his face red with anger. "You checked the airport, the private terminals?"

"Yes."

"Then she's probably still here in town. Did Remy have any other places around Charleston?"

"One of the daughters still has an apartment downtown. We're checking it out."

"Have our guy hack into the system and run her credit card. She could be at any of the hotels. She might be staying with a friend. Find her, dammit!"

"Yes sir!" Drummond said, leaving the room quickly and closing the door to Lacroix's office at his girlfriend's house. It was actually one of his, but he had been letting the woman stay here since he was first sent away.

She peaked her head in the door. "You done with business?"

Lacroix tried to calm himself and nodded for her to come in. She was dressed in a short silk robe, clearly with nothing on beneath. She came over and sat on his lap. "It's been too long, baby," she whispered in his ear.

He knew she had been seeing two other guys on the side while he was locked up, but at this point, tonight anyway, he'd let that pass and deal with it later.

He pulled her close. "Yes, it's been too damn long!"

Brenda Dellahousaye sat in the back of the plushly appointed sedan as her man, Broussard, drove down the darkened highway. They were on their way to Hilton Head to stay at the condo her deceased husband had purchased for their "wild child" daughter, Ophelia. Broussard had convinced her she needed to get away. Lacroix would not give up now. Her failed attempt at taking him out first had failed miserably and she was now the hunted.

Her mind raced with the high emotions that a near-death experience can muster. The bile rose in her throat as she remembered how close she had come to a painful end at the hands of Lacroix's killers. She hadn't had time to even think about next steps and how to respond. For now, survival was the most critical issue. Broussard had arranged for a small contingent of trained security men to come to Hilton Head and, hopefully, set up an impenetrable barrier that even Lacroix and his men would have trouble breaching.

The two dead men in the closet of her beach house bedroom had already been disposed of, so she would not have any issues with the local cops. Her daughter, Ophelia, was supposed to be on her way back to New York. Armed security had also been arranged for both girls, and both had been warned to be on high alert.

The sane twin daughter, Ida, who wanted nothing to do with the family business, had been very perturbed with this disruption in her otherwise normal life. Brenda had talked to her personally and pleaded with her to be careful. She felt she could trust Ida to be smart and keep alert for dangers.

Ophelia was another matter. When it came to good judgement, she had definitely been dealt a weak hand. The latest boyfriend, Streak... she cringed when she even thought about the loser, would be no help in keeping O safe. She would have to rely on Broussard's judgement and his hired team of former mercenaries and Special Forces operatives to keep them all alive until she could deal with Xander Lacroix.

As her stress and fear continued to fade, her thoughts became filled with how best to back all that her husband Remy and his father, Asa, had built. Xander Lacroix was a trusted associate in Remy's organization, but he was also an opportunist, and when Remy was killed, he moved quickly to take over most of the profitable businesses the Dellahousaye's had built.

When Remy had first abandoned her for the young, soon-to-be second wife, he had left her with a considerable settlement to live out the rest of her life in relative comfort. *'Relative' was the key word*, she thought as they continued south to Hilton Head. It wasn't long before the financial demands of the two twins, particularly Ophelia, and her own excessive lifestyle, began to put strains on the financial resources she had been left with.

With Remy gone, it became clear she needed to take the initiative to reclaim what was rightfully the Dellahousaye's and also secure her own financial future and those of her daughters.

She was concerned the remote island of Hilton Head was too far from the fight ahead in Charleston, but Broussard had convinced her otherwise. *We'll see*, she thought.

CHAPTER FOURTEEN

Sheriff Stokes was having a hard time keeping his temper under control with the murder suspect, Lando Tern. His deputy had cleaned and bandaged the man's broken nose, but he clearly needed to be taken to the hospital for a doctor to look at the damage.

Stokes' early discussions with the man had not gone well. Tern refused to answer any questions without a lawyer present. He had been given his Miranda Rights and allowed to call an attorney, but Stokes continued to press him for any knowledge of the dead girl in Dugganville. He steadfastly denied ever knowing her.

Tern did continue to threaten the department with all manner of lawsuits related to his injuries and detainment. He was definitely focused on Alex Frank and the assault in the bar he claimed nearly killed him. The old sheriff was grateful he had sent Alex home. This would not have gone well with the two of them together here in the interrogation room.

They had run the sheet on Lando Tern, and he was a habitual abuser of law and order. His list of past arrests, convictions and imprisonments was jaw-dropping. Numerous charges for drug offenses, assault, attempted murder, drunk driving... the list went on. *How in hell is this guy not in prison?* Stokes mused as he looked across the table at the man.

The bulky bandage across the bridge of his now displaced nose did not hide the bruising and swelling around both eyes. Splatters of blood were all over his clothes, his arms and hands, despite the deputy's best efforts.

One of the sheriff's men knocked on the door and stuck his head in. "The attorney is here."

Stokes nodded and said, "Let him in."

After a few brief formalities, Tern's lawyer informed the sheriff he would need time alone with his client. Stokes agreed and stood to leave the room. He looked down at the lawyer. "You need to know we have clear evidence your client has been in an affair with the married woman we found dead in Dugganville this morning. We also know he made inappropriate advances toward another married woman this afternoon at a nearby shopping center. There seems to be a pattern here that we will indeed get to the bottom of."

The lawyer listened as Tern whispered something in his ear. "Sheriff Stokes, again, I need time with Mr. Tern to fully understand the situation. From what little you've just told me, I assume you have no intention of holding my client or charging him with any crime."

"That would be an incorrect assumption, sir," Stokes said. "When you've had your little talk, we will definitely want to get more questions answered from your client.

The lawyer replied, "Mr. Tern clearly needs medical care."

"And he will get it as soon as we are through questioning him tonight," Stokes said. "We're on your clock now, counselor, so I suggest you get moving. I'm ready when you are."

Alex found Hanna sitting in one of the old Adirondacks chairs on the sand behind the house, dozing. He sat down in another next to her and took in the wide view of the dark beach and ocean. A bonfire a few houses down left a trail of smoke drifting by. He was glad to see Hanna didn't have a glass of wine on the arm of her chair. She had been very conscious lately about cutting back.

His cell phone chimed to alert him that a text message had come in. The sound caused Hanna to stir and start coming back from her nap. He looked at the screen. It was from Pepper Stokes. *Tern has a lawyer. We're not making much progress. You sure about this affair with the Combes woman?*

Hanna said, "Welcome back," her voice drowsy. "You okay?"

"I'm fine," he answered, knowing in truth he was far from it. He had almost gotten himself fired on his first day on the job. He had seriously injured a potential suspect in a murder trial, let alone a gangster who would likely be seeking revenge.

Hanna got out of her chair with a few moans from stiff muscles. She came over and sat down on his lap and put her head on his shoulder. "I appreciate you defending my honor, Deputy Frank."

He wrapped his arms around her and pulled her closer. "This guy is bad news."

"I know, he totally creeped me out today," she said, wiping the hair away from her face. "Do you still think he killed that woman in Dugganville?"

"Pepper's got him on ice right now. We'll see what he learns tonight."

"Why do you think he came after me?" she asked.

Alex thought for a moment. It could have been totally random. On the other hand, Tern was connected with the Dellahousayes and Xander Lacroix, who all had serious issues to address with both himself and Hanna. "We'll find out," he finally said.

He texted back to Stokes. *Gilly is a good source.*

Pepper Stokes came back into the interrogation room when he was told Lando Tern's lawyer was ready to proceed. It was past midnight now, and he was anxious to get this over with.

"Sheriff Stokes," the lawyer began before he could even sit down, "we're going to file a criminal complaint against your deputy who assaulted my client tonight."

Stokes knew this was coming. "Don't waste your time. This guy didn't tell you there are multiple witnesses who say he threw the first punch."

The lawyer looked over at Tern, who just kept staring back hard at Stokes.

"Let's get down to business here," Stokes said. "We have a very reliable source who tells us, Mr. Tern, that you *do* know the deceased, Ally Combes, and that you've been having a romantic affair with her for some time. Now, you can continue to deny this, but lying to me now is not going to help your case down the road. How long you been seeing her?"

Tern hesitated, looked over at his lawyer and then leaned back in his chair. "Guess I do remember seeing her a few times. I hang out with a lot of women, Sheriff. Hard to keep 'em all straight."

"You must be quite the player, Mr. Tern," Stokes continued. "When was the last time you saw her?"

"Not sure. Maybe a couple of weeks ago."

"Where were you last night?"

"Lots of places... down at the Shamrock, mostly. Got home around 11."

"You happen to go into Dugganville last night?" Stokes asked.

Tern seemed to ponder the question, then said, "Not that I recall."

"Not that you recall," Stokes repeated. "Anybody can vouch for your time at the Shamrock?"

"Bartender there. Name's Gilda."

"You make a habit of approaching women in parking lots, Mr. Tern?"

"Don't know what you're talkin' about."

"Sure you do. You came on to a woman down at the grocery store this afternoon. Is that how you meet all your women?"

"Wife of your deputy, you mean," Tern fired back. "Asshole nearly killed me. I was just trying to help her with her bags."

"Yeah, right," Stokes replied, shaking his head in frustration. "Look counselor, it's late. We'll pick this up in the morning. Your client is free to go. Mr. Tern, we need you to stay in town where we can find you. Write down your address and cell on this pad for me." He pushed it across the table.

"We're still going to file that complaint in the morning," the lawyer said.

"Be my guest!" Stokes replied. "Mr. Tern, let me give you some advice. We find you anywhere near the woman you accosted earlier today or give my deputy any trouble, and I will personally haul your ass back in here."

Tern started to protest, but his lawyer grabbed him by the arm to silence him.

"We're done here," Stokes said. "Get the hell outta my sight!"

CHAPTER FIFTEEN

Senator Jordan Hayes took his coffee strong and black. He savored the first sip as he sat in a coffee shop in downtown Charleston. There were two other customers at a table across the room, a single barista behind the counter. His hand shook as he tried to take another drink from his cup. He was not looking forward to this meeting.

The call from Xander Lacroix had come in late last night. He insisted they meet this morning. Hayes had protested about meeting in public, but Lacroix had made it very clear he was not open to other options.

He had done *work* for the Dellahousaye family for many years and was close to the deceased patriarch, Asa. Working with Remy after the old man's passing had been easier as the man had a front of legitimate businesses to shield scrutiny of their more nefarious pursuits. The relationship had been very profitable.

Soon after Remy's demise, Lacroix had reached out to continue the "consulting" work on behalf of his newly acquired businesses. The actual nature of the work was more of influence, using Hayes' connections to resolve issues and create new opportunities. Again, he had been compensated handsomely. The fact that he was also doing work for Lacroix's chief rival now, Brenda Dellahousaye, seemed a minor inconvenience for Hayes.

Lacroix would certainly be unhappy to learn of that connection and the fact Hayes had worked on her behalf to try to block Lacroix's release granted by a corrupt judge here in South Carolina. But such was the delicate nature of his firm's work, he mused, as he waited for Lacroix to arrive.

He had his driver and security man just outside in the car, but he wasn't necessarily concerned about any physical danger meeting with the gangster, but more in what the man was going to ask him to do.

The bell on the door chimed and Hayes looked over to see Lacroix's man come through first. He took a quick scan of the place and then turned to inform his boss it was safe to come in.

Hayes stood and greeted his client, offering him the other seat across the small table. Drummond went to the counter to order coffees.

"Morning, Senator," Lacroix began as they shook hands. The gangster was dressed elegantly in a well-tailored blue suit, a crisp white shirt and red and blue striped silk tie. His hair had obviously been freshly styled.

"Welcome back to the world, Xander," Hayes said.

"Thank you. It was quite nice waking up this morning in a real bed with no bars on the windows."

"I can only imagine," Hayes said, holding his coffee cup with two hands to keep from shaking as he took another sip. "What can I help you with?"

Lacroix leaned forward and glared into Hayes' eyes. "First, it pained me to learn you were working behind the scenes to expose the judge who granted my release."

Hayes blanched and felt a rush of fear sweep through him.

"Don't worry, Senator," Lacroix whispered, "it's business. I understand."

His words did little to comfort Hayes, who placed his cup down before he spilled the whole drink.

"I was also not surprised to learn you were working on behalf of Brenda Dellahousaye."

Hayes put his hand up in protest, but before he could reply, Lacroix said, "Again, Senator. It's just business. But, I do need your help and I'm sure you'll be willing to do so." He paused while Drummond handed him a cup of coffee and then moved over to sit a few tables away, staring menacingly at the ex-senator.

"Anything, Xander." Hayes managed to say without choking.

"I'm sure you know Brenda and I are having a little disagreement.'

"A disagreement?"

"Let's not get into the details," Lacroix said. "I need to speak personally with Brenda, and she seems to have disappeared. I thought you might be able to help me find her."

"Disappeared?" Hayes replied, thinking through his last conversation with her. He realized he was in a precarious position with both clients at this point. "She's not at either of the homes?" he asked, buying time, trying to think through how best to respond.

"Her cell phone has apparently been turned off, too."

"That's certainly odd."

"I know you speak frequently with Brenda. I thought you might be able to help track her down. We have some serious business to discuss."

I'm sure you do! Hayes thought. "I did speak to her a couple of days ago, Xander. I thought she was here in South Carolina, out at the beach house."

Lacroix shook his head. "We thought she might be visiting one of the daughters. Any idea where the two of them are residing these days?"

Hayes thought for a moment. He knew he would have to comply with Lacroix's request. To do otherwise could prove very dangerous. "I hear Ida is up in Boston at school."

"Yes, we know where to find her there," Lacroix said. "And the other crazy one?"

"Well, I know she has a place here in Charleston, but I think she's living up in New York right now. I've visited Brenda and Ophelia down at the girl's place in Hilton Head. Those would be the only other residences I can think of."

Lacroix's attention perked-up. "Can you tell me where in Hilton Head?"

Hayes gave him the name of the condominium but couldn't remember the unit number.

"You've been very helpful, Senator. Thank you!" Lacroix said, standing to leave. "Let me give you some advice, Jordan."

"Certainly."

"I think it would be in your best interest to terminate your business relationship with Mrs. Dellahousaye. The conflict of interest is very concerning to me."

Hayes swallowed hard but tried to appear calm in his practiced manner. "Of course, Xander," he managed to say, standing to shake the man's hand. He watched as the gangster and his goon left the shop. He sat back down and took a long drink from his coffee, his hands starting to shake so hard he spilled half of it down his white shirt and tie. *Damn!*

CHAPTER SIXTEEN

Alex walked into the *Andrews Diner* on the main street in Dugganville. He'd grown up going there with his parents and brother. He was greeted by the proprietor, Lucy. She came up and gave him a warm hug, then stood back.

"My, aren't you handsome in this new deputy get-up!"

"Enough, Lucy. How you been?"

"Great, son. Missed you around here. Heard you're married now and staying up on Pawleys. Good to have you back close."

"Thanks, Lucy."

"The usual?"

"Sure," Alex said with a smile, then walked over and took a seat in an empty booth. Lucy brought over a cup of steaming coffee. "You heard about Ally?" she asked.

"That's why I'm here," Alex replied. What's everybody saying?"

"Alex, I knew the girl pretty well. She used to come in a lot, working across the street at the hardware. Always was such a nice girl. Then, about a year ago, it was like night and day. The few times I did see her back here, almost didn't recognize her. Looked like she'd been through hell and back."

"What do you think happened?"

"Some folks think she got into drugs. She started seeing this bad dude who's tied up in all that. Felt so bad for Boyne."

"You get a name of this guy?" Alex asked, picking up his coffee cup and taking a first sip.

"Lanny or Lando something, I think."

"You ever talk to Boyne about all this?"

She thought for a moment. "He sits at the counter most days for lunch," she said, motioning behind her. Been pretty quiet these past few months. Everyone's been talking about this affair Ally's been having. Boyne's been trying to keep his head down."

"How bad is this drug stuff getting around here, Lucy?" he asked.

She shook her head in disgust. "Lot of young people getting hooked early. Hear the high school is just a mess of drugs and overdoses. A couple kids have died. It breaks my heart."

"Any idea who else is involved with this Lando guy?"

"I hate to say it, Alex, but word is, Boyne Combes is hip deep in all of it."

Alex nodded, thinking about his old friend.

"Let me go check on your eggs," she said. "Be right back."

The bell hanging on the door rattled and Alex looked up to see his father walk in with his wife, Ella. Both got a big smile on their face when they saw him. They came over and gave him a hug before sitting in the booth to join him.

"Small world," Alex said.

"Small town," Ella replied.

She looked remarkably well put together, Alex thought, for so early in the morning. She and the Skipper were typically out late over at *Gilly's* most nights.

"What brings you back to town, boy?" Skipper asked.

"Workin' on the Ally Combes case."

"Just a damn shame," Ella said, as Lucy walked up with two more cups of coffee.

"Already got your order goin'," Lucy said. "How you been, Ella? Still puttin' up with this crusty ole shrimper?"

Ella laughed, reaching for her coffee with hands dappled in age spots and nails painted bright peach.

Skipper said, "Get the hell back in the kitchen and make sure my eggs are done right. You hear me, woman?"

Lucy walked away chuckling.

"You got any idea why she ended up under that tower yet?" Skipper asked.

"No, a couple of leads, but still trying to sort it out."

Ella said, "Why in the world would she be up there in the first place?"

"Used to go up there and make-out when we was kids," Skipper said.

"With who?" Ella demanded and then elbowed him in the ribs.

Skipper looked away out the window, shaking his head.

Alex lowered his voice and leaned across the table. "I'm hearing Boyne's caught up in a new drug ring operating around here. You getting wind of that, Pop?"

He nodded. "Hear he's about to lose the hardware to the bank. Must need the cash."

"You ever hear of a guy named Lando Tern around here?" Alex asked.

Both Skipper and Ella shook their heads *no*. Skipper said, "I'll ask around with some of the boys."

"Thanks, Pop. How you two doing?" Alex asked. "Haven't seen you since the wedding, Ella."

"Besides your old man giving me more gray hair every day, just fine," she replied.

Alex couldn't help but laugh as he looked back at her deep red dyed hair.

Ella said, "You heard Adrienne's back in Florida?"

Alex nodded. "Hope they work it out for Scotty's sake."

"He's a good kid," Skipper said, turning back toward the door to the kitchen. "Lucy! Where the hell are my eggs?" He looked down at the ugly scar on the top of Alex's left hand. "How you doin' with that?" he asked.

"Still some pain now and then. Haven't got all the mobility back yet.

"Glad you put them sonsabitches in the ground!" Skipper growled.

Alex left some cash on the table and got up to leave after they had all finished their breakfast. "My treat today."

"Thank you, son."

"Thanks Deputy!" Ella said with her big bright smile.

Alex was halfway to the door when I man walked in he didn't recognize. He was a hard-faced man, deep wrinkles and sunken eyes beneath a shaved head tanned and scarred by the sun. He was walking by to go out when the stranger said, "So you're the guy who took my job."

Alex turned in surprise. "Excuse me?"

"You're the one Pepper brought in when he canned my ass."

"Who are you?" Alex asked, still puzzled.

"Name's Ingalls. I suggest you watch your back, rookie."

Alex turned and squared off with the man. "You got something to say, get it out."

"I was you, I'd be looking for a new career opportunity, fast."

"I'm not going anywhere," Alex said, defiantly, looking over and seeing Skipper watching the confrontation with a glare as if he was about to step in. Alex held up a hand to suggest he stay put. "Pepper tells me you were running with a bad crowd."

"None of your business, rookie," Ingalls said, then moved on to take a seat at the counter.

"Right," Alex said to himself as he watched the man move away. He nodded to the Skipper that all was okay and then tipped his hat as he turned to leave.

Alex walked into the Combes' Hardware. He saw Boyne standing at the cash register helping a customer check out. He came around and waited until the customer left the store. Combes saw him approaching.

"Hey, Alex," he said tentatively.

"Morning, Boyne. You got a minute?"

Combes looked around the store and yelled to another man to take the register. "Let's go out back."

Alex followed him through the store and then out the big open door to the storage area and garage. They came out on the alley along the river and started down toward the docks. The morning sun had burned off the low fog. The dark current moved slowly toward the bay and ocean. The alley was heavily shaded with tall trees, and gulls flew past over the river in random chaos, screeching at each other. The commercial docks up ahead were half-empty with fisherman and crabbers and shrimpers out for the day.

"You got any word on Ally yet?" Combes asked. The man's voice was shrouded in deep sadness.

"Couple leads I wanted to ask you about," Alex said as they continued along. "I think you know a man named Lando Tern." Alex noticed his step falter a bit.

"Yeah, I know him."

"I know this is tough, Boyne, but I hear he was seeing your wife."

"Seeing my wife...?" Combes repeated, then, "you mean screwing her?"

"Hey, I'm sorry..."

"No, it's okay," Combes broke in. "Actually, no, it's not okay!"

Alex watched him stop and look out over the river. His face was drawn and his eyes watered, near tears. "It's my fault, Alex."

"How's that?"

"Tern was in the store. We were doing some business. Ally came by and I introduced them to each other. Later in the day, I come around a corner and this guy is back making moves on my wife."

Alex thought about Tern and Hanna. His right fist clenched, and he still felt the pain in his finger joints from the punch he'd thrown into the man's face. "What kind of business?" he asked.

Combes looked back at him, wiping away the moisture in his eyes. "What?"

"What business were you doing with Tern?" Alex asked again.

He hesitated, his eyes looking down, then said, "Just another salesman. Can't remember what he was pitching."

"It was drugs, wasn't it, Boyne?"

They stared at each other for a few moments, then Combes said, "Don't know what you're talkin' about."

Alex said, "Let me be straight with you. Word is you got mixed up with the Lacroix crime family and the drug ring operating out here. You gonna look me in the eye and tell me I'm wrong?"

Combes turned and started walking back to the store. "I got nothin' more to say."

Alex followed along. "I can bring you in, Boyne. We can sit your ass down in front of the sheriff and have this out. We've been friends a long time. I wanted to give you a chance to be upfront with me."

"Like I said, got nothin' more to say!"

"Boyne, wait," Alex said, reaching for his friend's arm. "I want to find out what happened to Ally."

"The bastard killed her, Alex!"

"You mean Tern?"

Combes nodded, the tears coming freely now, streaking down over his flushed face. "This has been going on for a long time. He got her hooked on something, not sure what, but I hardly knew her anymore."

"I'm sorry, man," Alex said.

"She'd been going out most nights, not coming back sometimes for a couple days. Always said she was staying with a friend, but she knew I was on to the whole thing. I just kept trying to get her some help, but she wouldn't listen."

"Look, Boyne, we're turning the screws on the guy. You can help us."

Combes started walking again, shaking his head. "Can't do it, Alex."

"Why not? Don't you want to help us take this guy down?"

"You know these guys," Combes said, "I'll get my ass thrown off that tower next."

"How deep are you in with Tern and Lacroix?"

Combes hesitated, then turned back again. "We talkin' friends here or official business?"

"I want to help you, Boyne."

"I'm probably gonna lose the damn store, Alex. I'm so far behind with the bank, don't know how I'll ever get caught up."

"So, you've been working on the side with the Lacroix outfit?"

Combes took a deep breath and wiped his hand across his tear-stained face. "They been runnin' shipments up the river here. I've been helping with distribution inland." He paused and let out another deep breath. "I don't want to go to jail, Alex."

Alex stared at his friend then looked away as an old crab boat drifted by in the river, the noisy outboard leaving a trail of smoke behind on the water. He turned back. "Let me talk to Pepper."

"He'll want me to testify?"

"I imagine."

"They'll kill me, Alex!" Combes pleaded. "You know these guys!"

"Not if we take 'em down first," Alex said.

Combes seemed to ponder Alex's promise. "You gotta help me with this, man."

"I'll do everything I can," Alex said. "I need to get Pepper in on this."

They kept on along the river, back to the hardware store. Boyne Combes said, "You remember the night that guy took a cheap shot at you in the regionals, broke your leg at the goal line?"

"Still remember the pain if that's what you mean," Alex replied, remembering the cool Friday night on the football field at Dugganville High School. The injury ruined any chance he had at a college scholarship, though there weren't any strong schools looking at him, anyway.

Boyne continued, "And you remember I took that sonofabitch's head off. Got thrown out of the damn game."

They kept walking awhile in silence, then Alex responded, "I got your back, Boyne."

CHAPTER SEVENTEEN

Hanna got out of her car at the law office and reached back for her bag. When she turned, she almost screamed. A man stood no more than two feet away. His face was heavily bandaged across the nose, his eyes nearly swollen shut. It took just a moment, but she recognized the oily swept-back hair and realized it was the man who had accosted her the previous day at the grocery store.

This time, her first reaction was anger, not fear.

"Hello, pretty lady," Lando Tern said.

Hanna moved closer. "I don't know what you think you're doing, but I'm not up for your nonsense!" She started to walk up to the office entrance. Tern grabbed her by the arm. "Just wanted to apologize, ma'am."

"Let go of me!" Hanna shouted, pulling her arm away.

"Let me at least buy you a cup of coffee to say how sorry I am."

"Are you kidding me?" Hanna said, backing away.

Another car pulled into the parking lot and one of her partners got out. Kelly Waldron was a tall and well-fed ex-marine who stayed in shape at age 57 with martial arts classes every other day.

"There a problem here?" Waldron said, walking up behind Hanna.

She waited for Tern to reply, but he stood there silent, staring back at her with a broad smile revealing large white teeth.

"Think you need to leave, son," Waldron said, no question about the threat in his voice.

Tern looked back through slits for eyes. "Don't want no trouble, sir. Just stopped by to pay my respects."

"You need to leave, now!" Hanna demanded.

Tern started backing away, but before he turned to go to his car, he said, "See you down the road, pretty lady."

Hanna was furious. She was tempted to run over and throw another hard right into his broken nose. She was sure Alex would approve. *Alex! This is not going to sit well,* she thought as she watched Tern get into his Cadillac and drive away.

She was tempted not to tell him, but when Alex called mid-morning to ask about plans for the weekend with Skipper and Ella, Hanna filled him in on Lando Tern's earlier visit. She expected to hear him explode in anger on the other end of the line. Instead, there was just silence.

"Alex?

"Sheriff Stokes and I made it very clear to this guy there would be no repeat of yesterday's scene. He hasn't been released two hours and he's in your face again?"

"I took care of it," Hanna said, trying to calm him. "I just thought you should know."

"He didn't hurt you?"

"He grabbed my arm..."

"What!"

"I told you, I took care of it."

"Hanna, I need to go," Alex said quickly.

"Please don't go off on this guy again!" she pleaded, but he had ended the call. She sat back in her office chair and turned to look out the window across the marshes to Pawley's Island. Several thoughts crossed her mind. *How does he know I work here? How long has he been following me? What does he want?*

Alex ended the call with Hanna, his blood pressure rising in anger. He was standing to go share the latest on Lando Tern with the sheriff when Deputy Gallagher walked in. He glared back at Alex as he walked over to his desk.

As he was sitting down, Gallagher yelled across the floor, "Hey, rookie, hear you got your ass sued first day on the job. Nice work!"

A couple other deputies sitting nearby chuckled. Alex ignored the comment and walked back down the hall to Pepper Stokes office. He knocked on the door frame. "Got a minute?"

Stokes waved him in. "Close the door and have a seat." The old sheriff looked like he hadn't slept all night, which was close to the truth. "What you got?"

Alex shared the information on Lando Tern harassing Hanna again.

Stokes shook his head in disgust. "Why am I not surprised? This guy has no moral compass. We got a serious problem here, Alex."

"Exactly," Alex replied. "I want to bring him back in."

Stokes frowned. "Not a good idea. Don't want you trying to take this guy's head off again. Already got your ass in a sling over last night."

"There's more, Pepper," Alex said. "I stopped by to see Boyne Combes down in Dugganville this morning. He confirmed Tern was running around with his wife. Sounds like he got her hooked on something and she just went off the deep end with this guy."

"And now he's makin' a run at Hanna," Stokes said.

"And I don't think this is random, Pepper," Alex continued. "He followed her to the grocery store yesterday. He knew where she worked. He's obviously got an agenda."

"An agenda?"

"The guy is working for Lacroix. I think they're trying to get back at me through Hanna. This is gonna go south fast, Pepper."

"Okay, I'll get Tern back in here this morning," Stokes said.

"There's more," Alex said. "Combes told me this morning he's been helping Tern and the drug ring down there. They're bringing product up the river from offshore, and Boyne's been helping with distribution."

"He just told you that?" Stokes asked in surprise.

"We're old friends. He needs help. The business is going under, and he was desperate. He's willing to help bring down Lacroix and this whole bunch if we can protect him."

"You think he deserves a deal?"

"I do."

Stokes rubbed his hands through his scruffy hair and leaned back. "He's puttin' a big target on his ass."

"He really wants to take Tern down. He's convinced he killed his wife."

Stokes nodded, considering the situation. "Alright, bring Combes in. Let's have a talk. I'll have one of the others get on Tern, get him back as well."

Alex stood to leave. "Oh, I ran into your old deputy, Ingalls, over at Lucy's this morning. Didn't seem real pleased to see me."

"He's a total prick, Alex, I told you that. And he's hip-deep with this Lacroix mess. You be careful with this guy."

Hanna ended a conference call with a client and got up to go to the kitchen for another cup of coffee. Her cell buzzed and she reached for it on her desk. She looked at the screen and saw "Unknown Caller." She let the call go to voicemail and left the phone on her desk to go get the coffee.

When she got back, there was a chime on her cell that the caller had left a voicemail. She sat down and pressed the button to listen. As soon as she heard the voice, a chill prickled across her skin.

"Hello, pretty lady. Just wanted to say how nice it was to see ya this mornin'. My, you looked good in that blue dress."

Hanna stopped the message. She was tempted to delete it she was so angry, but she pressed the screen again.

"Don't see why we couldn't be better *friends*, ma'am, if you know what I mean. See you down the road, pretty lady."

Hanna ended the message and slammed the phone down. A sense of dread rushed through her. She felt violated just having this guy's call on her phone. For all she knew, he could be watching her office right now. She got up and walked to the front of the office and looked out across the parking lot and as far as she could see in both directions. There was no sign of Tern's Cadillac.

"Everything okay, Hanna?" her partner Waldron said, walking up behind her.

"That creep just left me a very unpleasant voicemail." Just saying it made her cringe again.

"Alex should run this guy in," Waldron said.

"He's already on it," Hanna replied, looking down the street again. "He's the one who rearranged the guy's face last night."

"Didn't seem to do much good."

"No... no it didn't," she said, trying to regain her composure.

"You let me know if he comes around again."

"I will, trust me."

"None of my business, Hanna, but do you carry?"

"A gun?"

"Yeah."

"She shook her head. "Never had the urge."

"Might be a good time to reconsider," Waldron said, then smiled and walked back down the hall.

CHAPTER EIGHTEEN

Brenda Dellahousaye sat on a deeply cushioned chair on the lanai of her daughter's condominium in Hilton Head. She'd gotten no sleep the past night and the coffee was doing little to help her feel better. The condo looked out over a marina filled with big sailboats and cruisers and then off across the marshes behind the island.

She was still trying to stop from shaking after her near-death experience the previous night when Lacroix's men had been only moments from killing her. Her emotions swung hard between total fear and unchecked rage.

She reached for her phone and pressed for a number in her contacts. In a few moments, she heard the voice of the former senator, Jordan Hayes.

"Good morning, Brenda," came Hayes' tentative greeting.

She didn't bother with pleasantries. "I need help, Jordan! Lacroix tried to kill me last night!"

"What!" There was silence for a few moments, then, "Brenda, this is way beyond the scope of our..."

She cut in, "You're not listening!"

"What do you expect me to do?" Hayes protested.

"You need to lean on the right people to put this guy back in jail, dammit!" she demanded.

She heard Hayes take a deep breath on the other end of the call. "Brenda, please, I can't…"

"Jordan! Listen to me! This has to stop. I'm afraid for my girls as well. You must know someone in the Justice Department or the FBI who can take this guy off the streets."

"Let me see what I can do," Hayes said, tentatively.

"That's not good enough, Jordan!" she yelled into the phone. "I have enough on you to leak to the Feds. You'd never work another day in Washington if you don't end up in jail."

"Brenda, please," Hayes pleaded. "Let me get back to you."

Ophelia Dellahousaye had a long-standing commitment to doing exactly the opposite of what her mother asked her to do. The frantic request for her and her boyfriend to return to New York went in one ear and out the other.

As she sat in the deep-cushioned sofa in the living room of her condo in downtown Charleston dressed in shorts and a sleeveless t-shirt from a Rolling Stones concert, she thought about the threat from some of her father's past associates. She knew her father, Remy, was tied up with some bad actors, as was her grandfather, Asa. None of that had really affected her life previously, other than the money and lifestyle their illegal gains had provided.

The boyfriend, Streak, was passed out in the bedroom. *One joint too many as usual,* she thought.

She stood and walked to the wall of windows, looking out across the skyline of Charleston and the Cooper River beyond all the way out to the Atlantic. The majestic Ravenel Bridge spanned the river heading across to Mt. Pleasant. A steady stream of cars headed in both directions and looked like ants from this far away.

Her phone rang and she looked at the screen. It was her mother calling, presumably from Hilton Head. She sent the call to voicemail. *Not in the mood!*

She was walking back to the kitchen to get a Diet Coke when a knock at the door surprised her. *Who in hell even knows we're here? Probably the building super.*

She opened the door and stepped back in surprise at the sight of two men dressed all in black with masks hiding their faces. Both had guns in their hands, pointing at the floor. The guns had silencers screwed onto the barrels.

Ophelia backed away slowly as they came in and closed the door behind them.

"Where's the boyfriend?" the man on the right asked in a low, menacing voice.

She gestured to the closed bedroom door. The other man went over and pushed through the door, coming out with a groggy Streak a few moments later.

"What do you want?" Ophelia managed to say, her body trembling, her voice breaking.

"If you do what we ask, we won't hurt you."

"What the hell..." Streak mumbled, his red plaid boxer shorts hanging low, his bare upper body revealing a canvas of tattoos.

The man holding his arm turned and slapped him hard across the face, knocking him to the floor. "Shut-up!"

Ophelia screamed out, "Please, don't hurt him!"

"Get up and get dressed!" the first man said. "Where's your mother, Ophelia?"

She was struggling to control the fear that was coursing through her veins. She thought she might be sick, and she staggered, trying to steady herself.

"Where's your mother!" he yelled out again.

"I don't know..." she whispered, barely able to speak.

He came toward her slowly, the gun coming up, and pointed now directly at her forehead. "I won't ask again."

She kept backing up until she hit a low coffee table and fell over, knocking over a half-empty cup of coffee before falling to the floor.

"Get up!"

She pulled herself up slowly, holding on to the couch for support. He came over and held the silenced gun barrel firmly against the middle of her forehead.

"She's in Hilton Head... my place on the island down there."

He lowered his arm, pointing the gun at the floor again and then turned to his associate. "Get him dressed."

Streak managed to get to his feet, rubbing his jaw, his long hair hanging down in his face. Ophelia watched as he shook his head, seemingly confused, probably still stoned, she thought. He started toward the bedroom, then turned quickly and rushed toward the man who hit him. "You asshole...!"

The man caught him square on the side of the face with a vicious punch that sent him to the floor again, then leaned over him, lifted the silenced weapon, and put one round into his forehead. The gun made only a soft spit of a sound.

Ophelia screamed as she saw the bullet explode into Streak's head. He lurched back on the floor and then fell still, his eyes open, pleading and then vacant.

CHAPTER NINETEEN

Alex pulled into the drive of Hanna's law office in the Charleston County Sheriff's cruiser. He saw her silver Honda parked in the shade of a group of tall pines. He reached for the sack of sandwiches he had grabbed at a shop up the road and walked over to the front entrance. The heat was building to its mid-day crescendo. Two crows in the trees squawked down at him. He looked out across the marshes behind the office and saw a man and a young boy on the deck of a flats boat casting for redfish in one of the channels.

The receptionist greeted him and let him into the back-office hallway. He watched Hanna look up and smile tentatively as he walked in. "You doin okay?" he asked, coming over and laying the sandwich bag down on the small round conference table.

"Been better," Hanna said, walking around her desk and falling into his outstretched arms. They held each other close, then she lifted her face to kiss him. "Thanks for lunch."

They sat across from each other. Hanna pushed at a few buttons on the screen of her phone and then played the voicemail Lando Tern had left for her.

Alex felt his temper flare again as he listened to the irritating southern drawl. He suddenly lost his appetite and pushed his chair back. "That's enough! I need to go find this guy."

"No, please don't!" she pleaded. "You're in enough trouble."

He took a deep breath to try to calm himself. He looked across at Hanna's face and could see how upset she was. "Pepper already has a team out to round him up."

"Good, let them do it."

"I think this is all part of Lacroix's plan to get back at me now that he's out of prison."

"You really think so?" she replied.

"Tern knows too much about where you're going, where you work. This is all orchestrated."

"What do they want?"

"Lacroix probably wants my head after we took him down and sent him away."

"He could have done that a long time ago."

Alex thought for a moment, then said, "I think this is personal with Lacroix. I think he wants to personally get back at me."

"You mean kill you?" she said, her eyes wide in disbelief.

"I don't know, but we have to assume the worst." He pulled out the sandwiches and pushed one across the table to Hanna.

She brushed the hair back behind her ears, then closed her eyes and sighed. "When are we going to be through with the Dellahousayes and all their crazy people?"

"They're like rats on a ship. You throw one overboard and ten more come out."

Hanna took a small bite from the sandwich as Alex unwrapped his. She swallowed and said, "My partner here, Kelly, asked if I carry a gun. Do you think I need to?"

Alex shook his head. "More often than not, it's more dangerous having a gun with you than carrying it for protection in the rare case you might need it. You've spent enough time shooting at the range with me, so you know how to handle a gun, but I'm just not sure."

"This Tern guy really scares me," she said.

"I know. We'll try to get him out of circulation as soon as we can. Hopefully, they've already picked him up." He thought more about protection for Hanna. Lando Tern may well have killed Ally Combes and his past record was troubling. "I've got the 9mm you've shot before back at the house. I'll go by and bring it back for you before I go back on duty."

"Thank you," she said with a note of relief.

Alex came out of the beach house after retrieving the gun. As he walked over to his cruiser, he saw a note stuck under the wiper blade. He pulled it out and read... *Tell the pretty lady hello for me. LT*"

His anger flared and he looked around in all directions for any sign of Tern. He walked down the drive toward the main road. It was empty in both directions. As he walked back, his senses were on high alert. *Is Tern watching from cover somewhere?*

He unbuckled the strap over his service revolver. When he got back to the cruiser, he pulled out his phone and called Sheriff Stokes.

"Whatta you got, Alex?"

"Any news on Tern?" he asked, knowing the answer.

"Sent the boys out to Asa D's old fish camp. Someone's staying there, but no sign of our guy."

"Well, he's been here at Hanna's beach house in the past few minutes. Left a note on my window while I was inside."

"Let me try to get both bridges covered before he gets off the island," Stokes said. "Not sure who's nearby. I'll call you back."

Alex put his phone in his pocket and looked around the property. Tall pines and live oak shaded the heavy wild scrub all around the clearing. He walked around to the front of the house and down to the beach. A few sunbathers were gathered to the south but no sign of anyone else.

As he turned back to the house, he stopped short. There was a woman sitting up in the dunes on one of the Adirondack chairs around the fire pit. Her red hair was striking, and it seemed strange she would be wearing a long dress on such a hot day. "Hello!" he yelled, starting up to the house. He looked to the north again quickly to see if anyone else was about. When he looked back, the woman was gone.

He started running slowly in the loose sand, looking in all directions for any sign of the woman. Nothing. He suddenly remembered Hanna's description of the ghost she'd been seeing these past years, her great-grandmother. *What was her name... Amanda?*

He had never doubted Hanna's retelling of her encounters with the spirit. She had shown him the picture of her and the family up in the dining room taken in the 1860s at the old plantation house over near Georgetown. He had just never expected to see her. He got up to the fire pit, and again, there was no sign of the woman.

He looked down at the arm of the chair. Someone had left a blossom from the hydrangea bush up near the house. It was one of Hanna's favorite flowers. He reached down and grabbed it, taking it with him as he started back around the house.

His thoughts returned to Lando Tern. *This has got to stop!*

As Alex drove back to Hanna's office, he kept thinking about Xander Lacroix. *If the man wanted revenge, why is he playing around with Tern and all his nonsense? Why doesn't he just come after me?*

When he walked back into Hanna's office, she ended a call and put the phone back on her desk. He reached out and handed her the hydrangea bloom.

"Well, how thoughtful," she said, smiling up at him.

"It's not from me."

A worried look came across her face.

"No, not Tern. I saw Amanda," Alex said.

"What?"

"Your grandmother."

"You're kidding."

"I went back to the house to get something, and she was sitting down at the fire pit. By the time I got up there, she was gone. She left this for you, I imagine."

Hanna stood and came around the desk. "Isn't it incredible?"

"I never doubted you, but to really see her," Alex said.

"Let me get some water for this." She walked out and came back with a bowl of water and put the flower in it on her desk.

"I think she's my guardian angel," Hanna said.

Alex considered whether to worry Hanna anymore about Tern and the note he'd left. She needed to know. "Tern was at the house. He left this note." He handed it to her. As she read it, he took the 9mm semiautomatic out of his backpack and laid it on Hanna's desk.

She looked up, shaking her head. "This guy is really creeping me out."

He slid the gun across her desk. "I think you need to keep this with you. There's a magazine with fifteen rounds. Leave it loaded and keep the safety on, of course. You know how to handle it, but please be careful."

She handed the note back to him. "Pepper had any luck tracking him down?"

"Sounds like he may be staying out at the Dellahousaye fish camp." He watched her cringe as he knew the dark memories she had from a terrible night at his father's camp when they had taken down Asa Dellahousaye. "I need to get back on duty. Obviously, you'll call if this guy shows his face again."

"You'll be the first to know," she said, managing to smile.

He hugged her and kissed her on the cheek as he turned to leave. "I'm glad you have a guardian angel," he said.

"I have two," Hanna replied.

CHAPTER TWENTY

Alex drove back into Dugganville and pulled up in front of *Combes Hardware*. Inside, he was directed to the back and found Boyne Combes at his desk sorting through paperwork. He looked up when Alex knocked on the door jam.

"Hey, Alex."

"Spoke with the sheriff," Alex began. "He wants to talk to you."

Combes hesitated. "You guys can really protect me?"

Alex tried not to let his doubts show. "We need to move quickly here and get these guys off the street. Can you come down to the department this afternoon?"

Combes looked at the calendar on his desk. "I can be there in about an hour."

"I'll meet you there."

"Thanks, Alex... I think."

The fire tower loomed above the tall trees in the park. Alex pulled the cruiser to a stop in the parking area nearby and got out. Tree frogs screeched in the cover above and the smell of diesel gas and old fish drifted up from the river. The crime scene tape was still fluttering in the light breeze at the base of the tower. He walked over and looked up at the tall structure of crisscrossing stairs and the lookout platform at the top.

He went through the fence gate and walked around the base of the tower again, scouring the grass for any signs or evidence that might have been missed. He knew the forensics team had scrubbed the area, but he just needed to try again. He came around to the steps and started up.

Halfway up, he rose above the tree line and could see out across the broad panorama of woods, marshes, and the river out to the ocean. The sky was a deep blue with high clouds drifting slowly above. Three more flights and he reached the top of the stairs. Walking out onto the platform, he paused to catch his breath. He held onto the iron rail to steady himself, looking down cautiously. He had never been good with heights and again felt the rush of goosebumps across the skin of his arms.

He turned and pushed open the door into the observation room. The air was stale and hot. Walking in, he moved slowly around the perimeter. The glass windows hadn't been cleaned in years, and several panes were cracked. He looked down at the old wooden desk and the stains they had seen earlier. *Have to ask Pepper what they found here,* he thought.

He came back out and looked down at the lawn below where Ally Combes had been found. He thought again about what they found in her hand. *Why is a woman with a condom in her hand jumping to her death?*

He started down the steps. Two flights below, he stopped to look out over the vista out to the ocean again before he got below the tree line. He reached for the rail and then pulled back when he saw a small spot of something on the rusted metal. He looked closer. *It almost looks like blood,* he thought. He made a mental note to also ask the sheriff if the investigators had found this.

He thought about it for a moment. If Ally Combes had hit the rail when she fell, it could be her blood. The more he considered the situation, it seemed unlikely if she had jumped to her death in a suicide attempt that she would have fallen this close to the stairs. But, if she had been pushed over the top rail, she may well have tumbled close to the tower steps and struck herself on the way down.

As he continued down, he looked for more blood traces but found none. Back on the ground, he walked over to where they had found Ally. He looked up to the top of the tower. He estimated she was about eight feet out from the top rail, a distance that seemed to make sense if she had jumped out to her death. But, if she had fallen more closely to the stairs and hit herself part-way down, it could have propelled her out and away. He would have to also ask Pepper if there was any other trauma, cuts or bruising that could have been caused by hitting the rail as she fell.

As he turned to go back to his car, another department cruiser pulled into the lot and parked beside his. Gallagher got out alone and started toward Alex.

"What the hell you doing?" he barked.

"Just following up," Alex replied, trying to push back his frustration with his fellow deputy.

"Pepper put me in charge of this!" Gallagher said, facing off with Alex now and blocking his way.

"Okay, what did the forensics team find?"

"None of your damn business, rookie."

Alex tried to remain calm. "I thought we were on the same team here, Gallagher."

"Don't need a rookie messin' up our investigation."

Alex was tempted to remind the man that he had considerably more experience with this type of investigation with his time at the Charleston PD and later with the FBI, but knew Gallagher was aware of this. Alex shook his head in disgust. "Guess I'll just have to share what I found here with the sheriff."

"What's that?" Gallagher demanded.

Alex managed a thin smile, then said, "None of your damn business."

He pushed past Gallagher and saw him glaring back at him as he got into his cruiser and pulled out of the lot.

CHAPTER TWENTY-ONE

When they pulled the hood off her head, Ophelia Dellahousaye squinted at the bright light and held her arm over her eyes. She had been in the back seat of a car for what seemed like hours. One of the men who had taken her, and shot her boyfriend, sat beside her and kept her lying flat on the seat so passersby couldn't see her. She had pleaded with them to let her go, but neither man spoke the entire way.

She was still trembling with fear, the images of Streak's death printed indelibly on her brain. One of the killers took her by the arm and pulled her away from the car. As her eyes adjusted, she saw a rustic old house ahead built up on stilts. The place was surrounded by heavy woods. A wide wooden stairway led up the front to a deck and the front door to the place.

"Do not think about running," the man said behind her. "There's nothing but gators and snakes for miles in any direction."

She looked past the house and saw a wide bay with brown water surrounded on all sides by a thick blanket of trees and scrub. There was a dock with a small boat tied up. There were no other houses or boats visible on or around the water.

The man pushed her up the steps. She stumbled and caught herself, scraping her hands on the worn wooden boards.

"C'mon, let's go!" the man demanded.

At the top of the stairs, he came around and opened the door to let her in. The second man followed them. The place was sparsely furnished. An old stone fireplace was set in against the wall to the right, a small kitchen to the left with an old wood table and four chairs. Windows around all sides let in some light, but the room was dark and musty smelling.

"Take her in the back bedroom," the last man said.

They both had put masks back on before taking hers off. He pulled her along now and back through a narrow door into a small room that had a twin bed with a bare mattress. There was one small window looking out at the dense trees and the marsh beyond.

"This will go much easier if you keep your mouth shut," he said before closing the door behind him.

Ophelia looked around at the grim setting, faded wood walls, and the floor dusty and littered with crumpled paper and other trash. She sat carefully down on the bed and tried to gather herself. *What is going on here? What do these guys want?*

She had been thinking about nothing else on the long ride from Charleston, other than Streak's gruesome death. She kept coming back to one conclusion. They were going to use her to get to her mother.

She had already revealed her location down on Hilton Head. She wondered if they had taken her, or worse, had she met the same fate as her boyfriend.

She got up and tried to walk quietly to the window, though several of the old boards squeaked as she stepped on them. She got to the window and looked out. There was no sign of help or human contact in any direction. She tried to lift the window, but it was firmly shut and wouldn't budge. She turned and looked around the bleak room and wondered if she would ever walk out of this house alive.

Brenda Dellahousaye's man, Carmen, closed the door to the condo behind him as he left her alone. He had just briefed her on the security precautions in place to prevent Xander Lacroix and his men from breaching their perimeter. It gave her little comfort.

She went into the kitchen and pulled a bottle of wine out of the refrigerator. She found the corkscrew in a drawer and opened the bottle, pouring a glass half-full. She walked back out to the living room and sank down into the soft couch. Through the sliding glass doors, she could see sailboats and cruisers tied up in the marina and the marshes surrounding the back side of Hilton Head beyond.

Her ex-husband, Remy, had bought this place for their daughter, Ophelia. She was supposedly going to work on her painting, and she opened a gallery to show her work, but it never made enough money to cover expenses. She ended up spending more time with a couple she met on the island who moved in with her.

She was holding out hope she would hear back from the ex-senator with news the Justice Department or the Feds would arrest Lacroix again. Hayes had seemed less than excited to help her, but she did have enough dirt on him to have him put away in Federal prison for the rest of his life. She loved leverage.

But she also knew that Hayes was as ruthless as they come and would do anything to survive. *Would he team up with Lacroix to take her out?*

Her cell buzzed in the kitchen, and she got up quickly to go check the call. The screen said, "Unknown Caller", but she felt compelled to answer.

"Yes," she said tentatively as she walked back into the living room.

There was silence for a moment, then a voice screamed out, a voice she knew too well. "Mama! I'm sorry! I'm so sorry!"

"Ophelia!"

A fear that only a mother could muster for her child swept through her.

Another voice came on the phone and calmly said, "Mrs. D, you've probably figured out we have your daughter."

"Don't hurt her!" Brenda yelled out. "I'll do anything!"

"Yes, ma'am, you will. You'll do exactly as we say."

"Anything!"

"Mr. Lacroix would like to meet with you personally."

"What?" Where?" she stammered in full panic.

"A car will be coming for you in a few minutes," the man said, his voice deep and assured. "Tell the goons to stand down. If they try anything, you will not see your daughter again. Am I clear?"

"Yes, of course.

In the background, she heard O scream out again. "They killed Streak! They killed him!"

Brenda felt her stomach lurch. She cursed herself for thinking she could take Lacroix on. "Please don't hurt her! I'll do whatever you want." She heard the call click off. "Hello! Hello!" She threw the phone down on the couch and it bounced and landed on the floor.

The sun was still high over the trees to the west. As the car she was riding in came around the private terminal at the small Hilton Head airport, she saw a jet parked with the door swung open and steps leading up. The man beside her in the backseat held a gun to her side and had not spoken a word since she had gotten in at the condo, nor had the driver.

Carmen Broussard and his men had indeed stood down when she explained what was happening. He tried to convince her to fight back, but she insisted she couldn't risk her daughter's life.

The car pulled to a stop next to the ramp stairs to the plane. The driver got out and opened her door. She looked at the man next to her and he nodded for her to get out. Her legs were weak from fear, and she almost fell when she tried to stand. The driver reached for her arm and pulled her up the stairs.

When she ducked her head to go inside the cabin of the jet, she stopped in surprise. Sitting in the first seat was the old senator, Jordan Hayes.

"Hello, Brenda."

Chapter Twenty-Two

Hanna looked at the time on her cell. She was surprised to see it was almost 4 o'clock. She called Alex and he picked up on the third ring.

"Hello, counselor," she heard him say. It had become one of their fond greetings.

"I just looked at the time and there's no way I'm getting home for dinner. I've got a court hearing in the morning and I'm nowhere near ready."

"Not a problem," Alex said. "I'm on my way back down to the department to meet with Pepper. We'll probably be there a good while.

"How's the Combes case coming?" she asked.

"I've got a lot to tell you," Alex replied, "but not now. I'm just pulling in."

"We'll catch up tonight."

"Are you there alone?" he asked.

"My partner will be here for a while. We'll make sure the place is locked tight if he leaves."

"Call when you're ready to leave and I'll come over."

"Not necessary," she said.

"Just the same, I'd feel better."

"We'll see how late it is. I'll call you later."

"Love you!" she heard him say before he clicked off.

When Alex walked into the Deputy's Room. Gallagher apparently wasn't back yet. In fact, no one else was back from patrol. The shift ended at five. He walked straight back to the hall to Sheriff Stokes' office. He found him looking through some evidence reports. He looked up when Alex filled his doorway.

"Come in. Take a seat," Stokes said.

"You get the report back on the Combes case?

"Sure did." He slid a stack of papers across the table to Alex. "Take a look."

"What about the stains on the desk up in the tower?" Alex asked.

"It appears Ms. Combes had intimate knowledge with someone of the male persuasion."

"On the desk?"

"Appears so," Stokes replied.

Alex tried to connect the random pieces of information. "So, Ally has sex with someone, walks outside and jumps to her death with a condom in her hand."

"Or was helped over the rail by her lover..." Stokes continued.

Alex cut in, "Or someone not very happy with how she had just spent her last minutes on the top of the fire tower."

"Like her husband," Stokes said.

"Who should be here any minute."

Pepper Stokes stood and walked to the file cabinet against the far wall. He opened the top drawer and pulled out a half-empty bottle of Jameson Irish Whiskey and a coffee mug with an inscription that read, *"Put up your hands!"* He turned to Alex. "Join me?"

"A bit early for me, Pepper."

Stokes poured a generous amount into the cup and put the bottle back before coming over to sit behind his desk again. "So, we're about to interview a man who can help us bring down the Lacroix drug ring, and he may also be the prime suspect in what's looking like a murder case."

Alex said, "I went back to the tower this afternoon, trying to get my head around what might have happened. Your star deputy, Gallagher, was there and not too happy about me sniffing around."

Stokes scowled. "Don't get me started. We get through this mess in Dugganville, I'll want your help in cleaning this place up."

The phone on the desk buzzed. Stokes answered and said, "Bring him back."

Alex and Sheriff Pepper Stokes sat across from Boyne Combes in a small interrogation room. The man was clearly nervous and agitated, sweat pouring off his forehead, his hands shaking on the table.

Stokes began, "Mr. Combes, I want to thank you for offering to help with our investigation into drugs being run through our county. Deputy Frank here has told me you have some involvement in that, correct?"

"Yes sir," Combes managed, his voice breaking.

"We are prepared to offer you a deal in exchange for your assistance."

"What kind of deal?"

"I've spoken with the County Prosecutor, and we are prepared to offer you immunity in the case if you give us your full cooperation."

Combes nodded his head, cautiously, considering the offer. "And what guarantees would I have?"

"I've got it all official and in writing here from the prosecutor's office." He slid the document across the table. Combes chose not to read it, staring back at the sheriff.

"These guys don't play around," Combes said. "They find out, and I'm a dead man."

Alex said, "We can secure you in a safe house until we take the whole network down."

"What about my store?"

"You'll need to have someone take care of that for a while, Mr. Combes," Stokes said.

Combes sat still, looking back and forth between Alex and Stokes. Finally, he said, "What do I have to do?"

Alex replied, "We need names, locations, schedules, everything you can think of. When's the next shipment scheduled?"

"Tomorrow night."

"Good," Stokes said, "that gives us a little time to put this all together."

"We'll want to take down as many of the players as possible right away," Alex said. "Where do we start?"

"You know the guy, Lando Tern. He runs the overall operation in the area."

"Will he be there tomorrow night when the shipment comes in?" Stokes asked.

Combes nodded. "Always has been."

"Who else?" Alex asked.

Combes outlined the full operation for the delivery and who would be there. Alex wrote it all down, then asked, "How can we tie this back to Xander Lacroix? I doubt he'll be anywhere near this place."

"No, of course he's been locked up."

"So how do we bring him in on this?" Stokes asked.

"Tern repeatedly refers to *Mr. X* and his gang down in Charleston," Combes said. "When you take him down, you'll have to get him to turn on Lacroix."

Alex noticed his friend was having a hard time even saying the name of Lando Tern.

The sheriff went through several more questions until he was satisfied they had enough initially for the drug bust tomorrow night. Then, he switched gears. "Now, Mr. Combes, there have been some developments in the investigation of your wife's death."

Alex watched the color drain from Boyne Combes' face. "What developments?" he asked.

"I apologize if this is a bit difficult for you," Stokes began.

Combes nodded, shifting in his seat.

"It appears your wife was having sexual relations with someone up in that tower the night she died."

Alex watched the man's expression closely. He just stared back blankly.

Stokes continued. "We'll have DNA evidence soon that should tell us with who."

Combes' face turned angry. "I've told you she was runnin' around with Tern!"

"We may be able to prove he was up there with Ally when we get the DNA report back," Alex said.

"How long will that take?"

"Hard to say," the sheriff answered. "Depends on how backed-up the crime lab is."

"Boyne," Alex began, "was Ally on birth control?"

"What? No, we were trying to have a baby... at least before she got hooked up with Tern and..." He didn't finish the thought.

Stokes said, "Again, we're sorry for your loss. We're doing all we can to track this guy down. We get Tern tomorrow night, we'll be after him in your wife's case, also."

Combes blew out a big breath of air, shaking his head. "Thank you, Sheriff."

CHAPTER TWENTY-THREE

Hanna locked the door to the law offices behind her and felt the warm wind off the marshes on her cheeks as she turned to leave. The shadows of the falling day lay across the parking lot. Her car was the last left in the lot. She searched for her keys in her bag as she walked down the steps and then across the lot.

Her thoughts were occupied with details of her court appearance in the morning for one of her clients. She found the keys and pressed the button on the fob to unlock the door to the Honda. When she got in, the air was hot and stifling. She started the old Honda and then rolled down all the windows and turned the AC on Max.

There was little traffic on the road out to Highway 17. She turned up the radio and one of her favorite country songs greeted her, ... *"I'm the crazy ex-girlfriend."*

The two-lane road was lined with heavy pine forest with an occasional clearing for a small farm or the occasional business. It was another mile out to the main highway and her turn south toward Pawleys Island.

Something caught her attention and she looked up at her rearview mirror. A car was coming up fast behind her. She looked to the side mirror, and as the car approached, she could see it was the grill of a big Cadillac... *Lando Tern!*

She accelerated to sixty and looked again as the car sped toward her. Her emotions flared. She was beyond fear with this guy's harassment. She was pissed!

Reaching over for her bag, she pulled out the 9mm semiautomatic Alex had left for her, clicking off the safety with her thumb. She left it in the passenger seat within easy reach. Looking up again in her mirror, the car was nearly touching her rear bumper. She could see Tern's face now. He was grinning at her, and then he waved when he could see she was looking back.

She increased her speed to near 70 and her pursuer kept pace. She was sure he would ram her at any moment. With the windows open, the rushing air was buffeting the inside of the car. Her pulse was pounding, and she gripped hard on the steering wheel with both hands.

Hanna looked ahead and the stop sign at Highway 17 was about a half-mile up ahead. The car suddenly lurched forward, and she gasped as Tern bumped her from behind. Looking back, she saw his leering face again as he fell back a few yards.

"Alright, enough, asshole!" She slammed on her brakes and felt the impact of the Cadillac from behind as he tried to swerve to avoid her. Her car lurched to the left and she struggled to keep it from veering off into the ditch. She hit the gravel on the far shoulder and the car started to spin, but she pulled back hard to the right and got control. She heard a crush of metal and breaking glass and looked back in her mirror to see Tern's car careening off the trunk of a big pine and spinning sideways before coming to a stop in the ditch, the car resting now at a precarious angle.

She slammed on her breaks and pulled to a stop on the right shoulder. She reached for the gun and jumped out, the adrenaline pumping through her veins. She was so angry, she felt her cheeks flush hot.

Tern's car was about 100 yards back and she started running. She held the gun at her side, facing down. Her mind was buzzing with anger. She couldn't see the man through the glare of the shattered windshield.

As she got closer, she slowed to a walk and started looking around the car for Lando Tern. She approached cautiously, raising the gun now and pointing it at the side door of the car. The driver's side window was open, and as she came alongside, she saw Tern slumped over, his head on the steering wheel. There was blood flowing from a cut on his forehead, leaking onto the bandages from the broken nose Alex had given him.

She hesitated for a moment, not sure what to do. She looked back at her own car and then in both directions up and down the road, but no one was approaching. She turned back in surprise when the man groaned and started to move. She came closer and aimed the gun through the window. "I don't know what the hell you're trying to prove...!" she yelled out.

Tern fell back against the seat and then touched the blood on his face. He looked at his bloody hand and then out at Hanna. "Hey, pretty lady."

"What's the matter with you?" she yelled again. She quickly took in the crumbled condition of the Cadillac. *It's not going anywhere.*

She looked back when Tern said, "You havin' a nice day, pretty lady?"

"What?" She couldn't believe what she was hearing.

"I could really use a drink," he said, reaching up to his bloody face again. "You wanna join me?"

Hanna started backing away. *This guy is truly crazy!* She saw him fumbling with his seat belt harness. She kept the gun pointing at the car but kept moving back toward the Honda. She turned and saw the crumpled back bumper of her own car, but knew she could still drive it.

When she looked back at the Cadillac, Tern was obscured by the reflection from the sun off the windshield. She pulled her phone from her pocket and quickly got to the screen for Alex's number.

She was at the Honda's open door when he answered the call.

"Hey, what's up?" she heard him say.

"I need help!" she said, looking back at Tern's car. He still wasn't getting out. She jumped into the Honda, slammed the door, and started driving away.

"Hanna! What's going on?"

"It's Tern!" she finally managed.

"Where are you?" Alex yelled out.

"He tried to run me off the road! I finally slammed on my brakes and ran him off into the trees."

"Where?" Alex demanded.

"Just down the road from my office. He's hurt."

"Get out of there!"

"I'm just driving away," she said, looking back in her mirror, still no sign of the man. She heard him yelling at someone nearby.

"Hanna, we're on the way! I want you to come straight here to the department. I'll tell Pepper you're coming.

"He's a maniac, Alex!" she said.

"Just get away from there." She could tell he was running and breathing heavily. "Pepper, Hanna's on her way here now!" she heard him yell. "I'm going after Tern!"

Alex pressed the accelerator down on the cruiser and saw the speedometer edge above 80 as he raced down Highway 17. He had his emergency lights on and siren wailing. Cars were pulling over to get out of his way. Up ahead, he saw the familiar shape of Hanna's silver Honda approaching. He opened the window and waved as he passed. She managed a tentative wave back as she pulled onto the shoulder of the far lane across the median.

He looked back in his side mirror and saw her pull back out and continue on toward the Sheriff's Department. He had to slow for an approaching red light but pressed on the emergency horn to alert approaching drivers. He managed his way through the intersection and then sped up again.

In two minutes, he turned right onto the road to Hanna's office. Immediately, he saw Tern's wrecked Cadillac up ahead on the left, no sign of the man around the car. He skidded the cruiser to a stop on the gravel shoulder just short of the other car across the road. He pulled his weapon as he got out.

There was heavy front-end damage to the big Cadillac. The windshield was shattered, and he couldn't see in. He approached cautiously from the side, his gun pointed out at the open driver's window. "Tern, put your hands where I can see them!"

He inched closer and then was far enough to see into the car. There was no sign of the man. He checked to make sure there was no one in the front or back of the car. He turned quickly and surveyed the area. The woods were heavy on both sides of the road.

A car approached from the east and slowed as it passed, staring at Alex with his gun out, the wrecked car, the sheriff's cruiser on the far side, emergency lights still on. Alex signaled for the man to keep moving.

He walked around the car, going down into the ditch it was resting in and then along the far side. Again, no sign of anyone. He looked again up and down the road and then behind him into the woods. *No one.*

Coming back around to the driver's side open window, he peered in. Right away, he saw blood on the white steering wheel and white leather seats. Hanna said he'd been hurt. *Where the hell is he?*

He holstered his weapon and went back to the cruiser. He called into the dispatcher on the radio, asking for backup and a wrecker for the car. Reaching for his cell, he called Hanna's number. She picked up on the second ring.

"Did you find him?" she asked.

"No, he's gone."

"Gone!"

"No sign of him... except for the blood in the car. He must have run off, or he may have flagged down another driver."

"Ohmigod," he heard her say. "I hope he doesn't hurt anyone else!"

"You get to the department yet?"

"Just pulling in."

"Wait there," he said. "I need to get an alert out to the local hospitals and other cops in the area. I'll be back there as soon as I can. Stay there with Pepper."

"Okay, I will," Hanna said. "Please be careful!"

CHAPTER TWENTY-FOUR

As the plane accelerated down the runway and then lifted off effortlessly into the sky now tinged with pink clouds in the fading light of day, Brenda Dellahousaye looked across at Jordan Hayes.

"You mind telling me what the hell you're doing here?" she demanded.

"I was going to ask you the same thing," Hayes replied.

"It's Lacroix," she said. "He's got Ophelia!"

Hayes pursed his lips, then said, "His goons picked me up before we flew down here."

"What's he doing?"

"I don't know," Hayes replied, staring back, his face grim with concern. "Where have they taken your daughter?"

Brenda shook her head. "They called me, and I heard her yelling out for me. They've killed her boyfriend!"

Hayes gasped, the color draining from his face. "I assume they took your phone, too."

She nodded. "Where's he taking us?"

"I have no idea, but I'm not looking forward to finding out."

Ophelia lay back on the dirty mattress, the rusted box springs creaking beneath her. Images of her boyfriend's violent death haunted her thoughts. She placed her right arm over her face trying to shut out the memories.

She heard the door creak open and sat up quickly. One of the men, still dressed in black with his face covered, came in. He walked toward her, and she pulled her feet up onto the mattress, pushing back against the wall.

"Please, don't hurt me!" she pleaded. "I'll do anything! What do you want?"

The man stopped a few feet away from the bed. She flinched when he said, "Where is your sister?"

"What?" she said, suddenly confused.

"Where is your sister, Ida?" he demanded.

She thought for a moment, trying to sort out what was happening to her. *What do they want? Where is Mother?*

"Where is she?" the man asked again through the slit in the mask across his mouth.

"She's at school... up in Boston."

"Where?" he said, pulling a long knife from a scabbard on his belt.

"No, please...!"

"Give me the address!" He twirled the big knife in his hand.

Ophelia felt like she might be sick. "Please, no..."

"Tell me where she is?" he said again, placing the knife near the side of her face.

She gave him the address to Ida's apartment.

Without comment, the man turned and left the room.

Her heart was pounding. Her stomach lurched as the nausea flared. She moaned and lay over on her side on the bed. *Ida! I'm so sorry!*

Ida Dellahousaye was coming home from her last class of the day. She was meeting her boyfriend for dinner in an hour and needed to shower. She walked along past the brick row houses on the busy street, cars parked in every available space. A man approached, walking a little terrier dog. She stood to the side to let them pass and then kept on toward her apartment building, just up on the next block.

She thought about the phone message she had received earlier from her mother. She had tried to call her back twice, but there was no answer. *Please be careful! About what?* she thought as she came up to her building.

A car door opened suddenly in front of her. She stepped aside in surprise as a man got out and then grabbed her by the arm. Before she could react or yell out, he pulled her into the back of the car.

"What are you doing?" she screamed as she fell across the seat. She struggled to sit up and pushed away. "Leave me alone!"

The car pulled away and she saw the man driving up front. She tried the door, but it was locked. "Stop the car!" she yelled.

The man next to her calmly said, "This will go much easier, Ms. Dellahousaye, if you just calm down."

"Who are you?" she demanded. He was a bulky man, seeming to take most of the back seat. He was dressed in black jeans and a black t-shirt. His face was obscured by a black ball cap and pulled low over sunglasses. She looked up and the man in front was dressed similarly. "Where are we going?" she yelled out. "Stop the car!"

"Like I said," the man replied, "you need to calm down."

She lashed out and slapped him hard across the face. His hat flew off, and the glasses were knocked askew.

Before she could hit him again, his right hand flew up and the back of it caught her across the jaw, knocking her back against the window of the door. Pain flared through her face, and she cried out.

"Settle the bitch down!" she heard the man in front demand.

Then, suddenly, there was a gun pointed at her nose. She pressed back against the door. "No...!"

"I won't ask again," the man hissed, straightening his glasses back in place and reaching for his hat with his other hand.

She heard him click off the safety of the black gun pointed at her face. *Dear God!*

"I thought you were going to take care of this, Jordan!" Brenda said, pointing at the ex-senator, her voice desperate and rising.

"I made a few calls," Hayes replied. "I was waiting to hear back from two different people in the Justice Department and one at the Bureau when these guys burst in and grabbed me."

"So, someone must have tipped off Lacroix," she said.

She watched him nod back. She was surprised how *diminished* he looked. *The once-powerful senator was now afraid for his life*, she thought.

She was afraid, too... for herself, for her daughters.

CHAPTER TWENTY-FIVE

Alex got out of his cruiser in the parking lot of the Sheriff's Department outside Dugganville. He looked over and saw Hanna's silver Honda parked in the next row. His anger flared when he saw the crumpled rear bumper.

Tern had simply disappeared. Two other units had responded to the crash site and spread out looking for the man. The car was being towed in for further inspection. Alex was still concerned that Tern had commandeered another vehicle and some other motorist may be in danger.

He was walking toward the building when he heard, "Hey, rookie!"

He turned and saw Deputy Gallagher coming towards him from another cruiser. He ignored the man and kept on to the entrance.

"Hey, Frank!"

Alex turned again, "What do you want?"

"Heard your missus got sideways with this Lando guy."

"Right."

"How'd she get mixed up with that dude?"

Alex was quickly losing what little patience he had. "She isn't *mixed up* with him! He's been stalking her, and we're dealing with it."

"Sounds like you're not dealing with it very well," Gallagher said, an irritating smile spread across his face."

Alex had had enough. He grabbed Gallagher by the shirt front and threw him back against the car they were standing beside. "I don't have time right now to deal with your bullshit! But, trust me, I *will* find time soon!" He pushed away.

"Looking forward to it, rookie," Gallagher said, straightening his shirt.

Alex found Hanna sitting in Sheriff Stokes' office. He had apparently stepped out. She stood when she saw him come in.

"Did you find him?" Hanna asked.

He shook his head. "Seems to have just disappeared. We've got people out looking, but I'm afraid he got another car."

"I hope he didn't hurt someone."

"We've got alerts out to the area hospitals. There was a lot of blood in his car. He must be injured pretty badly." Hanna blanched, and Alex pulled her into his arms. "You okay?"

She didn't answer at first, her face buried in his neck. She leaned back. "He bumped me from behind and nearly killed me. I slammed on my brakes, and he veered off into the woods."

"The car looks nearly totaled," Alex said.

"I pulled the gun on him."

"Really!"

"He was still in the car, unconscious at first. I didn't know what he would do. He had a bad cut on his face. When he started coming to, I thought I better get out there. That's when I called you."

Pepper Stokes walked in. "Nothing yet on finding this guy," he said, coming around his desk and sitting down. "Hanna filled me in. We need to get this idiot off the street!"

"Hopefully, he'll show up at our little rendezvous tomorrow night," Alex said.

"What's that?" Hanna asked.

Stokes said, "Our man Tern seems to be heading up a new round of drug running here in the county. We've got a lead on taking them down. I'm bettin' he'll be there."

Alex reached around Hanna's waist and said, "How about I get you home?"

Hanna tried to keep her hand from shaking when she poured the wine into a glass on her kitchen counter. She was still off kilter from her run-in with Lando Tern.

Just one, she thought as she took the first sip.

Alex came down from upstairs, where he had just changed out of his uniform. He was barefoot with a blue polo shirt over blue jean shorts. He sat down beside Hanna at the kitchen counter. She offered him a glass of the wine, but he declined. "I may have to go back out tonight if anything else turns up."

"What are we going to do about this maniac?" Hanna asked.

"If we don't take him down tomorrow night, I may have to pay a visit to our friend, Mr. Lacroix, down in Charleston."

"You really want to go anywhere near that killer again?" she said, her voice hesitant and pained.

"This has got to stop, sooner or later," Alex said. "If we get Tern, there's going to be someone else. I doubt Lacroix is going to stop coming after me."

"You hungry?" she asked.

He shook his head.

"What's happening in the case over in Dugganville?"

Alex stood and walked to the sink, reached for a glass in the cupboard, and poured some water. He stood opposite the island from Hanna. "Some new evidence today makes it look pretty clear this was no suicide."

"Really!"

"Ally Combes was up in that tower with someone... probably had sex up there before she fell to her death."

Hanna said, "Seems like an odd place to climb all the way up there."

"Who knows what people are into or why," Alex said. "We found a condom in her closed fist after the fall, not something you'd expect if she jumped to her death as a suicide attempt."

Hanna scowled, trying to make sense of the situation. "Who do you think she was up there with?"

"This Tern guy is the prime suspect. We know they were having an affair."

"But, why would he kill her?"

He shook his head. "We don't know. Maybe it was an accident. Maybe she was getting too close to this drug operation Tern is running."

"What about the husband?" she asked. "Jealousy is a powerful thing."

"We're sure looking at that, too," Alex said. "Just doesn't seem to fit the man I know. We've been friends for years. He told me they were trying to have a baby before she got tangled up with Tern."

"This is so sad!" Hanna lamented.

"Hey, it's been a crazy long day," Alex said. "I was thinking about a swim."

Hanna looked surprised. "Do you know how cold that water is?"

"Exactly!" Alex replied.

"I'll watch," she said, reaching for the bottle of wine and her glass. So *much for just one.*

Alex took the first step into the cool Atlantic water and almost changed his mind. The sun was down now and lights in the houses up and down the beach sparkled back along the dune line along with a vast canopy of stars above.

He had made a fire in the pit up by the house, and Hanna was waiting for him there. He looked back and could just make out her form in the light of the small fire.

He took another step out into the ocean and then made up his mind he was just going to do it. Several more steps out, he dove into a low swell coming at him. The icy water cut into him like a thousand knives, but he took a strong stroke to dive deeper. It was even colder along the bottom. When he came up, he gasped for air and yelled out, "Whoa!"

He dove back under again, and this time, the water seemed more tolerable. He took several strokes before coming up again, breathless and shivering. These evening swims had always been a great source of escape for him, washing away the troubling events and stresses of the day.

He turned back to the beach, chest-high in water now. Another swell caught him from behind and almost knocked him off his feet. He steadied himself and continued on toward shore.

When he looked up to the house, he was surprised to see that Hanna wasn't sitting in the Adirondack chair where he had left her. He started walking more quickly, pushing hard through the deep water, alarms of concern going off in his brain. He reached shore and started running. "Hanna!"

The sand was loose, and it was difficult making his way. His breath was coming hard as he rushed toward the house. He yelled out again, "Hanna!"

He looked in both directions and up on the deck along the back of the house. No sign. He tried not to let his panic cloud his judgement, but in the back of his mind, he couldn't block the thought that Tern had come back for her.

As he reached the fire pit, he stopped short, trying to catch his breath. "Hanna!"

His heart leapt when she came out on the back porch and answered, "What, I'm up here."

"Ohmigod," he said. "I thought…"

"What?" Hanna asked as she walked to the steps, a bowl of popcorn in her hand.

He managed to collect himself enough to say, "Nothing, I just... no, it's nothing." He didn't want to alarm her again about Tern.

"No dinner tonight," she said as she came around and sat back on the chair, "but I thought this might do." She reached the bowl out to him.

He held his hand up and said, "No, I'm fine right now."

He sunk down into the chair beside her, his heartbeat slowing and breath flowing more freely.

"How was the water?" Hanna asked.

He suddenly realized he was cold and reached for the towel he'd hung on the back of the chair. "Like bathwater!" he lied.

"Right."

CHAPTER TWENTY-SIX

The next morning came much too soon.

Hanna woke to the sound of birds squawking outside the windows. The familiar pounding in her head from too much red wine the night before caused her to pull the pillow over her head. She moaned softly.

She felt Alex stir beside her, but kept the pillow pressed tightly down on her face, hoping that somehow it would chase away the dull ache in her brain.

"Morning, hon," she heard him say in a groggy voice.

Pulling the pillow away, she squinted at the bright morning light coming in from outside. She rolled over and pressed herself into Alex's arms and legs, her face on his bare chest. "Sorry I woke you," she said.

He leaned over and checked the time on his cell phone on the nightstand. The alarm went off just as he picked it up and Hanna flinched in surprise.

"What time is it?" she asked.

"7:30."

She remembered her court case and all she had scheduled today. Pulling away, she pushed back the sheet and blanket and turned to sit on the side of the bed. She felt his hand rubbing her back through the old Duke t-shirt she was wearing. "I need to get in the shower."

"You go first," Alex said, pulling the covers up over his head.

She found the aspirin in the medicine cabinet over the sink and shook out two. She couldn't remember if she'd taken any the night before. *Sure doesn't feel like it,* she thought, rubbing her temples and then rinsing the pills down with a drink from the faucet. The hot pounding of the water from the showerhead against her forehead offered some early relief, and she closed her eyes and felt the water splash into her and drip down her body. *Just one glass,* she thought... *right!*

Alex came down the stairs dressed for work in his uniform. He came over and kissed her on the cheek before turning to pour a cup of coffee.

"Love a man in uniform," Hanna said, smiling back at him.

"Should have kept my old Army stuff."

"No kidding!" Hanna said.

He saw that she was dressed for work in blue slacks and a white silk blouse. The jacket to the suit hung behind her on the chair. A half-empty bowl of cereal sat on the kitchen island.

"Time for breakfast?" she asked.

"No, I need to run." He went over to the pantry and came out with a protein bar. "Want one?"

"No thanks," she replied. "You ready to go then?"

He nodded.

"I'll walk out with you."

Alex watched as she collected her purse and the leather bag she kept all her files and laptop in. He followed her out the front door of the house and locked it behind them. He was just turning to go down the stairs when he heard Hanna yell out, "Alex!"

He glanced down quickly and saw her standing beside her car. There was something on the front windshield and he watched as she stepped back and away. "What is it?" he said, running now.

As he came up, she reached out her arm to stop him. He was close enough now he could see the lifeless carcass of a raccoon splayed out across the glass. The face of the animal was frozen in the last painful moment of death, its teeth bared and eyes wide in terror.

"Oh, Alex! It's awful!" Hanna whispered.

He immediately thought of Lando Tern as he looked around the perimeter. Nothing else seemed out of place. He walked up and pulled the animal off the car by the tail, then threw it into the bushes. "I'll bury it later," he said, flaring in anger.

Gallagher glared at him as he walked up to his desk. Alex returned the favor as he reached for a pile of phone messages. On the top was a note from the sheriff, "See me."

He walked up to Stokes' open office door and was waved in. "Whattaya got, boss?" he asked.

"Armed car-jacking called in last night after you left," Stokes began, gesturing to a chair for Alex to take a seat. Woman pulled up to a stop sign about a mile from the wreck. Guy who fits Tern's description comes out of the woods with a gun. Leaves her there, no injuries."

"Thank God for that," Alex replied. "Any sign of the car yet today?"

"No, but we have all state and local agencies on full alert to find it."

Alex said, "The asshole came by Hanna's again last night."

"You saw him?" Stokes asked in surprise.

"No, but he left a calling card on Hanna's car."

"What?"

"Dead raccoon. Probably picked it up on the road out to the island somewhere."

Stokes looked out the window in disgust. "This guy truly has a screw loose."

"Ah, yeah!" Alex replied. "Nothing more from the crime lab on the Combes case?"

"No, probably won't hear for a while on that DNA trace. Always takes forever."

Alex got up and walked over to the window and leaned against the sill, looking back at his boss. "What are you thinking about the drug bust tonight?"

"I called in the Feds. DEA needs to be involved with this," Stokes replied.

"I thought you wanted to take Tern and the rest of this outfit down," Alex said, sarcastically.

"I know," Stokes agreed. "If there's a way to screw this up, bring in a bunch of damn Feds!"

"Who you working with?"

"Man named Rohrsuch."

"Yeah, I know him," Alex said. "Good man."

"He wants the FBI in on this, too. Your old friend, Will Foster and the DEA guy will be out here a bit later to put this together."

"Not sure I'd call him a friend," Alex replied, pushing back all the negative memories about his last days with the Bureau. Foster had actually gone to bat for him to help save his job, but it wasn't enough. The D.C. brass had had enough of his "cowboy" antics, as they had called it.

"Who you gonna use here from the Department?" Alex asked.

"Not sure. Let's wait til we talk to the Feds."

"I sure don't want Gallagher out there if he has to cover *my* back," Alex said.

"We're gonna need everyone in on this," Stokes said. "We'll deal with Gallagher down the road."

Hanna came out of the courthouse with her client. They conferred for a few minutes on the sidewalk about next steps on the case. The judge had ruled in their favor on the motion she had filed in the divorce proceedings for this woman who lived near her on the island, but there was much more ahead.

The woman hugged her and left. Hanna started down the street to her own car and immediately started scanning the area for any sign of Lando Tern. She had to leave her gun with the guard in the courthouse before she could enter, but she had it back in her bag now.

She walked up to her car and grimaced as she looked at the damage to the rear-end. She'd had the car nearly ten years and it almost seemed like part of her. There just never seemed to be any good reason to spend money on a new car even though her former husband could certainly afford it and was always after her to trade in the old Honda. He didn't think it looked good for her to be driving around town in a late model used car he could barely fit in. Ben always had a nice European sports car of some sort. His last was a Jaguar that had been sold at auction after his death to help pay her bills. The Porsche he had bought for their son, Jonathan, had been spared. She couldn't bring herself to take away the kid's pride and joy.

There was no sign of Tern or any other threats. She got in and pulled out into traffic. A couple of miles down the road, she saw the turn to Dugganville and, on a whim, steered the Honda off in that direction. She hadn't seen Alex's father or crazy wife, Ella, since the wedding at the beach. She had come to truly love them in these past couple of years, and with her own father so far away in Atlanta, Skipper and Ella Frank were her closest family.

As she drove down the narrow highway out to Dugganville, she thought about her father, Allen Moss. He was still hard at work as senior partner at his law firm in Atlanta. He should have retired years ago. He certainly didn't need the money and his heart was on its last legs, she feared.

His second wife, Martha, was still a constant thorn in her side. The latest episode with the woman had been a tearful late-night phone call from her complaining about her father's work schedule and neglect of their marriage... *and on and on.* Hanna had little patience for the social-climbing, arrogant, self-centered...! She stopped herself and saw her turn coming up ahead.

As she came into town, she saw the looming structure of the fire tower pushing up through the trees. The sad thought of the poor woman who just died there continued to gnaw at her. As she drove by the park, she saw the yellow crime scene tape staked out on the lawn at the base of the tower. She had to look away.

Driving through the old downtown strip, she always marveled at the quaint little village that her husband had grown up in. She tried to imagine young Alex hanging out here with his friends. Then, she thought of the crazy ex-wife, Adrienne. *Thank goodness, she's back in Florida!*

Driving along the river now, she looked out at the shrimp boats and charter fishing boats lined up along the wharf. A block further on, she came up to Skipper Frank's house, a low white ranch nestled up in the woods on a small incline across the street from the river. Skipper's own boat, the *Maggie Mae,* rested on the calm waters at a pier across from the house. The big outrigger booms were pulled up and the old nets hanging to dry.

She pulled her car up on the shoulder in front of the house and started up the narrow stone walk to the front screened porch. Ella came out before she could get there, the door slamming behind her.

"Hanna, damn, woman! It's so good to see you!"

Alex's new stepmother wrapped her in an enormous hug and then kissed her on the cheek. "Hi Ella, just in the neighborhood and wanted to stop by to say hello."

Ella stood back. "My, you look good, girl!" she gushed.

"Had a court date today. Have to get dolled up every now and then," Hanna replied.

"Come on in! Got time for a drink?" Ella said, pulling her by the arm.

When they walked into the kitchen, Skipper Frank looked up in surprise.

Hanna was equally taken aback. He had a big bandage wrapped around his head with a spot of blood showing through on his forehead.

"Hanna!" The old shrimper got up slowly and came over to embrace her. "How you doin' darlin'?"

"I'm fine, but what happened to you?"

"The old coot lost his balance and fell off the *Maggie Mae* yesterday," Ella said.

"That's enough, woman!" Skipper snapped.

"Hadn't been for his deckhand, he'd still be out there like shark bait floatin' on the salt," Ella said, clearly agitated with her spouse.

"You okay, Skipper?" Hanna asked."

"Just a bump on the noggin. Nothin' serious."

"Damn near killed yourself, you old fool," Ella scolded. "He wouldn't call Alex. Didn't want to worry him."

"Get you a drink, honey?" Skipper asked, walking to the refrigerator. "Got a pitcher of Bloody Mary's goin'. Takes the edge off this headache!" He rubbed at his bandage.

She thought of her own morning hangover headache and said, "No, thanks, a bit early for me."

144

"How 'bout some lemonade?" Ella asked.
"Perfect!"

The three of them sat in the shade at the redwood picnic table on the back porch behind the house. Hanna noticed the Skipper was struggling with his balance when they came out. She knew Alex was really concerned about his mental faculties, but this seemed something new. *Maybe it was just the bump on the head*, she thought.

Ella took a drink from her Bloody Mary, then began, "You heard about the murder here in town? Alex tell you about it?"

"The Combes girl, yes, he did."

"Damn shame," Skipper said. "Known the Combes family since I was a kid. Alex ran with Boyne Combes his whole life before he moved away for the service. Sounds like the wife started runnin' with a bad crowd."

"Is Alex still working on the case?" Ella asked.

Hanna nodded. "He can't tell me a lot, but they might have a suspect." She chose not to get into her problems with the prime suspect, Lando Tern.

"No way Boyne kilt his own wife!" Skipper declared.

"Like I said, Alex can only tell me so much."

Ella changed the subject, "I was just telling Alex we need to have you two out for dinner, maybe this weekend."

"Love to," Hanna said. "You just tell me what we can bring."

"Saturday night, then?" Ella said. "How 'bout 6:00?"

"We'll be here unless Alex has something come up with work. I'll check on his schedule and we'll let you know."

Skipper said, "You seen your Grandmomma's ghost again lately?"

Hanna had shared her past encounters with Amanda Paltierre with them. They both had their own stories of close encounters with spirits. Skipper claimed the previous owner of the *Maggie Mae,* who died in an accident out on the boat years ago, still haunted the vessel. "The old bastard'll sneak up on me when I least expect it!" he had said.

"You just drink too much whiskey when you're out there!" Ella said. "You imagine all sorts of nonsense."

"Whatever!" the Skipper said in resignation.

Hanna said, "Well, yes, I did have another moment with her just the other day. And Alex saw her yesterday, down at the beach. She left a flower for me on the chair by the firepit."

"I'll be damned!" Ella said.

"I think she's my guardian angel."

"Well, I sure hope so," Ella answered before taking a big swallow from her drink.

CHAPTER TWENTY-SEVEN

Xander Lacroix watched the plane touch down as he sat in the back of his car on the tarmac of the small municipal airport, just north of the city of Charleston. A flock of gulls on the end of the runway flushed as the plane powered down and turned onto the taxiway and back toward the hangars.

His man in front, Cal Drummond, said, "What's the plan?"

"Tell the pilot I'm coming onboard."

The plane pulled to a stop about 50 yards away from the car, and Lacroix listened as the engines slowed and then stopped. Drummond got out and opened the door for him. The Carolina heat met him full force as he got out and started toward the plane. He watched the door open, and the stairs lowered. He patted his chest reflexively and felt the gun he carried in a shoulder holster under his sports jacket.

He climbed the steps slowly, cherishing the moment that was about to come. As he came into the plane, he saw Brenda Dellahousaye and Jordan Hayes standing in the aisle. Their faces were struck with fear when they saw him.

"Sit down!" he demanded, pulling the gun and holding it in his right hand pointed at the floor. Both of his captives quickly sat across from each other, facing him.

"Xander..." Hayes began.

"Shut-up!" Lacroix yelled.

"You've got this all wrong," Hayes persisted.

"What have I got wrong? That you tried to block my release from prison? That you were calling in the Feds to get me sent back? Did I get that wrong, *Senator*?"

Brenda broke in. "Where's my daughter?" she said, her voice cracking and weak.

"I'll deal with you in a minute," Lacroix said, his eyes still fixed on Hayes. "You politicians are something else. Your hand is always out. You'll take money from anybody with no sense of loyalty or commitment.

"Xander, please..." Hayes pleaded

"No! People think we're the crooks. We're just running a business. It's you assholes supposedly running this country. You could care less about your constituents. It's about money and power. How *powerful* do you feel right now, *Senator*?" Lacroix said, raising the gun and pointing it at Hayes' face.

Hayes shrunk back in his seat; a hand extended as if that would prevent a bullet from taking his head off. "Please, I beg you!"

Lacroix started laughing. "This is priceless. I wish I had this on video to share with all the people in D.C. who cringed in fear when the great Senator Jordan Hayes walked into the room or loomed over them in a hearing in the committee chambers. What a joy that would be!"

"Xander, I want to make this right," Hayes pleaded.

"Oh, we're going to make it right." He turned to his man, who was standing behind him in the aisle. "Take him out to the other car."

Drummond squeezed by and pulled Hayes up from his seat and then pushed him past Lacroix and off the plane.

Lacroix turned back to Brenda Dellahousaye, then sat across from her.

"Where is Ophelia?" Brenda stammered, her hands clenched and shaking in her lap.

"We have Ida, too," he said, calmly. He watched her eyes open wide in panic. "Yes, I have both your dear twin daughters."

"Please, they have nothing to do with this!"

"No, but you do, Brenda," he said, leaning across the aisle. She pressed back against the window. "I'm not out of jail two minutes and you try to have my head blown off."

She didn't respond.

My associates tell me you have an intricate plan coming together to steal everything I've worked for."

"It was never yours!" Brenda yelled. "Asa and Remy..."

"Shut-up!" he screamed. "I worked my ass off for those two, nearly got killed on multiple occasions for them. Went to prison. And what have you done? Sat back in your big houses and cars and did nothing! Nothing!"

She was crying now, the tears flowing freely down her cheeks. "Xander, please don't hurt the girls," she whimpered.

He watched in delight as his rival shook with fear in front of him. "I can't let this sort of thing go unpunished, Brenda. It's bad for business. What would people think of me?"

"Just let them go!" she pleaded.

He stood and put the gun back in the holster under his coat. "Get up!"

"What are you going to do?" she cried out, wiping at the tears on her face.

"I won't ask again."

Drummond came back on the plane. Lacroix turned to him and said, "Get her in the car!"

CHAPTER TWENTY-EIGHT

Alex parked in the alley along the river behind *Combes Hardware*. He walked through the back door. One of the workers came up, an older gentleman dressed in jeans and a blue vest over a white polo shirt.

"Can I help you, sir?"

"I need to speak with Boyne," Alex said.

"Let me go find him."

Alex looked around the storage area of the store and then checked his phone for any messages or emails. Combes came in after a minute.

"Alex."

"Morning, Boyne. Need a minute."

"Let's go outside," Combes said.

They started down along the river and Alex asked, "You got anything more on the delivery tonight?"

He watched his old friend stop and look in both directions, then turn and say, "Boat's coming in around midnight. They'll pull up here behind the store. They use my truck there to transport inland, down to Charleston."

Alex looked at the old panel truck with *"Combes Hardware Since 1952"* painted on the side. "How many guys come in with the shipment?" he asked.

"Usually three."

"Will Tern be here?"

"Always has in the past."

"You're sure about the timing tonight?" Alex asked.

"One of Tern's guys called me this morning."

Alex looked down the alley and then back in the other direction at the back of the line of old brick buildings for the businesses along the main street in Dugganville. He had grown up playing here along the river as a kid and not much had changed. "I assume these guys are armed."

"Heavily."

"The sheriff has called in the DEA and the FBI to help on this." Alex watched his friend's face, and he seemed relieved. "They're gonna want to talk to you later today, but not here. I'll call you to let you know when and where."

"Okay," Combes said tentatively. "Alex, you need to make this look like I'm going down, too. These guys can't think I set them up."

"We'll take care of that."

Alex looked up and saw the familiar faces of FBI Special Agent Will Foster and Sharron Fairfield come into the office. They spotted him right away and came over. Foster reached out his hand as Alex stood to meet them.

"Nice look, Alex," Foster said, appraising the new uniform. They shook hands, then Fairfield came around and gave him a hug.

"Good to see you, Alex," she said. "Didn't take you long to get your feet on the ground."

"Nice to see you, too," he said, then looked over and saw Gallagher and one other deputy watching them closely. "Let's go in the back."

Pepper Stokes joined them in the small conference room. Pleasantries were exchanged. They had all worked together on past cases.

As they sat around the table, Stokes asked, "When is the DEA guy coming?"

"Rohrsuch will be here shortly," Foster replied.

Fairfield smiled at the sheriff and asked, "How's your new deputy working out?"

Stokes shook his head, "Never a dull moment with this boy around."

"Don't we know!" Foster said.

"Okay," Alex said impatiently, "can we get down to it?" He started to fill them in when the door opened, and Gallagher leaned his head in.

"Sheriff, there's a guy up front to see you."

"Send him back."

Gallagher eyed the gathering around the table for a moment, then closed the door.

A minute later, Drug Enforcement Agency Special Agent Rohrsuch let himself into the room. Introductions were made, and they all sat down again.

Alex continued to brief the group on his earlier discussion with Boyne Combes. When he was done, Rohrsuch asked, "What kind of back-up can you provide, Sheriff?"

"Myself and four deputies. You tell me where you need us."

"DEA will take the lead on this, right Will?"

Foster nodded.

"Can we get this Combes guy away from the store this afternoon to run through this?" Rohrsuch asked.

"Where do you want him?" Alex asked.

"We need to get him out away from town. Don't want a bunch of Feds crawling around the store all day."

"How about Hanna's place out on the island?" Fairfield said.

"That should work," Alex said. "Pretty quiet out there. What time?"

The DEA man looked at his watch. "Let's say 2 p.m."

"Let me call him," Alex said, standing to leave the room.

When he came back, he listened in as the team discussed the take-down plan.

Rohrsuch said, "Sheriff, I don't want any of your patrol cars anywhere near that store. We need your people positioned outside of town at all possible exit routes."

"Will do," Stokes said. "Let me suggest one thing, though. Our man, Combes, is real scared and twitchy about this bust. I'm afraid if we don't have someone in there with him, anything could happen. Alex and him go way back. I think we should get Alex in there, plain-clothed, of course."

Rohrsuch thought about the request for a moment, then turned to Foster and Fairfield. "What do y'all think?"

"Makes sense to me," Foster replied.

"Agree," responded Agent Fairfield.

"Tern knows my face, so I'll have to stay out of sight," Alex said.

"Of course," said Rohrsuch, "but I think we need someone inside the store who can respond quickly and also keep our guy settled."

Alex met Boyne Combes as he pulled his car in and parked behind Hanna's house. There were two Sheriff's Department cruisers and two unmarked cars from the FBI and DEA teams. All the cars were screened from view all around by the heavy forest and shrub surrounding the house.

Combes got out and shook his head, "You call in the whole damn Army?"

"Damn near!' Alex replied. "Come on in."

Alex watched as Combes seemed taken aback by the assemblage of law enforcement sitting around the island in the kitchen. He placed his hand on his friend's back and introduced him to everyone, including Sheriff Stokes, who he had already met with down at the Department.

"Sit down, Mr. Combes, "Rohrsuch said, and Boyne took one of the empty chairs. "Alex has already shared what you've told him about the drug run tonight. We have a few more questions."

"Okay," Combes said, looking around at all the faces staring at him.

"What kind of boat will these guys be coming in on?"

"Usually, it's a shrimp boat. Not one of our local guys. Comes down from somewhere north, I believe. Name of the boat is *Sandblaster*."

"Okay, good," Rohrsuch said. "Do you know who they take delivery from offshore?"

"No, they never let me in on that."

"Right," he replied, looking at his notes.

Will Foster said, "You ever get names of any of these guys?"

"No, only the head guy, Lando Tern," Combes replied, a stern look on his face.

"And he's always there for these deliveries?" Pepper Stokes asked in his gravelly voice.

Combes nodded.

Alex said, "What kind of weapons do they carry?"

Combes thought for a moment. "There's always one guy up on the bow of the shrimp boat with a semiautomatic rifle. The others have handguns on their belts."

"And you always take the delivery by yourself?" asked Rohrsuch.

"Yes, and I drive the truck down to Charleston right after they leave. Tern or one of his guys usually ride with me to make sure I get there. It's a warehouse down on the waterfront." He gave them the address.

"We'll have one of the teams follow and have our people in Charleston nearby to take down all the people on that end," Foster said. "It's possible they'll be tipped off if Tern and his men are in custody and don't send along some predetermined confirmation the delivery is on its way."

Rohrsuch asked, "Do you know if they send any sort of advance signal?"

"No," Combes replied.

"Are we all clear here?" Rohrsuch asked, looking around the group for any further questions. When there were none, he turned to Alex. "I want you to get into civilian clothes and go back to the store with Mr. Combes. Stay out of sight as much as you can in case Tern or any of his people are checking the place out before the delivery."

"Will do," Alex replied, rising to go upstairs. "Boyne, wait for me, and I'll ride back with you. Don't want my cruiser over near the store."

Boyne Combes looked around at all the faces in the room. "And you people are sure you can keep my ass safe?"

Rohrsuch responded first. "We'll do everything we can to make it look like you're going down in the bust, too."

Foster continued, "And we'll keep up that pretense until we have everyone in custody, including Xander Lacroix."

Combes did not look particularly convinced.

CHAPTER TWENTY-NINE

Ida Dellahousaye screamed in pain as she was pulled from the back of the car. "Let go of me!"

The man who had sat beside her in the car during the ride from the small airport continued to pull her toward an old shack built up on pilings along the edge of a marsh. The place was surrounded by heavy woods. She looked up and saw the sun low through the trees, orange and flickering as the wind ruffled with leaves and vines. The air smelled dank and earthy.

She was led up the front steps of the old place and then pushed through the door into a large room, open to a peaked ceiling, walls and roof all faded lumber. The windows were dirty and cracked. A dilapidated kitchen was in the far corner, and a few pieces of ragged furniture were scattered about. Two doors were closed against the wall to the left. It reminded her of where she was taken after being abducted a couple years ago in a crazy scheme she still couldn't come to grips with. *Such is the life of the daughter of a mob boss!* she thought, trying to calm her nerves.

A man stood up as they came in. He was dressed all in black with a black mask that he pulled down over his face when he saw them. Ida saw the handgun on his hip and a knife in a scabbard on the other.

Her own captors had not bothered to cover their faces, she thought. She had tried to keep her panic in check on the long plane ride and then again in the car. *What the hell is going on!*

One of the doors opened and Ida gasped as her mother was pushed into the room.

"Ida!" she heard her mother shout out and watched as she pulled herself away and ran toward her. She felt the tight embrace of her mother's arms around her. When she pushed back, she saw a face flushed with tears and eyes that showed real fear.

"Momma, please, what do these men want?" she whispered.

Before Brenda could answer, the man who had dragged Ida in said, "Mr. Lacroix wants to deal with all of you personally. He'll be out later this evening after he takes care of some other business."

Ida saw another man walk out of the open door and realized it was Senator Hayes. She knew his grandson from school, and he was an old family friend. She had never seen him look so rumpled... and defeated.

"Hello, Ida," Hayes said, walking up next to Brenda.

"Senator..." Ida said, tentatively. "Are you mixed up with these men?"

"If you mean, do they work for me? No, I'm here as you are at Xander Lacroix's request.

Ida heard someone yelling in the other room behind the last closed door. She knew at once it was her twin sister, Ophelia. *Ohmigod!*

The yelling intensified. "Unlock me, you big goon!"

A moment later, O came rushing out, followed by her captor.

"Ida, I'm so sorry!" O pleaded. "They made me tell them how to find you! I thought they were going to kill me!

Brenda Dellahousaye rounded up both daughters in her arms, and the three women held each other close in the center of the room.

"Okay, let's break it up!" the man, who seemed to be in charge when Ida arrived, said. He turned to the other who had just arrived. "Put the women in one room and the D.C. guy in the other." Then, he turned back. "If we have any trouble at all from any of you, I will not hesitate to personally put a bullet in your kneecaps until Mr. Lacroix arrives. Is that clear?"

"Why can't you let the girls go?" pleaded Brenda. "You have me! You have what you want!"

"Mr. Lacroix made it very clear that he doesn't want any more Dellahousayes around to betray him the next time."

"Please, no...!" Brenda cried out.

The man slapped her hard and she staggered back. "I want no more trouble from any of you! Let's go!"

Everyone nodded, except for Ida. She had had enough. *They're probably going to kill us anyway!* She rushed the closest man and reached for the gun on his belt.

He moved with practiced grace and blocked her attack, then spun and backhanded her hard against the side of her face. She fell back and hit her head on the wood floor, sliding to a stop up against the wall. Her face was on fire with pain. She opened her eyes to see the man pulling his gun and walking nearer. Then, suddenly, the gun was pointed at her right knee. She heard her mother yell out.

"Please, God, no!" The man in black pinned her arms to hold her back.

Ida sat up and pushed her back up against the wall as the man towered above her, the gun still aimed at her leg.

She closed her eyes and screamed as a deafening gunshot exploded in the room.

But, there was no pain.

Ida opened her eyes, expecting the worst, only to see her attacker falling to the floor beside her. There were three more explosions of sound and then the front door burst open. She tried to crawl away from the chaos as she saw three men dressed in tactical assault gear with helmets and big guns rushing in. Her mother and sister fell to one side, and the senator dove for cover behind an old couch.

There was yelling and then more gunfire.

Then, all was quiet. The air was heavy with the smell of gunpowder.

For a moment, all Ida could hear was her labored breathing. She scanned the room quickly and saw only the three men standing who had just rushed in. One yelled out orders to check the other rooms.

Ida got to her feet, her pulse pounding and her face still burning from the blow she'd received. Her mother and Ophelia cautiously got to their feet. Then, she saw the senator crawling out from behind the couch.

"Is it clear?" Hayes asked, struggling to get to his feet.

"Senator, my name is Jacobs," the man from the tactical assault team said. "I'm with the South Carolina State Police. We received word from your people in D.C. that you had been abducted. They've been able to track your journey from there from the GPS app on your Apple Watch."

"My watch!" Hayes said. "They took our phones, but..."

"It has the same function as your iPhone." He turned to one of his men. "Radio in the medical team. Let's get some help for these people!"

Ida saw her mother and sister fall down into the dingy couch, both their heads falling back in relief and exhaustion. She walked over and sat beside O, then pulled her into her arms.

"I'm so sorry," Ophelia said, tears flowing in gasping sobs.

Brenda reached around and hugged both of her daughters. She was struggling to get her breath.

Ida felt her mother's face against her neck, wet with tears. She looked around at the police unit clearing rooms, yelling into radios, disarming weapons, checking the bodies of Lacroix's men on the floor.

"We need to get out of here!" she said.

CHAPTER THIRTY

Alex was driving back to the hardware store in Dugganville in his truck when his cell phone went off. He took the call from Pepper Stokes. "Pepper, what have you got?"

"Alex, we just received an update from the State Police guy I know down in Charleston. Xander Lacroix abducted Brenda Dellahousaye, her two daughters, and the old senator, Hayes."

"You're kidding me!" Alex said, thinking that Lacroix had clearly gone off the deep end after his release.

"Lacroix's guys were holding them out at the old fish camp where we took down Asa. You remember?"

"How could I forget," Alex replied, remembering the night they came in guns blazing to get Hanna. "So, what's happening?"

"The senator's crew found out he'd been taken, tracked his cell or watch or some damned thing, and the State Police tactical division followed them out there and got them back."

"Had to be pretty rough," Alex said.

"Yeah, three of Lacroix's men are in the morgue."

"All the Dellahousayes and Hayes are safe?"

"Yeah," Stokes said. "Lacroix was coming back tonight to deal with them all personally. In other words, turn out their lights."

"So, Brenda D almost got herself and her daughters killed over all this," Alex said. "Maybe she'll learn a good lesson."

"Lacroix is not going to give up," Stokes replied. "And he's not through with you, either. Keep your head up!"

"Will do, boss."

Alex pulled his truck up in front of his father's house and turned off the engine. He didn't want to park his own car anywhere near the hardware. The sun was falling now below the tree line to the west. The sunset sky was edged with patterns of red and purple, jet streams of passing planes streaking high above. Riggings from the *Maggie Mae* down at the docks clanged in the light wind still pushing up the river.

His old house was dark, and he figured Skipper and Ella were down at *Gilly's* for their nightly gathering. Hanna had told him about his father's fall on the boat, and he knew he needed to have another tough conversation with the crusty old knucklehead.

He pushed those thoughts aside and reached for his service weapon on the seat beside him. There was one magazine loaded with fifteen rounds. He reached into the glovebox and got three more magazines, all fully loaded. He put the gun and the loaded magazines in a backpack.

He opened the door and stepped out, the sounds and smells of the Low Country shrimper's town catching him full on. It took him back to so many memories, pulling up to this same spot as a teenager and then later as a man. He was glad that Hanna had taken the time to come out and check on his father and new bride. *It's always a new adventure with those two.*

Alex walked down the back alley along the river downtown to avoid being seen by anyone associated with Lacroix, Lando Tern, or any of their cohorts. The river was quiet now, most of the boats in for the day. The smells of diesel and fish and shrimp fresh out of the Gulf pressed into his nostrils.

The anticipation of the drug bust crept back into his thoughts and he kept thinking through all the eventualities and things that could possibly go wrong.

His friend, Boyne Combes, was a train wreck and he knew there was little hope he would be able to keep his act together tonight. His wife had been found dead on the ground at the base of the fire tower. Her affair with the drug dealer and Lacroix bad guy, Lando Tern, had ruined his life. He was a logical suspect as a jealous husband for the death of his wife, and now, he was forced to cooperate with law enforcement in taking down a drug ring where he had been a major cog in the wheel and would very likely end up dead if his complicity was revealed.

He walked through the big garage door at the back of the hardware store. The place was well organized and tidy. Alex thought to himself that he had to give Combes credit for still being able to run a tight ship, even if it was failing and about to go under.

He walked around a row of high shelving units and turned toward the front of the store, then stopped short when he nearly ran into Ingalls, the cop that Sheriff Stokes had fired.

"What the hell you doin' here, Frank?" Ingalls said in surprise, backing up a few steps and looking past Alex to see if anyone else was coming in.

"I might ask the same question."

Both men eyed each other.

Alex could see Ingalls was stressed, anxious, about to go off. *No doubt he's here as part of the drug delivery?* Alex thought.

Ingalls said, "You off duty?"

"Boyne's an old friend. Had some news about his wife's death I wanted to share," Alex replied, watching as Ingalls started reaching behind his back with his right hand.

Alex reached out with a lightning thrust and caught Ingalls around the neck and pushed him back hard against the boxes of shelves behind him. The man grunted in surprise, still trying to reach for something behind him... *his gun!*

Alex drove his right knee up hard into Ingalls groin and stood back as the man screamed out and then fell to his knees, holding his crotch and moaning.

Boyne Combes came around the corner. "What the hell!"

Ingalls turned his twisted face to Combes and croaked, "You're a dead man!"

"Get some zip ties!" Alex yelled, grabbing Ingalls by the neck of his shirt and throwing him prone to the ground on his face. He knelt down with a knee on the man's back. "Go!" he yelled to Combes.

The hardware man stared back for a moment, fear etched across his face, then ran back into the store.

Alex struggled to keep Ingalls down. He was still writhing in pain from the blow he'd delivered. "Seems Pepper was right for firing your ass!" Alex said.

"You have no idea what you're getting into, Frank!"

Alex pulled the back of Ingalls shirt up and found the gun in a holster on the back of his belt. It was a short barrel 45 caliber revolver. He pulled it out, checked to make sure the safety was on and pushed it down into the waistband of the back of his pants.

Combes came back in, tearing open a plastic package of zip ties. Alex pulled Ingalls' hands behind his back. "Tie him up, Boyne!"

Combes leaned down and quickly secured a long white zip tie around Ingalls' wrists.

"You are so dead, Combes!" Ingalls hissed.

"Now his legs," Alex ordered, and Combes quickly moved down and wrapped Ingalls ankles together, then stood.

"Jesus, Alex!" Combes said. "What the hell do we do now?"

"Shut up, Boyne!" Alex said, getting to his feet. "How many people are working out front?"

"Just one cashier."

"Make sure no one else gets back out here," Alex said, then looked down at Ingalls. "How long you been on the pad for Lacroix?"

"Go to hell!"

"Your buddy, Gallagher, is on this, too, right?"

Ingalls was struggling to turn over, still flinching in pain, his knees pulled up now in a fetal position. "Like I said..."

"We'll have to ice you down for a while," Alex muttered to himself, thinking through how to handle this complication. He leaned down and checked Ingalls' pockets. He found his cell and touched the screen. There was a text message waiting to be opened. He touched the link. "Report when you've checked out the store."

The number was a Charleston area code. "Who are you reporting to?" Alex asked, looking down at Ingalls. No reply. "You working for Lando?" Again, Ingalls didn't answer.

Alex looked at the string of messages on the phone. One caught his eye, likely from Tern. "Can't trust Combes. Get over there this afternoon and check everything out." He went back to the bottom of the messages and typed, "All clear."

Alex turned to Boyne Combes. "You got someplace we can lock this guy up?"

"This is bad, Alex! Real bad!" Combes said, his voice edged with fear. "No way this doesn't get back to Tern and Lacroix."

"You are dead!" Ingalls yelled out.

"Where can we put him!" Alex demanded.

Combes hesitated, looking around, clearly panic-stricken.

"Boyne!" Alex yelled.

"My office. Let's taken him over here to my office. We can lock it up."

"I'll do it," Alex said. "Go get something we can cover his mouth with."

CHAPTER THIRTY-ONE

Hanna pulled into her drive off Springs Avenue. The old Pawleys Island historic landmark sign indicating the heritage of the house and the ownership of her ancestors, the Paltierres, dating back to the early 1800s, stood to one side. She often found tourists stopped here on the road to read the sign and peeking down the tree-lined drive to see the house. On occasion, she would stop and talk with the people, giving them some additional historical background on the place. She often thought about the day in the 1860s when her great-grandmother, Amanda, had said goodbye to her new husband, Captain Atwell, at the end of this drive. In her journal, she wrote about watching him ride away down this road on his horse, the next battles of the Civil War looming ahead.

Today, there was no one about and she was tired and not in the mood to engage with anyone. She pulled to a stop in her normal spot under the late afternoon shade of a massive live oak tree. She was also hyper-aware of the continued harassment by Lando Tern and of his most recent visit here, even this morning to leave the dead raccoon on her car.

She scanned the area around the back of the house before getting out, then reached for her bag, looking inside to make sure she knew where to reach for the gun Alex had given her.

She opened the door and got out, letting the salt air and light breeze from the ocean wash over her.

Again, she thought about her great-grandmother, Amanda. Maybe it was the old sign up at the road. *I wonder if she's ever just watching me?*

Her low shoes crunched in the loose gravel. She was reaching in her purse for her keys as she walked up the steps.

"Hello, pretty lady!"

She jolted in surprise and turned quickly to see Lando Tern standing at the bottom of the stairs. He must have been hiding in the bushes, she thought, quickly looking around for any sign of help. She was four steps above Tern. He started up toward her. His face was heavily bandaged from the broken nose Alex had given him and the head wound from the car accident.

"Been lookin' forward to seeing you again, pretty lady," he said, taking another step up.

Hanna kept backing up the stairs, then reached into her purse. She dropped the bag on the deck at the top and pulled the gun out, and with both hands, pointed the barrel directly at Tern's chest.

Tern stopped and put up his right hand. "Whoa, slow down here."

Hanna tried with all her will to keep her hands from shaking. A cold chill swept through her body. She clicked off the safety on the side of the gun. "Leave now, or I *will* shoot you!" she yelled out.

Tern stepped back down to the stone path, his hand still up in protest. His eyes were lit with a crazed stare. "This doesn't have to be so hard, Hanna. I just wanted you and me to be friends."

She cringed and shook her head to steady herself. "All I want is to see you walking back down that driveway... and if you ever come back, I will not hesitate to put a bullet in you!"

Tern just stood there, staring back, a wide grin on his face. He started to turn, then stopped and rushed up the stairs.

Hanna pulled the trigger and the gunshot exploded, echoing through the trees. The round hit the step to the side of Tern's left foot and the wood shattered. Tern stopped immediately, both hands up in protest now. "Easy! Easy!"

"Back away!" Hanna yelled, the fear replaced now with a flush of anger. "Back away or the next one won't miss!"

Tern smiled again through the bruises and swelling on his face, then started backing away. "You're a tough lady, Hanna. I like that."

His grin was infuriating, and Hanna resisted the temptation to plant another round at his feet. She watched as he continued to back away down the drive, then he disappeared around the bend in the bushes and trees.

Her heart was pounding, and she tried to catch her breath, lowering the gun. Keeping an eye on the driveway, she reached down and found her cell in her bag.

She pressed through to her phone screen and called Alex. She heard his voice come on, clearly troubled and rushed. "Hey, what's happening?"

Hanna took a deep breath. "It's Tern. He was just here."

"Where are you?"

"At the house."

"Is he gone?"

"I almost had to shoot him!"

"Are you okay?" Alex said, "Is he gone?"

"Yes, I think so. He headed back out to the road."

"Let me call someone in," Alex said, quickly. "Maybe they can seal off the bridges. Go inside and lock every door and window. I'll get someone over there right away. I can't come right now, but I'll get someone to you."

"Where are you?" she asked, unlocking the door as she kept an eye on the drive, holding the phone to her ear with her shoulder.

"I'm over in Dugganville. Something's coming down. I can't get back for a while."

"Okay..."

"Just stay there until I can get a unit over there."

"I will."

"I almost had to shoot him, Alex!" she said, her voice quivering now as she thought about how close she had come to actually shooting a man. She got inside and closed and locked the door behind her. Looking out the window, there was still no sign of Tern.

"If he comes back and somehow gets in the house, do not hesitate to put him down! You have every legal right to protect yourself. Am I clear?" Alex demanded.

"Yes... yes." She walked over to the kitchen counter and put the gun down. She could still smell the gunpowder from the shot she'd taken. Her hand shook as she pulled it away. "When can you get home?" she asked.

"It may be late."

Hanna finished going through the house and checking all the windows and doors. She had the gun with her again, her index finger along the barrel of the weapon. When she came back into the kitchen, she went to the back door and looked out the window again. Still no sign of Tern, but she knew he could be anywhere out there.

The low wail of a siren caught her attention. It quickly grew louder and then she saw a Sheriff's patrol car pull into the drive, its emergency lights flashing. She felt a wave of relief when Pepper Stokes got out on the passenger side, then a deputy who had been driving. The deputy started off into the brush, his gun drawn now, looking for Tern. The sheriff came up the steps and she unlocked the door to let him in.

"Pepper!" she said in relief, reaching out to give him a hug.

The old sheriff returned the embrace, then pulled back. "You okay?"

"Not really…"

"Alex said you almost had to park a round in this guy."

She nodded.

"We got the bridges sealed. No sign yet. He may have gotten off the island already or might even have come by boat, tied up out back on the marshes. We'll keep looking."

"Thank you," she said, some sense of comfort and relief beginning to come back. "Come in." She backed away and walked back into the kitchen. "Alex said something's going down over in Dugganville."

Stokes sat at the granite counter island. "Tern and his boys are bringin' a load of drugs in tonight. I got Alex over there now. Got a bunch of Feds helpin' us."

"So, Tern's gonna be there?" Hanna asked.

"We think so."

"Good! That means he won't be out here!"

"Look," Stokes said. "I'm gonna be a little short of personnel tonight with this bust and all, but I will have someone come by regularly tonight to keep an eye out and be close."

"Thank you," she said, then reached for the gun on the counter. "I'll take care of it myself if I have to!"

CHAPTER THIRTY-TWO

Will Foster walked down the hall in the FBI offices in downtown Charleston. He ended the call on his cell with his superior back in D.C. and opened the door to the conference room on the right. Inside, he saw Brenda Dellahousaye and ex-senator, Jordan Hayes, sitting at the small table. He sat across from them, watching their expressions closely. Both looked like they had just stayed up seven nights without sleep and had the worst nightmares in their lives.

"Hello, my name is Will Foster. I'm in charge of FBI operations in this region."

Hayes said, "Yes, Mr. Foster, we've met previously."

Foster nodded, then said, "I do recall your association with the terrorist, Bassam Al Zahrani." Hayes started to protest, but he cut him off. "We're not here to talk about that, Senator."

"Where are my daughters?" Brenda asked.

"They're down the hall, Ms. Dellahousaye. They're fine."

"We need protection from Xander Lacroix!" she pleaded. "He was going to kill us all."

Foster looked at the fear on her face and couldn't help but think how complicit she was in this entire affair and the war she had started with Lacroix. The Dellahousaye family had cut a wide swath of corruption and death across the country ever since the patriarch, Asa, had risen to prominence in the crime world nearly fifty years earlier. With Asa and his son, Remy, both dead and buried, the FBI and other law enforcement agencies had turned their attention to Xander Lacroix and a few other smaller offshoots trying to capitalize on the Dellahousaye's demise. Now, Remy's ex-wife was actively trying to regain the family's stake in the vast illicit business empire and had nearly gotten herself and her family killed in doing so.

"Ms. Dellahousaye, I find it quite interesting that you're looking for protection when our sources tell us you have a contract out on Mr. Lacroix," Foster said, sitting back and weighing her expression and response. When Brenda looked back with a wide-eyed, panicked stare, he continued, "And apparently, the assassin you sent after Lacroix failed in his first attempt."

She managed to gather her composure enough to say, "I don't know where you're getting your information or who your so-called sources are, but I have no idea what you're talking about."

"Of course, you don't," Foster said, shaking his head and releasing a deep sigh. "And Senator, you have to fill us in on how you got involved in this whole mess."

Hayes looked over at Brenda and she glared back, her nostrils flaring. He turned back to Foster. "My firm does some work for Ms. Dellahousaye's family. I, unfortunately, was in the wrong place at the wrong time.

Foster nodded without replying, waiting for the man to continue.

Hayes finally said, "I have to agree with Brenda. This gangster, Lacroix, plans to kill us. We need the protection of the Bureau and any other law enforcement agencies that can be drawn in to help."

"And why would he want to kill you, *Mr.* Hayes?" Foster said, making a point of not using his D.C. title. "We understand Xander Lacroix is or was one of your clients and in fact, you and your influential connections were instrumental in getting him released from prison early."

Brenda Dellahousaye stood up, an enraged look on her face. Her chair was knocked over and fell back against the wall. "You did what?" she screamed. Her already tangled hair fell across her face and her hands trembled as she tried to brush it aside.

Foster thought he was going to have to go around the table to keep her away from Hayes. He stood quickly and held out a hand. "Please sit down, Ms. Dellahousaye!" She kept staring down at Hayes, ready to pounce and gouge out his eyes as far as Foster could tell. "I said, *sit down!*"

She stepped back and then looked behind her for her chair, pulling it upright and then sitting much further away from Hayes this time.

"Special Agent Foster," Hayes began, his practiced charm and manner returning. "This is all a huge misunderstanding."

"And how is that?" Foster replied.

"My firm has many clients around the globe. While it may be true that someone in our firm may have done some work for Lacroix or one of his businesses, I can assure you there has been nothing unethical..."

Foster cut-in, impatient with the bullshit. "Nothing unethical? Bribing judges, accepting kickbacks, committing fraud," Foster said, leaning in and staring hard at the ex-senator.

"This is ridiculous!" Hayes shouted. "I demand to have my attorney present!"

"You're not being charged with any crime, Mr. Hayes... yet. You were lucky enough to be rescued by the State Police of South Carolina before Xander Lacroix and his henchmen could have you taken off the board. And I have to agree with Ms. Dellahousaye, Lacroix will not back away from sending his killers after you again."

"And what is the FBI going to do about that?" Brenda interjected.

Foster was beyond losing his patience but tried to remain calm. "It's not our job to provide personal protection."

"You're not going to leave us unprotected?" she pleaded.

"Actually, I'm waiting on a callback from the Justice Department on what charges will be filed in both of your cases."

"Charges!" Hayes said, his face all blustery and senatorial.

"We're going to hold both of you here for now until we can finalize our point of view on your cases."

"You can't be serious," Brenda said. "What about my girls?"

"As far as we know, they've done nothing wrong," Foster replied.

"But they need protection!"

"I'm going to have you all held in protective custody until we get this sorted out," Foster said.

"You're putting us in jail!" Brenda said, her hands gripping the table hard.

"I want my lawyer!" Hayes demanded.

"You can make a phone call in a minute, Mr. Hayes," Foster said. "But I would like both of you to think about cooperating in our efforts to bring Xander Lacroix to justice. I can say with confidence that your cooperation will be looked upon favorably by both the FBI and the Justice Department."

"Where are you taking us?" Hayes asked.

"We have a suite of rooms at a hotel down the street where we will keep you under guard until we have some clarity around all this." Foster stood to end the meeting. I'll have your cell phones brought in so that you can reach out to your attorneys or whoever else you need to call. I would strongly advise against directing any further actions against Xander Lacroix. Let us take that from here, but we will talk again later this afternoon, and I strongly encourage you to be prepared to offer assistance in those efforts."

Ida Dellahousaye sat on a couch on one end of a large conference room. She looked across at her sister, Ophelia, sitting at the long table staring out the window at the skyline of downtown Charleston. As with most twins, Ida had come to not even think about the fact that she was staring at her exact double. O's hair was cut shorter and colored with streaks of blonde to highlight their rich brown curls, and her choice of clothes was always drastically different.

Ida took a deep breath to continue to try to calm herself. The abduction on the street in front of her apartment in Boston and the trip down here to South Carolina with her captors had more than unnerved her. She could still feel the chill of fear prickling through her veins, even though she was sitting in the protective watch of the FBI.

If anything, she was more angry now than scared. Her mother was obsessed with the Dellahousaye fortune and past business dealings. Her obsession had almost gotten them all killed. Ida knew her mother had more than enough money to live comfortably for the rest of her life. But, for Brenda Dellahousaye, there was never enough, Ida thought. It wasn't that she really wanted more homes or cars or anything. It was more jealousy than greed. Her mother was jealous of anyone who possessed something that had once belonged to the Dellahousayes. It was as if she was trying to reclaim her once vaunted position as the matriarch of the Dellahousaye empire.

Her parent's divorce had nearly sent her mother off the deep end, and then again, Ida thought, apparently it did. She was apoplectic when her ex-husband remarried. The young new wife quickly took over all of Brenda Dellahousaye's social status and perks. When her father and the new wife were murdered by

Lacroix's men, she had seen her mother become almost gleeful at the news.

And then there was her sister. Ida had learned that Ophelia's boyfriend had been shot and killed right in front of her and the shock of it was still written all over O's face. She couldn't imagine how terrifying it all must have been.

Ida got up and walked over to the table and stood behind her sister's chair. She reached out and started massaging her shoulders. Ophelia leaned her head back and closed her eyes. "How are you doing, O?" She felt her sister's body relax and release a deep sigh.

"I feel like I've had my insides ripped out! I can't stop seeing it."

"I know. I know," she said, trying to soothe her twin's raw emotions.

"These people are crazy!" Ophelia said. "They just shot him like he was an animal that needed to be put down."

"We're lucky we didn't get the same treatment. Our dear mother did her best to get us all shot. I don't know where we'd be right now if the police hadn't been tipped off by the senator's people."

"What's going to happen to us?" Ophelia said, turning her chair to face her sister.

"I wish I knew."

CHAPTER THIRTY-THREE

Alex checked the ropes he and Boyne Combes had used to tie the rogue ex-cop Ingalls to a chair in the back office of the hardware store. They had also secured a gag to keep the man quiet during the upcoming bust. He and Sheriff Stokes decided not to try to transport the prisoner back to the jail, risking being seen by any of Lacroix's men.

Ingalls struggled to get free but was held fast. He moaned something unintelligible through the gag, his eyes flared in anger. Alex checked the man's cell again and there were no further texts or calls from Tern. He nodded for Combes to come outside with him. They locked the office door, and both walked back into the storage area of the store. Alex said, "How you holding up?"

Combes looked back with a dazed expression, then said, "There's no way we keep Lacroix from finding out about me helping you guys. There's no place I can hide they won't find me. I don't care if they're all in jail after this. Lacroix will still send somebody after me."

Alex knew his friend was right, but also knew he had to keep the man's emotions in check. "We'll worry about that after tonight. You understand?"

Combes stared back but didn't respond.

Alex checked his watch. It was nearing six o'clock. There was still at least six hours before the boat would arrive with the shipment. He gave Combes a hard stare. "Why didn't you tell me Ingalls was involved here?"

"He hasn't been in the past. This is the first time."

"You better be straight with me Boyne," Alex said firmly. "I've got no tolerance for any more surprises tonight."

"I swear to you, Alex!"

Xander Lacroix stood looking into the mirror above the sink in the bathroom at his office. His face was stoic, his hair recently trimmed. The complexion of his skin was pasty white from his long incarceration. The white dress shirt he'd been wearing all day was open at the neck.

The image of himself staring back blurred as his thoughts returned to the phone call he had just taken. Somehow Hayes' people had worked with the cops to track the senator and the Dellahousaye women to the fish camp. The assault had taken the lives of three of his men. His captives had been freed. Brenda Dellahousaye was free to continue her war with him, or at the least in protective custody of the Feds.

He looked down and saw a heavy ceramic soap dish next to the sink. A slow burn of fury was building in his gut. He reached down, grabbed the dish and threw it as hard as he could into the mirror. The glass exploded into thousands of spiky shards, crashing around him, one even slicing into his cheek before it fell to the floor.

His breath was coming hard now as he tried to calm himself. He saw a drop of blood hit the counter next to the sink, then another. There was a box of tissues beside the sink, and he grabbed a handful and held them against his cheek to stem the flow. His mind was racing with conflicting thoughts. He knew he needed to think clearly. Time was of the essence.

Clearly, the Feds will connect him to the Hayes and Dellahousaye abductions. Surely, they had them in custody somewhere trying to sort all this out. They would be coming for him at any time. He had a safe house in the country north of town he was sure no one would be able to find him at, and he knew he needed to leave now.

But there was other business to be dealt with, too. The drug delivery up in Dugganville tonight would be the biggest shipment they'd ever taken. He wasn't entirely confident in the crazy bastard, Lando Tern, running the operation, but he didn't have other options now.

Tern had also been tasked with taking out the lawyer and the cop who had helped put him away. He had been tempted during his time away to move on both of them, but in the end, he decided he wanted to personally administer the final revenge on Alex Frank and his wife.

Tern had been trying to get into both their heads before setting them up to be taken out. From the reports he was getting, the man had been doing a damn poor job of it.

Lacroix reached for his phone. Lando Tern answered on the second ring.

"Yeah boss."

"How we doing on the delivery tonight?"

"Everything is on schedule. No complications."

Tern's arrogant voice darkened Lacroix's mood even more.

"Boss, I know about the boys going down out at the fish camp. What the hell's going on?"

"Where'd you hear about that?"

"I tried to get in touch out there. When there was no answer. I couldn't get hold of any of them. I went out the back way by boat to check it out. There were cops everywhere. I snuck around a little, saw them taking our guys out on a stretcher. The cops took Hayes and the women away."

"I know, you idiot!" Lacroix barked into the phone. His anger on full tilt again. "We all need to get out of town after the Dugganville delivery tonight. I'm coming down there. I want you to round up the lawyer and the cop and have them there when I get there... no later than eleven."

Tern didn't respond.

"Did you hear me?" Lacroix yelled.

"Sure, Mr. Lacroix. I'll take care of it."

Lando Tern clicked off the phone and sat back in the cushioned seat of his center cockpit backcountry boat. He was floating on the incoming tide in the marshes about half a mile from the fish camp.

Lacroix wants me to round up the woman and the cop, he mused. He thought about the last encounter he'd had with Hanna Walsh. He was hoping to have a little fun before delivering her to Lacroix, but that seemed out of the question now.

Damn, I thought she might actually shoot me! He chuckled at the thought of it. *After all the bad asses I've come up against, to get taken out by a woman like that. And then there's the cop to deal with,* he thought.

Tern touched the bandage across his nose and flinched at the pain. He had planned to deal with Alex Frank with his own brand of payback, ideally while he had his way with the man's wife in front of him.

He turned the key to start the boat's engine. *Maybe there's still time!*

CHAPTER THIRTY-FOUR

Deputy William Gallagher reached the last flight of steps to the top of the fire tower in Dugganville. He paused before making the final ascent to catch his breath and looked out over the treetops and distant marshes out to the Atlantic Ocean. A flock of buzzards flew in spirals high out to the west, likely eyeing some tasty bit of roadkill below. A shrimp boat was making its way slowly up the river into town, nets hanging to dry on the large booms. The shrill screeching of tree frogs echoed through the high branches.

He had parked two blocks over in a quiet neighborhood away from the river, not wanting to draw attention to his presence here in the park. He ducked low behind the rail when he saw another department cruiser turn the corner down to the left and drive by. *Probably that new asshole, Frank,* he thought. *Hometown boy! That idiot Stokes has him working the drug bust tonight.*

With his heart rate returning to normal, he started up the stairs. At the top, he walked around the perimeter, holding on to the rail to steady himself, gloves on his hands to prevent any further prints left behind. When he reached the spot where Ally Combes had spent her last moments on earth before falling to her death, he stopped and looked down. His head spun with dizziness, and he gripped the rail harder.

The yellow crime scene tape bordered the area where Ally had been found. A piece of the tape had come loose from a stake and blew out sideways in the wind. He breathed in deep again, trying to catch his breath. He thought about what must have been going through Ally's mind in those final seconds.

He walked around and into the glass observation room. The door creaked as he pushed it open. The old desk sat against the far wall. The image of Ally Combes on the desk came to him. *When will the DNA evidence come back?* he thought.

He walked around the perimeter, looking down and along the wood rail beneath the windows for any possible clues or evidence that might have been overlooked. He knew the crime scene techs had gone over the place extensively, but he needed to be sure.

Reassuring himself there was nothing more to be found, he walked back out along the platform and looked out across the view of Dugganville and the Low Country swamps surrounding it. His thoughts returned to Ally Combes and her deadly spiral into the abyss of drugs and dangerous men.

Pepper Stokes pulled his Sheriff's Department cruiser to a stop in the parking lot beside *Gilly's Bar* in Dugganville. He got out and started toward the steps to the front entrance. The muted sounds of music played inside, a Cajun song he faintly remembered, and he started humming along as he walked up the steps.

As he opened the door, the familiar stale smell of beer and sweat greeted him and the music blared louder. The after-work crowd was here in full force. He saw Gilly behind the bar with his wife, trying to keep his customer's glasses and bottles full.

His old friend, Skipper Frank, and new wife, Ella, sat at their usual spot along the far end of the bar. They were both in deep conversation with three other men sitting and standing beside them. Ella was thumping one of the men on the chest with her index finger, trying to emphasize some point she was making. Stokes smiled as he thought about the good times he had spent over the years with the Skipper and before they were married, with Ella, with whom he'd had a brief and toxic affair.

He made his way through the crowd, stopping a couple of times to converse with other acquaintances. He came up behind Frank and tapped him on the shoulder. The Skipper turned and Stokes saw a big smile spread across his friend's face.

"Somebody called in the cavalry!" Skipped yelled out. "How the hell you doin', Pepper?" He reached out his hand and the two men shook.

"How are you, Skipper?"

"Never better!"

Ella turned and stood to give the sheriff a hug. "How have you been, you old coot?" she said, then sat back down and took a long pull on her beer bottle.

"Good evening Ella. You're looking beautiful as usual."

"You leave my wife alone, Pepper! She's mine now!"

Stokes eyed the bandage wrapped around Skipper's head. "What'd you do, fall off the barstool again?"

"No, fell on the boat, dammit!"

"Gettin' a little tipsy in your old age?"

"He tips over a lot!" Ella added, scolding her husband.

"Good to see you two," Stokes said. "Hey Skipper, I need a minute. Can we go outside?"

"What'd I do now?" Skipper growled. "Ain't kilt nobody in damn near a year," he said, grinning broadly.

"Just need a minute," Stokes replied.

Outside, the fresh air was a welcome break. Stokes waited as Skipper Frank came up to stand beside him at the patrol car.

"Whaddya need, Pepper?"

"Like to put you to work."

Skipper looked back with a puzzled stare.

"What're you doing tonight?"

"Drinkin' beers with my hot wife here at *Gilly's*. What does it look like?"

"Got a little operation comin' down tonight out on the salt. I'd like to have you out there to give us some eyes and ears on some bad guys coming up the river with a load of drugs."

"You serious?"

Stokes nodded. "We want to put a couple of DEA guys on the *Maggie Mae* with you. They'll monitor the approach of the boat and be out there to catch anyone trying to get away if we don't take them all down in town."

"Hell yes! Glad to help!"

"Suggest you put a lid on that last beer up there and get home and get sober. This is all comin' down around midnight. The DEA boys will be coming by your house around ten to give you time to get out on the water."

"I'm in, Pepper! Who are these pukes?"

"Bad bunch. Some of Xander Lacroix's gang."

"Been hearing about drugs coming in again since the Richards were taken down."

"You sure you're up for this?" Stokes asked, looking at his friend's bandaged head and unsteady bearing.

"I'm all in, Sheriff!"

FBI Special Agent Will Foster sat across from his partner, Sharron Fairfield, in the Charleston office as she looked up from the laptop on her desk. "We have Hayes and the Dellahousayes secured down the street?" he asked.

She nodded. "Just got the call back."

"What have you heard from the prosecutor's office?"

"This has gone high up on the Justice Department food chain."

"I'm sure because the honorable ex-senator Hayes is involved," Foster said. "Nothing like a little scandal to get D.C. all riled up."

"They're considering attempted murder charges against Brenda Delahoussaye for her moves to take out Lacroix. They're upfront though in admitting they don't have enough evidence yet for an indictment."

"And what about Hayes?"

"Bribing a federal judge, accessory to attempted murder, the list goes on."

"But it doesn't sound like we're going to have enough to hold them."

"No, I don't think so."

"Is the AG's office open to cutting a deal for cooperation in bringing down Lacroix?" Foster asked.

"Everything's still on the table, as far as I can tell."

"Good. We've got another call with the DEA boys in a few minutes to finalize plans for the bust tonight." Foster stood up to leave. "I'm going to need you out there somewhere."

"I've cleared my dance card," Fairfield said with a smile.

Brenda Dellahousaye fumed as she stared blankly at the television. Jordan Hayes had turned on network news to see if there was any coverage of their abduction and rescue. Her thoughts were stuck on the fact that she was literally locked up by the Feds with no access to a phone or computer to communicate with anyone, including her daughters, who were in another room down the hall of the hotel with their own guard stationed at the door. She was grateful for the protection because she knew Lacroix would now be obsessed with finding them... and killing them.

The thought of how close they had all come to a violent death at the hands of Xander Lacroix made her cringe. She got up and walked to the window of the hotel room and looked out at the vast skyline of downtown Charleston and the rivers beyond stretching out to the island where the first shots in the American Civil War had been fired on Ft. Sumter in 1861. None of this held any interest for her at the moment. She was consumed with plotting her next moves to protect them all from Lacroix, and possible indictment by the Justice Department.

The FBI had encouraged her and Hayes to cooperate in their investigation of Lacroix, and she was having trouble finding a reason why that wasn't a good idea. She had underestimated Lacroix and failed in her attempt to take him down. He was obviously madder than a hive of hornets at this point and would not stop until he had exacted his revenge. *And why did I think I could go up against a professional mob boss and killer?* she thought.

CHAPTER THIRTY-FIVE

Hanna walked down the steps from her beach house and felt the warm comfort of the sand around her bare feet. She walked past the circle of weathered Adirondack chairs around the stone fire pit and on down the path through the beach grass and low dunes to the ocean. The sun was low in the west behind the house now, and the light was casting its brilliant shades of colors across the sand and water and boats far offshore.

She carried her leather bag on her shoulder. The weight of the gun Alex had given her was noticeable and reassuring. When she reached the water's edge, she let the wash of the waves cover her feet and soak the bottom of her jeans.

A young couple walked toward her from the south, holding hands, laughing and kicking the surf as they came near. She walked a few steps back on the beach and allowed room for them to pass. "Evening," she said, as they went by.

Both turned and smiled back at her but didn't respond, too caught up in their own conversation.

Good for them, Hanna thought, thinking back many years when she had walked this beach with her new husband, Ben, both deeply in love and caught up in each other. *How quickly that all went south!*

She turned and looked back up at the house nestled in the dunes, a few lights visible through the windows as the light faded. She scanned the row of houses up down the beach in each direction for any sign of Lando Tern. The couple walking away now were the only people in sight.

Turning back to the ocean, she remembered a page in her great-grandmother, Amanda Paltierre's diary. She had seen a stranger walking on the beach, right here where she stood. The war had recently ended and there was always the threat of danger from retreating soldiers, outlaws, and carpetbaggers, as they called them back then. The stranger had stopped to look up at her on the back porch of the house. Amanda had carried a gun with her that day as well that she always kept close during and after the war.

It turned out the stranger had actually come from far away looking for her. Their ultimate fate was a love story that Hanna went back and reread often in the diary.

Something moving up on the deck of her house caught her attention. She squinted through the fading light and saw a woman standing there.

"Hello?" she yelled out. She started walking up the incline of the beach in front of the house. The woman moved closer along the rail on the deck and started waving a hand. As Hanna came closer, she stopped. She could see now the woman was the spirit or ghost of her great-grandmother. "Amanda!" she yelled.

She kept walking up through the narrow path and she could see more clearly now. The always bright and happy face she had seen on previous sightings was clearly troubled now.

When Hanna got to the fire pit, she stopped and looked up. The spirit of Amanda Paltierre was gone. From behind, she heard, "Hello, pretty lady."

Alex looked up from his phone, ending a call with Sheriff Stokes. His old man was going to be in on the bust, carrying DEA guys out on the water in a boat that wouldn't raise suspicion. He wasn't sure that was such a good idea considering his father's often tempestuous actions, but he would leave that up to the Sheriff to judge at this point.

Someone walked through the back garage door of the hardware store and Alex saw Deputy Gallagher come in.

"What are you doing here?" Alex asked. "We're trying to keep this low-key until tonight. We don't need a bunch of uniforms and patrol cars all over town."

"Just doin' my job, rookie."

"Stokes asked you to come down?"

"No, but I'm sure he'll have us involved somewhere tonight. I'm waiting to hear."

A muffled sound came from the locked office behind them. Ingalls was struggling to get loose again and trying to yell out for help. Alex was regretting his decision to keep the man here. He should have had someone from down at the department come over to pick him up. Again, he didn't think there should be a lot of cops in the area until this all went down.

"What was that?" Gallagher asked, looking over at the closed door.

Ingalls tried to call out again from inside.

Alex said, "Your old friend, ex-Deputy Ingalls, is in on this drug deal with Lacroix and his boys. He came by earlier and we had a little disagreement on how all this would go down. I decided it best to put him on ice until this is over." He watched the expression of Gallagher's face grow dark with concern.

"You've got him tied up in there?" Gallagher asked, starting toward the door.

"Let it be, Gallagher!" Alex said firmly, stepping in front of the man.

"You do not want him around here tonight, rookie," Gallagher said. "Let me take him down to the department and out of your hair."

Alex considered the offer for a moment. The last thing they needed was any of Lacroix's men who might happen to be nearby, seeing Gallagher being taken away in a patrol car. On the other hand, having Ingalls here was a complication that could create some issues when the bust actually went down.

"We need to hold him on charges for being part of this, Gallagher," Alex finally said.

"On what grounds?"

"He as much as admitted it to me at the same time he was pulling a gun on me."

"Ingalls?" Gallagher said, questioning.

Alex had doubts this was really much of a surprise to Gallagher. "I just got off the phone with Stokes. He agrees we need to come down hard on your old friend. It's why he got fired in the first place. Pepper just didn't have enough to bring him up on charges."

"Let me take him in," Gallagher offered again. "Get him out of your hair."

Warning bells were going off in Alex's ear, but he wasn't sure he had a better option. To cover himself and hold Gallagher accountable, he said, "Okay, bring your car around back here. I'll let Pepper know you're taking Ingalls into custody.

Hanna didn't bother to turn when she heard Lando Tern's voice close behind her. She bolted quickly for the stairs, her heart racing in her chest, her hand reaching desperately into her bag for the gun. She was halfway up the stairs when she felt Tern grab her right ankle in a vice-like grip. She stumbled and tried to catch her fall with one hand, the other still searching desperately for the gun. She ignored the pain from her fall as she crashed down hard onto the wooden steps.

As she turned to face her attacker, her hand found the cold metal grip of the gun. She pulled it out, instinctively clicking off the safety as Alex had trained her.

Tern was laughing as he came up and stood over her, his feet between her legs. "This doesn't have to be this hard, pretty lady. You might actually enjoy yourself."

His expression changed when he saw her pull the gun from her bag and point it at the center of his chest. He put both hands up and stepped back one stair below her. "Let's not get crazy here!" he said, the smile stretching out across his face again.

Hanna reached up with her left hand and pulled the slide back on the 9mm to load the first round. She let it slap back loudly to make a point. "I *will* shoot you!" she shouted, trying with all her will to steady her hands.

Tern stood for a moment, not responding, his smile still mocking her.

A hollow feeling came over her. A ringing in her ears started and grew louder, though there was no sound around. She felt her finger on the hard curve of the trigger. She knew if she pulled it back even the slightest, the shell would explode out of the barrel and blow a hole in this man's chest, probably even kill him.

He started to back away, moving down one more step, his hands still up in protest. "You really don't want to do that, pretty lady."

"If you call me that one more time, I *swear* I'll shoot you!"

Keeping the gun trained on the center of his chest, she managed to get to her feet. She backed up slowly to the top of the stairs.

Tern was now ten steps away. He dropped his arms and looked out to his left at the ocean. "Damn nice place you have here, Hanna," he said, looking back up the stairs.

"Leave! Now!" she shouted out into the fading light.

He turned as if he was going to walk back around the house, and then, in a quick move, he started up the steps, his smile gone now, only the look of a crazed attacker.

"Stop! Now!" Hanna yelled out, backing away ten steps on the deck. Her entire body was shaking now, and she was afraid she might drop the gun. She heard Tern coming up the steps, but she couldn't see him. His head came into view, then the rest of his body as he reached the top of the stairs.

"Drop the gun now, pretty lady." He hesitated a moment, looking down the barrel of Hanna's gun. Suddenly, he rushed at her, a long knife now visible in his right hand.

Hanna's mind went blank as she squeezed the trigger once, then again. The two loud explosions echoed out across the beach.

Tern spun to his right and staggered, then started backing up to the stairs. The knife fell from his hand and clattered on the wood deck. He fell back against the rail at the top of the stairs. His eyes had a look of astonishment, disbelief, then anger.

Hanna watched as he tried to take a step toward her, then lost his balance and fell backwards down the stairs. She could hear him thudding down the steps as he fell. Her breath was coming in frantic gasps. She lowered the gun, listening. Nothing.

She tried to gather her breath, calm herself. Slowly, she started toward the opening in the rail and the steps down. She pulled the gun up again, trained at the space where Tern had fallen.

She got far enough to look down. Even in the fading light, she could see he was gone.

Had he crawled into bushes beside the house? She listened to hear if there was any sound of him moving back around the house toward the road. All she could hear were birds squawking as they flew in from the marshes and the low rumble of waves down at the beach.

She ran to the back door and reached inside to turn on the outdoor lights, then hurried back to the top of the stairs. A spotlight on the corner eave of the house shown down on the bottom of the stairs out to the fire pit. There was no sign of Tern.

"Where are you!" she shouted out into the night.

Then, she heard someone rushing through the heavy bushes between the house next door.

"Hanna! Hanna! Are you alright?"

She recognized the voice of her neighbor. His name was John and he had been a close friend for years. "Stay back!" she yelled. "I don't know where he is!" She saw him come into the light.

"Hanna, I heard gunshots," he said. "What's going on? Are you okay?"

"John, please! I don't know where he is!"

He started up the stairs and she lowered the gun again.

In a moment, she was overcome with all that had just happened. She staggered back against the rail and then sank down to her knees. She clicked on the safety on the gun and laid it on the deck beside her.

"Hanna, what happened?" John said, coming up and kneeling beside her.

She looked up into his face, her mind racing. "I think I just killed a man."

CHAPTER THIRTY-SIX

There was no sign of Lando Tern.

Alex had taken Hanna's call after the shooting and got permission from Pepper Stokes to go back to the beach house. It was still hours before the drug bust. Another deputy in the area reached the old house on Pawleys Island before Alex got there. When he skidded to a stop in the gravel behind the house, he saw the other patrol car.

The deputy named Oliver came around the side of the house with his gun out in his right hand.

"Where's Hanna?" Alex demanded.

"She's up in the kitchen. She's okay, just a little shaken up."

"Have you got the guy?"

Oliver shook his head. "There's a blood trail at the bottom of the stairs that leads along the side of the house over there." He gestured to his right. "Then it's gone. I've been all over the property. Nothing. The knife he pulled on her is still up on the back deck."

"Thanks for getting here so quickly," Alex said. "Let me go check on Hanna."

He ran up the steps to the house and through the door. He saw Hanna sitting at the kitchen island, her head down in her hands, a cup of coffee steaming in front of her. The next-door neighbor, John, was standing at the other side of the island. Hanna looked up when she heard him come into the room.

"Alex!"

He rushed over and took her in his arms as she stood. She buried her face in his shoulder.

"I told him to stop! He just kept coming! He pulled a knife."

"It's okay," he said softly. He could feel her body start to shudder and then heard her sobs.

"I think I killed him!"

"He's not here, Hanna."

"I know I hit him!" she said, looking up at him, tears streaming down her cheeks now.

"He must have been able to get away," Alex said, turning to the neighbor. "Thank you for coming over."

"I heard the shots," John said.

"But you didn't see the guy?"

"No, he must have already gotten away.

Alex turned back to Hanna. "Since his car is wrecked, I have to believe he's coming in by boat. He could have docked at any of the piers out behind us here on the channel. I've already got our mobile unit out looking for him.

"Alex, I know I hit him with at least one of the shots. It spun him around and he fell back down the stairs. How can he just disappear?"

"I don't know," Alex replied. "The wound must not be severe, but he was bleeding. There's a blood trail out alongside the house, but then it stops, or we just can't find it. I have the other deputy out checking the piers."

Hanna looked at him in desperation. "I don't know what he would have done. He knocked me down and then pulled a knife. I told him to stop, but he just kept coming."

"You did the right thing," Alex said, pulling her close again and rubbing her back. "I don't want you staying here alone. I have to get back to Dugganville. You should come with me and stay with Ella at my father's house."

Hanna stepped back and rubbed her face to wipe away the tears. "Okay, let me grab a few things."

Ella met them at the door and took Hanna into her arms. "I'm so sorry, honey! Come on in."

Alex followed them into the house. "Thanks Ella, I really appreciate this."

"Wouldn't have it any other way."

"Hanna still has her gun if this guy somehow finds out she's over here. I doubt that's going to happen, but you need to be alert."

Ella said, "I got one of Skipper's shotguns loaded, too. We'll be ready if that asshole comes round."

Alex walked over to Hanna and hugged her, then whispered in her ear. "I'll be downtown here til past midnight, but I'll get back as soon as I can."

"Please be careful," Hanna said, then kissed him on the cheek.

Ella said, "So you know your old man is out on the salt with the Feds tonight trackin' down drug runners."

Alex nodded.

"The old coot's gonna get himself killed, I swear."

"He'll be okay," Alex replied. "Those DEA boys won't let anything happen to him."

It was close to 11 p.m. when Alex got back to the hardware store. He walked down the back alley and through the big garage door entrance. There were lights on in the storage area. The store had been closed since 9. He looked around and found no sign of Boyne Combes. Walking back into the store, all the lights were off.

"Boyne, you here?"

No response.

He heard some commotion back out in the storage room and turned back in that direction. Sheriff Stokes walked in from the alley with deputy Oliver.

"Where's Combes?" Stokes asked Alex.

"Just got back from dropping Hanna over at my old man's place. Came straight here. No sign of our man. I was afraid this was going to happen."

"Shit!" Stokes cursed. "You got his cell?"

"Let me try it." Alex pulled out his phone and found the number in his *Contacts*. He pressed the call. It rang four times before it went to voicemail. Alex waited for the tone. "Boyne, you need to get back down here. We can't get these guys if you're not here for the meet. Call me back!"

Stokes said, "Foster and the DEA guys will be down here any minute. We need to figure out Plan B fast."

"Plan B for what?" Will Foster said, walking in behind them.

Alex said, "Our man Combes here at the store is gone. We're trying to track him down." He watched for Foster's reaction. Sharron Fairfield walked in with two other men, including Rohrsuch, both with DEA logos on their jackets.

Foster said, "Let's all get inside where we're out of sight."

Alex led them back to Boyne Combes' office. Rohrsuch said, "Just checked with the team out on the shrimp trawler. No visual on the boat yet. Our radar has a boat tracked about five miles down from the mouth to the river. It's probably our guys."

They all gathered in the office. Foster asked, "How'd we lose Combes?"

"It's on me, Will," Alex said.

Pepper Stokes jumped in. "I told him he could leave for a bit. This Lando Tern guy showed up at Alex's wife's house again, went after her with a knife. She had to shoot him."

"Why am I just hearing about this?" Foster protested.

"My fault, Will," Stokes said. "We got a lot coming down here tonight."

"Okay, enough with the blame game," Foster said. "Alex, how's Hanna doing?"

"Really shook up, as you can imagine, but she did what she had to do."

"So, where's Tern?"

"He took at least one round. We tracked the blood trail as far as we could in the sand, but he's gone. We've got the marine unit out looking for him, and all state and local have an alert on the guy."

Fairfield asked, "Do you think he'll still show up here tonight?"

Alex thought for a moment. "Depends on how bad he's hurt."

Foster said, "These guys coming in are going to expect Boyne Combes to meet them. We have to be prepared to move fast to take them down before they spook at Combes not being here."

Alex said, "Let me go run by Boyne's house, see if I can't pick him up."

Stokes said, "Agree, but hurry up!"

Alex got back to his truck and started driving through town. He made the first turn and was driving past the park when something caught his eye. There was a car parked in the lot next to the old fire tower. He pulled in and turned off the truck. The lights went out and he got out, letting his eyes adjust to the dark.

He walked over to the car and looked in with a flashlight he had on his belt. The car was empty, but a cell phone lay on the passenger's seat. He opened the door and reached for the phone. The screen lit up when he touched it. There was a notice that there was a voicemail message from his number just a few minutes ago. It was Boyne Combes' phone.

Alex stepped away and looked around the area. He yelled out, "Boyne! You here?"

His eyes had adjusted enough he could see the shadowed structure of the fire tower through the dark off to his left. He started in that direction, then stopped short.

In the dim light, he saw the shape of something or someone lying at the base of the tower. He rushed over and knelt beside a lifeless body lying face up. He grabbed the flashlight and confirmed it was his friend. He checked for a pulse on both the man's neck and wrist. Nothing.

He leaned back and took a deep breath, then stood and looked up at the top of the tower, barely visible up in the treetops.

He reached for his own phone and dialed the Sheriff. "I found Combes. I'm over at the park. It looks like Boyne jumped from the tower... just like his wife."

CHAPTER THIRTY-SEVEN

Xander Lacroix stood on the back deck of the safe house they had fled to outside Charleston. With his cell phone to his ear, he gave his final instructions. An informant who had been instructed to watch the FBI offices had called earlier to alert him that the Feds had taken Brenda Dellahousaye, her daughters and Jordan Hayes to a hotel down the street. They were in guarded rooms on the sixth floor.

His next call was to his man running the drug run tonight. Lando Tern answered immediately.

"Yessir."

"You ready to go?" Lacroix asked.

"Everything is set, boss. Boat's comin' in on schedule for a midnight drop."

Lacroix could sense all was not right. "What's goin' on up there?"

Tern's voice broke a bit before he tried to speak again. "Like I said, we're ready."

"Tell me you've taken care of our attorney and the cop," he asked. "I want them out here at the safe house tonight."

"Not yet, boss, Not yet."

Lacroix exploded. "Why the hell not?"

"I'll take care of it," Tern said, his normally calm demeanor clearly rattled. "I'll round them both up after the deal goes down, then get them back down to you. That cool?"

"Just do it!" Lacroix ended the call.

Ida Dellahousaye was the first to hear a disturbance outside in the hotel hallway. Her sister, Ophelia, was asleep on the couch. She walked softly over to the door and peered out through the peephole. She couldn't see far enough in either direction. Then, she heard another noise, almost like a whispered thud, then a grunt and the sound of a man falling over.

As quietly as she could, she opened the door a crack and peered out. The guard who had been stationed outside her mother's room was lying prone on the carpet, not moving. Ida gasped and closed the door, trying to push back the panic that was rushing through her. She took two deep breaths then cracked open the door again.

The first thing she noticed was the leg of the guard who had been outside her door, lying off the left. Then, the door to her mother's room opened and she watched both her mother and the senator being let out by two men. They had guns with silenced barrels stuck in the backs of their captives.

Ida closed the door again and locked it.

"Ida, what is it?" Ophelia asked from behind.

"They just took mother!"

Brenda Dellahousaye felt the gun barrel pressed into the middle of her back as she and Jordan Hayes rode down the service elevator with the two men who had burst into their suite.

The doors opened and they were pushed out into a long hallway that smelled of laundry soap. The men pushed them both to the right. They passed a large room with rows of large washers and dryers, then a door to a big commercial kitchen. They came up to another door and one man pushed it open.

They were outside now in a back alley behind the hotel. A white van was parked a few feet away. One man opened the back doors, and then Brenda and Hayes were both pushed in. One man got in with them. The other went up, got in the driver's seat, started the van and began driving away.

The man in back picked up plastic zip ties lying on the floor of the van and pulled Brenda's wrists tight behind her back and secured them with one of the ties. She sat up against the side panel of the van as the man now secured Hayes' hands.

She was beyond fear now. She knew these were Lacroix's men and their fates were sealed. There would be no rescue this time. Her only concern was for Ida and Ophelia. "Where are my daughters?"

"Shut up!" yelled the man working on Hayes.

She made eye contact with the senator and the panic in his eyes was clear.

"Do something!" he pleaded. The man slapped him across the face.

"I said, shut up!"

Brenda thought how pathetic the once-powerful senator looked now.

Ida Dellahousaye peered out of her hotel room again. The men who had taken her mother had been gone for several minutes. Cautiously, she stepped outside and gasped when she saw the still bodies of both guards lying on the floor. She knelt by the first man and searched for a pulse. He was still alive. There was blood leaking from two wounds on the side of his head. She found a similar wound on the man outside her mother's door.

She pushed back a wave of nausea as her sister came up beside her. "What's going on? Where have they taken them?"

"Check to see if he has a phone," Ida demanded, pointing to the man outside their door. Ophelia rushed away and Ida began searching the pockets of the man lying beside her. She found his phone in his back pants pocket.

Quickly, she tried to pull up the phone app, but the cell was password protected, and she couldn't gain access.

Ida yelled over, "I can't get in. I need a password."

The phones in their rooms had been disconnected to prevent them from calling out. She stood and raced for the elevator. She turned to Ophelia and yelled, "Get back in the room and lock the door!"

She reached the elevator and waited impatiently for the doors to open. When it finally arrived, she rushed in and hit the button five times for the lobby. The elevator moved at a slow pace and Ida beat on the wall. When the doors finally opened again, she ran across the lobby. There was one woman working behind the counter.

"I need to call 911!" Ida screamed. "There's been a shooting up on the sixth floor! They've taken my mother!"

CHAPTER THIRTY-EIGHT

Lando Tern cursed as he pulled the wrap tighter on his upper arm. He sat in the cockpit of his boat just south of the mouth into the bay and river into Dugganville. The woman's first bullet had barely missed him. He felt the rush of air, not a whisker away from his ear. The second round caught him high on his right arm in the meaty part of his outside shoulder. It had stunned him enough that he lost his balance and fell down the steps of the beach house. *The fall nearly killed me!* he thought as he held one end of the bandage in his teeth and pulled the other with his good hand. His back and ribs ached from something he had pulled or broken in the fall. The small first aid kit in his boat had enough supplies to at least stem the flow of blood, but he knew he needed to get to a doctor soon.

He thought again about the other woman he'd seen for just a moment at the bottom of the stairs as he struggled to get up and run to the front of the house. Her red hair almost seemed on fire. When he got up, she was gone.

As he looked out into the dark of the night across the ocean and down into the wide bay into the river, he thought to himself, *How the hell did I let that bitch get the better of me again?*

The memory and images of the whole situation out at the beach house caused his blood to boil in fury. *No way in hell I thought she'd pull that trigger. Never again!*

His cell lit up and he checked the number on the screen. It was his man on the other boat. "How we doin', Amigo?" he said, then listened to learn that the shrimp boat with the shipment was approaching the inlet.

Tern looked around and saw the red and green navigation lights on an approaching boat about a mile away coming up the south shore. "We're clear here, Amigo. I'm heading upriver to the store. I'll call back with an all-clear." He ended the call and put his phone on the dash of the boat. He pressed the throttle forward and the boat powered up into the night.

Skipper Frank sat in the wheelhouse of the *Maggie Mae,* the throttle set low, booms and nets out as if they were really shrimping. The two DEA men were dressed in what would pass for deckhand clothes. Both were stationed up on the foredeck, scanning the horizon for approaching lights. Occasionally they would get a call and an update from the person monitoring radar.

He was having a grand time being out on the water with the Feds, tracking down badasses. *Haven't had this much fun with my clothes on in a long time,* he thought.

One of the DEA agents came back into the cabin. "We've got a small boat approaching from the southeast. Can you steer more out to the middle of the inlet so we can get a better look? Nothing too obvious."

Skipper corrected course. "How's that?"

The man scanned the horizon, then said, "Better, thanks." He went back to join his partner.

Skipper strained to see out ahead. His eyes weren't what they once were but, in a few moments, he picked up the nav lights of the approaching boat. *Should pass 'em a couple hundred yards to starboard,* he thought. "Damn drug-runnin' sonsabitches!" he murmured to himself.

Lando Tern saw the deck lights and navigation lights of the big shrimp boat up ahead. It wasn't uncommon to see shrimpers out at night in these waters. The boat was coming up off his starboard bow about a half-mile out. There were no other boat lights on the inlet or coming out from the river. There were a few lights from houses sparkling through the heavy woods on shore and out on the end of docks in the bay.

Continuing to steer with his knee, he reached for his cell phone and tapped out a text to his man onshore. "OK?"

There was a delay of a minute or so, then, "All clear."

Alex put Boyne Combes' phone back in his pocket after answering the text. He turned to Will Foster and Sheriff Stokes. "Looks like we're on."

Foster said, "I want everyone in position out of sight as we discussed. If the first boat gets in too far ahead of the second, we take him down quickly. Get his phone and we'll place a man on the pier next to the boat to avoid suspicion from his buddies coming in behind. Worst case, we've got both Coast Guard and DEA boats coming in behind them to block any escape from the inlet."

"I'll pull the hardware truck around into position where Boyne told me they take the delivery," Alex said.

"Go!" Foster replied, and Alex walked out the back door and down the alley to where the truck was parked. As he walked, he thought again about Hanna and how stressed and upset she must be about all that happened out at the beach. He had been on both ends of shootings and the shock and trauma were always a nightmare to deal with.

There's a special place in hell for a guy like Tern, he thought. He was fighting with his emotions between wanting to

The Fire Tower

exact the most painful and final revenge on Lando Tern and his professional discipline, which was screaming at him to follow the book. He still wasn't quite sure which side of the issue he would come out on.

Tern drifted in slow idle speed up the river toward Dugganville. The banks had narrowed as he left the inlet, and his speed was just enough to make headway against the slow current. A flock of egrets cast ghostly white shadows across the dark tree line to his left as they moved to their evening roost. A bull gator grunted his displeasure with the passing boat from shore. Mosquitos buzzed around his face, but he was too focused on the job that he paid no attention.

He didn't want to get too far out ahead of the big shrimp boat carrying the merchandise. They were about a half-mile behind him based on their last check-in and he knew he had about that far still to navigate up the river to town.

His cell phone lit up on the dash and buzzed with an incoming call. He could see on the caller ID it was the rogue cop, Gallagher. He'd tried earlier and Tern didn't pick up, too occupied with other issues... *like getting my head nearly blown off!*

"Yeah, what is it?"

The deputy answered back, "You've been made, man!"

"What!"

"Combes flopped to the cops. That asshole Frank and the Feds are waiting for you."

Tern felt a flush of anger, then let it pass, thinking hard on how best to respond. His mind raced through all the implications... delivering Lacroix's drug shipment, exacting his revenge on the cop and his wife, dealing with the snitch, Boyne Combes. The thought of it all was so delicious that he forgot about the pain that wracked his body.

Alex Frank is waiting for me! Perfect!

He reached down into a duffel bag at his feet and pulled out the semi-auto assault rifle he always took on jobs like this. He loaded a clip of ammunition and checked to see that he had four more clips in the bag. He pulled them out and put them in a backpack that he threw over his shoulder. He also grabbed a scabbard that held a long knife and pushed it down into his belt. He'd dropped another knife on the deck when the woman had tried to kill him. *I'll get it back, pretty lady!*

From the phone, he heard Gallagher, "Tern, are you there?" He clicked to end the call. The bandage wrapped across his broken nose had been bothering him all day. He'd almost forgotten about it after the episode with the Walsh woman out at the beach. He ripped the bandage off and threw it overboard, ignoring the flare of pain.

"Alex Frank! Perfect!"

CHAPTER THIRTY-NINE

Hanna sat out behind Skipper Frank's house at the old redwood picnic table with Ella. She had a half-empty glass of white wine sitting on the table in front of her. Ella was nursing a longneck bottle of Bud Light. Bugs flew in and out of the lights across the back of the house. The sounds of tree frogs and crickets split the night air.

She took another sip from the wine glass, her hand trembling a bit as she placed it back on the table. The echoes of gunshots still rang in her ears and the image of Tern coming at her with the knife sent another chill up her spine. She shook her head to clear her thoughts.

"You're gonna be okay, honey," Ella said. "It'll take some time."

"You know what's really bothering me the most?" Hanna said.

Ella stared back, taking another drink.

"I almost wish I had killed the man," she said. "He's still out there, and who knows who he'll hurt next."

"Pepper and Alex will get this asshole, honey, you just watch."

Hanna reached out and touched the 9 mm she had put on the table within close reach. "I won't miss the next time, Ella!"

Alex took his assigned position in the garage behind the first row of shelving units. He checked his weapon and touched the two extra magazines of ammunition in his pocket for reassurance. He put Boyne Combes phone on the shelf next to him in case there were any more incoming texts from Tern or the drug runners. He tried to slow his breathing and calm himself. He had been on many busts in his long career, and he always had the same sense of anticipation and nervousness.

He tried to keep focused on tonight's takedown, but he couldn't help but think back to another bust when he and his Charleston PD partner, Lonnie Smith, had gone into a bar downtown after the hitman named Caine. The deadly outcome still haunted his sleep.

Will Foster was stationed across the storage room from him. Two DEA agents were positioned outside the hardware store, hidden from sight in the alley. Foster had put Sharron Fairfield out on the street in a car to keep an eye on the front of the store in case any Lacroix reinforcements came in by car or on foot. Sheriff Stokes was just inside the store. They were all on the same radio frequency and Foster checked with everyone to make sure they were in position.

Alex was the last to respond. He put the radio down and looked out the back door. He could see about fifty yards down the river from where he was standing. The two DEA guys would get the first look at the boat or boats coming in. They were to let them land and start tying up before the takedown would initiate.

The plan was designed so that ideally, no gunfire would be exchanged, but everyone was prepared for the worst. The radio squawked and Alex listened as one of the DEA guys on the *Maggie Mae* called in to confirm a large shrimp boat had just passed, making its way up the river now. They could see three men onboard, though it was possible there were more below. They were sealing off the river now at the mouth of the inlet, and the Coast Guard and DEA boats offshore were also moving in.

CHAPTER FORTY

Skipper Frank held the *Maggie Mae* on course headed out to open water. One DEA agent in the wheelhouse with him said, "There's our boys."

"How do you know?" Skipper asked.

"Only boat within five miles on the radar."

"Why don't you guys just take 'em down out here?" Skipper asked, looking back down at his instruments and heading.

"We want the whole lot of them together at the store to make sure we get everyone involved."

"Right," Skipper said, thinking now about his son lying in wait up in town. He wished he could be down there with him to really get in on the action, but he knew their job was to be a spotter and to help block any attempted escape out of the river. He almost wished some of them would try. *I'd run the Maggie Mae right up their asses!*

Alex heard the radio scratch again in the earpiece he was wearing. The DEA agent positioned downriver from the store reported he could hear the first boat coming in, still just out of sight, maybe two hundred yards down.

He clicked the safety off on his weapon and felt another surge of adrenaline. He tried to push thoughts of Lonnie Smith aside. Instead, he wondered how Hanna was holding up. He was looking forward to his next encounter with the crazed Lando Tern.

Tern slowed the boat and eased it up alongside a pier and loading dock that ran across the back of an old warehouse. He had tied off the steering wheel with a piece of mooring line to keep the boat on course up the river the rest of the way to the hardware. He grabbed his backpack and the rifle and quietly jumped off the boat onto the pier, slipping into the shadows. The boat kept on as if nothing had happened.

Alex heard the DEA man report again that the first boat was now in sight, moving slowly up the middle of the river.

Will Foster came on. "We let this first guy land and wait as long as we can for the other boat to get in."

Alex pulled the slide back to load the first round in his pistol. He peered into the darkness for the first glimpse of the boat, hopefully, the one bringing Lando Tern into them.

Foster came on the radio again asking the DEA lookout for a report. There was no response. "Robert! Report! What's happening down there?"

Again, no response.

Tern let the man fall to the ground, wiping the blood clean from his knife on his pants. It had been easy to come up from behind, and going for the throat prevented any call out or sound. He pushed the pain wracking his body aside. He had more scores to settle.

He kept on up the back of the buildings along the river, staying in the shadows away from the few lights that had been left on. He watched his boat still motoring slowly ahead of him up the river.

So, where is Frank?

Foster tried again to reach the DEA lookout. "Robert, come in!" Silence echoed back. "Alex!"

"Go Will!" he quickly responded.

"Slip around and check on him. Let me know what the hell's going on."

Alex moved quickly to a side door to the storage room that emptied out to a narrow alley between the next building. He slipped out quietly and started toward the river, his gun held up in front of him with two hands.

A shadow slipped by the opening at the end of the alley. *Was it Robert the DEA guy?*

He kept moving forward, pressed against the brick wall to his left. There was no cover now between him and the alley along the river. He took two more steps and was about to peer around the corner when the deafening explosion of semi-automatic gunfire erupted. He flinched and fell to one knee. *What the hell!*

Two more bursts of gunfire, then shouting, both on the radio and from down the alley. As he looked around toward the open door at the back of the hardware, he saw a lone gunman firing again at the DEA agent stationed at the far side of the store.

Alex yelled out, "Tern!" and watched as the man spun around. They both made eye contact and Alex could clearly see the face of Lando Tern. He pulled back quickly behind the wall as Tern let off three more bursts. Bullets smashed into the walls on both sides of the narrow alley, chunks of brick and mortar flying all over.

He shielded his face, then leaned out far enough to be able to see again, his weapon pointed down toward Tern.

There was no sign of him, then gunfire started again inside the storage room. There was more shouting on the radio in his earpiece, but he was totally focused on where Tern had gone.

He inched along the wall, then clicked the transmit button on the radio. "Will, what's happening!"

No answer. More gunfire, this time single shots from pistols mixed in with the automatic rifle fire. He heard a man scream in pain and the gun battle continued. He heard Fairfield on the radio, "I'm coming in!"

CHAPTER FORTY-ONE

Hanna and Ella looked up toward town when they heard the first burst of weapons fire. "Ohmigod!" Hanna said, standing and listening. More gunfire.

"Alex!" she screamed, reaching down for her gun and then running down the steps from the back porch and around the house.

She heard Ella yelling behind her, "Hanna, please no!"

She reached the street along the river and kept on running on the shoulder of the road toward town, the gun in her right hand. Her feet thudded on the hard packed dirt, her breathing quickly becoming labored and short.

It was at least four blocks down to Main Street, where the hardware was located.

The gunfire continued and a sense of mind-numbing dread swept through her. *Alex!*

Alex crept up to the big opening into the storage room. The shooting suddenly slowed, intermittent shots coming now. More shouting. He peered around, his gun out in front. The first thing he could see in the dim light was the prone body of a man lying near the door into the store. *Pepper!*

There was another long burst of automatic fire from the left and he ducked back. When he looked back up, he saw Will Foster leaning out from behind some shelves returning fire.

"Will, I'm here!" he yelled out and they both made eye contact. Foster nodded and looked back to Alex's left.

Suddenly, it was quiet. Alex listened, his senses on full alert for any sign of Tern.

A loud splash in the river split the night. Alex turned and looked back down toward the smaller alley he'd just come out, and then to the black flow of the river, the ripples from the splash just barely coming into view.

"Tern!" he yelled, running back up along the river. He strained his eyes to see. There was hardly any light on the river. A few leaves drifted slowly near the bank by the alley. The river was about fifty yards wide in this part of town. There were other piers and boats docked across the far side. He strained to see any break in the water or sign of Tern.

He jumped when Will Foster came running up beside him, yelling into his radio, "The shooter is in the river! Take the shrimp boat down, now! Sharron, get someone over on the other side of the river!"

To Alex, he breathlessly said, "Pepper is down. Go check on him. Get an emergency team out here!"

Alex felt his heart sink as he thought about the fate of his old friend. He didn't want to let Lando Tern get away but forced himself to follow orders. He ran back into the storage area calling the 911 operator. As he reached the motionless body of Stokes, he knelt beside him and leaned down close to the man's face pressed against the concrete floor. "Pepper! Pepper! Talk to me!"

Stokes stirred, then tried to push himself over. Alex held him down. "Where are you hit?" He heard Stokes try to answer, but it came out as a garbled moan. "Stay still, we've got help coming!"

Behind him he heard, "Alex!" He turned to see Hanna running through the door from the store. She rushed over and fell to her knees beside him and the old sheriff. He noticed the gun in her right hand as she threw her other hand around his shoulder.

"You shouldn't be here!" he said, trying to control his emotions amid all the chaos.

"I heard the shooting," she said, trying to catch her breath. "How is he?"

"Can't tell how bad it is. A paramedics team is on the way."

"Is anyone else hurt?" she asked.

"One of the DEA guys. It looks pretty bad," he said. "It was Tern. I think he got away in the river."

"Oh, Lord no!" Hanna moaned.

Will Foster came over. "The units out on the water have secured the boat with the drugs," he said. "How bad?" he asked, looking down at the sheriff.

Alex responded, "He's still with us."

Lando Tern let the current pull him further downstream through town. He paddled as close to the far docks and boats as he could, keeping his head barely above water to breathe. There were few lights on. His body was on fire with pain from the gunshot wound on his arm and the fall he'd taken out at the beach house.

He forced himself to ignore the pain and let his mind linger on the fact that he had failed in getting Lacroix's drugs delivered and also failed in taking out the cop, Alex Frank. He was tempted to swim back and finish the job but was certain the place would be crawling with even more cops by now.

He still had the rifle in his hand but wasn't sure how it would operate after getting soaked in the river. The backpack with more ammunition was still on his shoulder. He was certain his boat had run into something upriver by now and the cops probably had it anyway.

He needed to get further downriver before he tried to get out. He could steal a car and get out of town later tonight when things cooled down. Thoughts of alligators and snakes crept into his brain, but he tried to ignore the threat. He knew he had let his anger at the cop and his wife get the best of him. Lacroix would not tolerate what he'd done. How many millions in drugs had just been confiscated? He would have to leave town, get far away as soon as he could.

But not until I deal with Alex Frank and the woman.

CHAPTER FORTY-TWO

The van pulled to a stop and the back door opened. Brenda Dellahousaye and Jordan Hayes were pulled to their feet and pushed out. Brenda saw an old farmhouse next to the driveway illuminated by a porch light and another on a tall pole out next to a barn. There were two other cars parked back by the barn.

She looked for any other lights or houses for possible help, but there were only dark woods to either side of the house and what looked to be a wide-open field across the road. They were pushed toward the front door. Brenda felt her heart thudding in her chest. She had tried to manage her panic on the long drive out to wherever they were by reassuring herself that the twins were safe.

One of their captors stepped forward and opened the door. She and Hayes entered a small living room, sparsely furnished, with no one there. Then, she heard the sound of someone approaching from down a hall to the left. Her heart sank when Xander Lacroix entered the room.

"Well, how nice of the two of you to stop by," Lacroix said. He was dressed casually in jeans and a blue golf shirt. His gray hair was combed back straight, and his dark eyes seemed clouded as if he was high on something.

Hayes said, "Xander, this is just a big misunderstanding..."

Lacroix broke in and stepped closer. "A misunderstanding!" He moved to within inches of Hayes' face. "A misunderstanding!" He threw a vicious punch into Hayes' gut and the man fell to his knees gasping for air.

Brenda cried out, "No, please...!"

Lacroix stepped back and then let loose a side kick that caught Hayes on the temple, sending him sprawling across the floor. He lay there moaning and mumbling something that was incomprehensible.

Lacroix turned to Brenda. "And what am I to do with you?" She started backing away and tripped on the leg of a chair, falling backwards onto an old couch. She sat there cowering, her mind racing for any inspired plan of escape.

"Xander," she began meekly, her pulse pounding and body literally shaking in fear. "There must be some way we can work this out." He walked over and loomed above her. She looked up and saw no sign of capitulation in his face.

With a slight smile curling up at one end of his mouth, he said, "Brenda, you made the first play in this hand. I don't know who you hired to take me out, but I hope you got your money back."

She didn't reply, looking nervously over at the senator who was still writhing on the floor.

"Look at me!" Lacroix screamed.

She flinched and looked back. This time he held a gun in his hand, the end of the barrel pointing directly at her forehead.

"You've cost me a lot, Brenda. Some of my best men are dead. The Feds came down on one of my drug deals tonight up on the coast, I'm sure because of all the distractions of dealing with you and Hayes." He looked down at the pathetic form of the once powerful Jordan Hayes, now lying in a fetal position, crying, saliva dripping from his mouth. "And now, just days after release from the pen, I've got the cops all over me because of this war you've started."

"Xander, please..." she began.

"No!" he screamed, and she shrunk further back into the couch. "What would you do if you were in my shoes, Brenda? You'd have me wiped off the face of the earth where I could never come after you." He leaned in and placed the gun inches from her forehead. "Wouldn't you!"

She was weeping uncontrollably now, her brain trying to block the thought of the pain she would feel when the first bullet split her forehead. She closed her eyes, waiting for the inevitable. *Please, just get it over with!*

She tensed when she heard the gun trigger click...but there was no pain. There was no explosion of the first bullet firing. All she could hear was Lacroix laughing.

She opened her eyes and he had backed away, the gun pointed down at his side now.

"Not here, Brenda. Not now. I just wanted to give you a little preview. Too much of a mess to clean up here."

She fought to catch her breath, to stop the tremors of fear racking her body.

"I think we'll take a boat ride, Brenda."

CHAPTER FORTY-THREE

Alex closed the doors to the ambulance with one of the paramedics and stood back as the blue and red lights splashed a kaleidoscope of colors against the brick wall of the hardware. Pepper Stokes had not regained consciousness. The emergency team had done a quick assessment, staunched the flow of blood from the bullet wounds and then determined the sheriff needed to be transferred to the hospital as soon as possible.

Another emergency team had taken the fallen DEA agent. His wounds seemed serious but not fatal.

Alex stepped back and leaned against the wall, feeling the quickened pace of his heart starting to settle in his chest. He looked down and saw blood on his hands and arms from helping the paramedics get Pepper on the stretcher. He shook his head and took a deep breath trying to gather his thoughts.

The drug deal had been halted. He assumed his father would be coming in soon from the bay on the *Maggie Mae* with the other DEA boat and the boat the drugs had been seized on.

Lando Tern had escaped and radio checks from the law enforcement officers looking for him here in Dugganville and the perimeter around it were providing no updates on his location. The man had gone off on a crazed killing spree and Alex knew he was surely one of the targets. *This is not over!* he thought.

His friend, Boyne Combes, was dead. He had either taken his own life in a fall from the old fire tower, or there was some other form of foul play up there. Alex thought through the events leading up to the drug bust. The rogue deputies, Gallagher and Ingalls, most likely had tipped off Tern and the boat coming in. Boyne Combes knew he'd been outed as cooperating with the authorities in the drug bust and that Xander Lacroix would have him on a hit list he would never be able to escape.

Will Foster had shared reports that Brenda Dellahousaye and the old senator had been abducted from the hotel downtown, most likely by Lacroix, as their personal battle escalated. They had also learned that two hired security officers had been badly wounded there. Alex had little doubt that Dellahousaye and Hayes may already be dead, or soon to suffer that fate. He found it hard to understand how the woman had been so foolish in trying to take down the ruthless Xander Lacroix. She obviously didn't know or was too obsessed to care about the risks.

Alex wondered about Boyne Combes again and his deceased wife, Ally. He still wasn't sure how Ally had fallen to her death. Had Boyne pushed her in a jealous rage and taken his own life now in remorse and with the surety that Lacroix and his goons would hunt him down eventually and kill him? She was having an affair with Lando Tern. What role had he played, if any, in her death?

And what about Lacroix? he thought. *Now that he was released from prison, how long until he comes after me and Hanna? He certainly has a score to settle.*

Alex had insisted Hanna go back to his father's house and stay there with Ella until he could get free and come over. One of the other deputies had given her a ride. She still had the gun he'd given her, and he urged her not to hesitate to use it again if Lando Tern happened to find his way over there. He looked down river and saw the green and red navigation lights on the front of the old shrimp boat, the *Maggie Mae*, coming back into town. The lights from the two other boats followed.

He pushed away from the wall and walked toward the edge of the pier behind *Combes Hardware*. A feeling of total exhaustion came over him and he squatted down and reached for the concrete to steady himself. Bowing his head, he closed his eyes and tried to clear his mind and focus on what he needed to do. He also said a silent prayer for his friend and boss, Pepper Stokes, who was near death and on his way to the hospital.

"You okay?"

Alex looked up and saw Will Foster walking from inside the hardware. He pushed himself up, groaning at the effort it took. "Been better."

"Crazy night," Foster said. "Still no sign of Tern."

"He can't be far," Alex said, looking down the river as his father's boat pulled into the slip in front of their house. He could see the outline of his father in the light of the pilot house. The DEA guys on board were scrambling to secure lines and get the boat tied up. He was sure his father was shouting a stream of orders and obscenities at them.

"Sorry about Stokes," Foster said. "I know the two of you have been friends for a long time."

"He's a tough old guy. We'll see."

"We're still trying to get a lead on Brenda Dellahousaye and Hayes," Foster said. "Lacroix is nowhere to be found."

"I doubt the two of them are long for this world, Will," Alex said. "He's not out of prison more than a couple days and we've got dead bodies everywhere, drug deals going down, total chaos. We need to take this guy down again."

"We're working on it," Foster said. "I still can't believe that judge let the guy out."

"He's gonna have to go underground after all this. I'm sure he's got a plan to disappear, probably out of the country."

"We've got the State Police looking, too. I had them check the old Dellahousaye fish camp, but everyone's cleared out."

Alex tried to think back on all the time he'd spent tracking down and battling with the Dellahousayes and then Lacroix after both Asa and Remy had been taken out. "You know, Lacroix has a boat downtown at one of the marinas. At least I think he still has it. Big cruiser."

"You think he might try to run?" Foster asked.

"Boat's big enough to get across to the Bahamas and from there, anywhere south."

Foster pulled out his phone. "Let me call your old boss at Charleston PD downtown."

Hanna took the glass of wine Ella had just poured for her, and the two of them walked from the kitchen into the front room. She knew Lando Tern was still on the loose and they had locked all the doors and checked the windows. She had Alex's gun in the bag over her shoulder, a magazine loaded and ready to fire.

I won't miss the next time! she thought to herself as she sat in an old, upholstered chair across from Ella. She noticed pictures of Alex and his older brother, Bobby, on the wall. They looked to both be grade school age. She smiled as she saw the younger face of her new husband. Bobby Frank had been killed in the war in Iraq. Alex had followed his brother and joined the service, suffering serious wounds himself over there.

"That's the *Maggie Mae* coming back in to tie up," Ella said, looking out the window. "Crazy old coot out there chasin' drug runners." She shook her head in disgust and then took a long pull from the cold bottle of beer she'd just opened.

"Alex said they took down the boat with the drugs," Hanna replied.

"Oh, I'll never hear the end of it now! He'll probably want to be off to *Gilly's* to tell all his buddies about it."

"Alex said he'd be here as soon as he can," Hanna said. "We'll get back up to the island and out of your hair."

"You're both welcome to stay tonight. Got the guest room made up."

"Thanks Ella, we'll see how late it is." She looked again at all the pictures on the wall next to her. There was one of Alex's mother standing with her two sons.

"She was a looker," Hanna heard Ella say, "the Skipper's first wife."

"Alex told me she was killed in a car accident when they were both in high school."

"That's right," Ella said. "Remember when it happened. Seems like yesterday. Whole town loved that woman. Still a stink about how that went down that night."

"What do you mean?" Hanna said, looking back.

"Investigators say she swerved to miss a deer or something late at night coming back into town based on the skid marks. She went off the road and hit a tree."

"Alex doesn't talk about it much."

"No, I imagine not. It was really tough on the boys and on the old Skipper. Tough to follow in the woman's footsteps."

Hanna smiled back at Ella and reached over to take her hand. "You're the best thing that's happened to Skipper Frank in a long time."

The woman smiled back and shook her head, looking out the window again at the shrimp boat down at the pier on the river. "Skipper still thinks some drunk ran her off the road that night. He's never stopped trying to find out who it was."

"Really," Hanna said, "Alex has never mentioned it."

"There were paint scrapes on the side of her car. Different color paint," Ella said.

Hanna heard footsteps out front and the door to the screen porch across the front of the house creaking open. She reached into her bag and found the grip of the gun. The knob turned, but the door was locked. Ella got up and went over, looking out the window in the door before unlocking it and letting Skipper Frank inside.

The grizzled old shrimper lumbered into the room. "Hello woman!" He gave Ella a big bear hug and then noticed Hanna.

"Well, hello Hanna!" Skipper said. "Wasn't expectin' you tonight."

Hanna got up from the chair and met him halfway, getting her own big hug. "Hear you're a big hero, taking down the drug runners," she said.

"Ah, piece a cake!" he said, reaching for Ella's beer and taking a long drink.

"I'll get you another," Ella said, walking back into the kitchen shaking her head.

"The *Maggie Mae* and the other boys on that DEA boat, well we had those rascals surrounded before they knew what hit 'em," Skipper said. "Heard there was some shootin' here in town. Everyone okay?"

"I went down to the hardware..."

"What?"

"I heard the shooting. Alex is down there."

"So, you go runnin' down to a gunfight!" Skipper said as Ella handed him a beer. "Damn, woman, that took some stones!"

"Alex is okay, but Pepper Stokes got hit with automatic rifle fire. It's pretty bad." She could see Skipper's expression turn deadly serious. She knew they had been friends for a long time.

"He gonna make it?"

"I don't know. They rushed him off to the hospital."

"Who was the shooter?" Skipper asked.

"This Lando Tern guy who's been giving us some trouble the last few days. He works for Xander Lacroix and was taking the lead on the drug deal."

"Did they get the sonofabitch?"

"No, he got away. Alex says they've got a lot of people out around town looking for him."

"Well, I hope he tries to come by here," Skipper said, plopping down on the couch and spilling some of his beer down the front of his shirt.

"Easy, Rambo," Ella teased, sitting down beside her husband and wrapping an arm around his shoulders. "Kinda sexy, you being this tough old lawman now!"

"Oh stop it, woman," Skipper said in disgust, but Hanna could tell he was enjoying it.

"Alex said he'd be coming by as soon as things get tied up down at the hardware store, and hopefully when they've found this Tern guy," Hanna said. "I didn't tell you, Ella, but he came out to the beach house earlier today and tried to attack me."

She pulled Alex's gun carefully out of her bag. "Alex gave me this earlier when the guy had bothered me a couple other times. This afternoon, he wouldn't back down and I don't know what would have happened, but I fired off a couple of rounds in defense. I guess I only wounded him, but now I wish I'd taken him down after what happened to Pepper."

"You did the best you could, honey," Ella said.

CHAPTER FORTY-FOUR

Alex waited for Hanna to pick up his call on her cell. He was driving over to the fire tower to check on the investigation into Boyne Combes' death. A State Police crime scene team was onsite.

Hanna answered, "Hey, are you on your way back?"

"No, I have a couple of other things I need to check in on here at the park where we found Boyne's body, and back at the office where I hope our rogue deputy, Gallagher, still has one of the bad guys in custody. His name is Ingalls and he's the one Pepper fired a while back. He's hip-deep in this drug ring. I have a bad feeling his old buddy Gallagher is in on it, too. I can't come up with any other way that Tern was tipped off about the bust tonight."

"Well, be careful," Hanna said. "The Skipper is back and feeling pretty good about the *Maggie Mae* helping out."

"Yeah, I saw him coming up the river. I hear he did a good job."

"Alex, I'm so sorry about tonight... your friend, Boyne, and now Pepper, too."

He paused for a moment and took a deep breath. "We need to find Tern and Lacroix. It all leads back to those two."

"We're okay here," Hanna said. "Skipper has his shotgun and he's hoping the bad guys stop by."

"Of course he is," Alex replied, managing a thin smile. He was pulling into the parking lot by the fire tower. Two State Police vehicles were still there. "I need to run. I'll call when I'm on my way back."

"I love you, Alex."

"I love you, too. I'll see you soon."

He got out and walked toward the gathering of crime scene investigators. An officer in uniform came toward him and introduced himself as Trooper Wayans."

"Alex Frank, Charleston County Sheriff's Department." He shook hands with the man. Alex looked beyond him and Boyne Combes' body was still on the ground. "What have you learned?"

Wayans turned and walked toward the rest of the team with Alex, then said, "Well, we can rule out suicide."

"How's that?"

"He's got a bullet hole in the back of his brain."

"What?"

"Small caliber. Close range. Probably a .22."

"We didn't have time to spend with the body earlier, except to check for vitals."

Wayans said, "Heard the drug bust went down okay."

Alex nodded but said, "Sheriff Stokes took a few rounds. He's in pretty bad shape."

"Sorry to hear that. We've got some of our troopers working with the locals and Feds to help find this Tern guy. Nothing yet as far as I've heard."

Alex knelt beside the lifeless body of his friend. Wayans leaned in next to him with a flashlight and pointed to the bullet wound at the back of the man's head. Alex looked up into the dark form of the fire tower above them. "Find anything up there?"

"Not sure he was ever up there. Forensics guys aren't seeing signs of trauma from a fall. He may have been shot here."

Alex thought for a moment. "Our guy Tern was out on a boat in the bay."

"No way it was self-inflicted from that angle behind," Wayans said.

Alex stood as the loose ends started coming together in his brain. "I may have something for you shortly. I need to get back down to the department."

Alex pulled into the parking lot behind the Sheriff's Department building at a little past one in the morning. A single pole lamp illuminated the area. There were two other department cruisers parked and three pick-up trucks. He could see lights on inside the building, which was not unusual. Before he got out, he pulled his service weapon and checked the magazine, which was full. Getting out, he placed the gun back in his holster and started toward the back door.

The night sky was clear above, the air cool. A dog barked down the street and he could hear music still playing, probably from a nearby house or car radio. A soft wind from the south pushed the tops of the tall pines in a slow cadence.

He reached the door and pulled his security card and held it against the electronic reader on the wall. The door clicked open, and he pulled it back to go in. Walking down a long hall past restrooms, the kitchen and a lounge area, he came into the main squad room where his desk and others were located. No one was in sight. The light to Sheriff Stokes' office was off. He pushed aside the troubling images of Pepper lying near death just a short time ago. He walked through the desks to a door on the far wall that led to the front reception area.

The duty officer for the night sat behind a long counter, reading something on the computer screen. It was a woman who Alex had met briefly a couple of days earlier, but he couldn't remember her name. She looked up in surprise when he came in.

"Oh... good evening."

"Hi, Alex Frank."

"Right, I remember, she said. My name is Castle... Mary."

"Sure, Mary....," Alex replied. "You heard about the sheriff?"

"I did," she said, standing. "Any news from the hospital?"

He shook his head. "Hey, did Gallagher bring in former-deputy Ingalls earlier tonight?"

She looked puzzled. "I just came on duty an hour ago. Haven't seen either of them."

"Nobody back in the holding cells?"

"Haven't looked."

"Let me know if you hear anything from the hospital," he said, leaning over to write his cell number on a message slip.

"Will do. How bad is he?"

"Not good, I'm afraid."

He walked back and down a hall to the holding cells. All of them were empty.

So, where did Gallagher take Ingalls? he thought, heading back to his desk. He was almost certain now that Gallagher was dirty and had probably worked with Ingalls to tip-off Tern about the drug raid.

He sat down and looked through the clutter, trying to think through what he should do next. There were several telephone message slips but nothing that he needed to deal with tonight.

He looked over at Gallagher's desk, then rose and walked over to it. He scanned the papers and files, noticed pictures of the deputy's wife and two small boys. He tried the drawers of the desk, but they were all locked.

Back at his own desk, he pulled out a phone book and looked for the listing for Gallagher's address, but there was nothing. He picked up the phone and buzzed the front desk.

Mary Castle answered, "Yes?"

"Do you have a cell and home address for Gallagher? I need to get in touch with him tonight."

"Yeah, just a second."

Alex could hear a drawer pulled, papers shuffling.

"Here we go," Castle said. She gave him the number and the address.

"Thanks Mary," Alex replied. "I'm headed back out. Again, call me if you hear anything from the hospital... and if Gallagher shows up, don't say anything to him, just call me."

"Will do, Deputy Frank."

Alex walked back out into the night air, the stress and chaos of the past day starting to catch up with him. He was exhausted and his body felt numb. He started toward his pick-up, reaching for his keys in his pocket. He climbed in and fired up the engine. There was country music playing loudly on the radio and he turned the volume down. As he was backing out, he noticed one of the other trucks was gone, but there were no more department cruisers in the lot.

He pulled out onto the main road and started toward the highway back to Dugganville. He reached for the contact information for Gallagher that Castle had given him. He pulled out his cell and called the number on the message slip. There were six rings before the call went to a voicemail message, ``This is Gallagher, leave a message."

After the beep, Alex said, "Gallagher, we need to talk." He left his cell number and ended the call.

The sign for Highway 17 came up and he turned south. The four-lane road was deserted in both directions at this late hour, then he noticed headlights pull out behind him from the same street he'd just come. At first, he didn't pay much attention but then, looking in his rearview mirror, he saw the vehicle coming up fast behind him. He was still driving in the left lane from the turn he'd made and pulled over to the right lane to let the driver pass. He didn't care how fast the vehicle was going, he was in no mood to pull over a speeder in the middle of the night on his way home.

Lights flashed in his rearview and he looked back. The vehicle was swerving over to the right lane, too, and was approaching quickly. As it came closer, he could tell it was a truck. The outline of two men could be seen riding inside. *What the hell?*

Before he could react, the big truck slammed into the rear of his own truck. Alex fought to keep control, the truck veering suddenly toward the shoulder and the ditch that ran beside it. He looked back in the mirror and saw the vehicle swerve suddenly out into the left lane then speed up alongside. Before he could do anything else, he watched as his pursuer swerved hard to the right crashing into his front quarter panel. He slammed on his brakes, but there was nothing he could do to prevent the truck from spinning to the right, tires squealing, as he headed over the gravel shoulder then down the embankment and a sudden jarring crash into the ditch. Water sprayed up on the windshield. His driver-side airbag exploded in his face. He felt the pain of the impact across his body from the shoulder harness. He sat there, stunned for a moment, the truck leaning at a precarious angle, nearly on its side.

Ahead, he saw his attackers pull to the side of the road. The reverse lights came on and the truck started backing up toward him. He reached to release the seat belt, then tried to open his door. It was jammed from the damage of the collision and wouldn't open. He slid across the console to the passenger seat, the pain from the impact screaming back at him. The brake lights went on in the truck coming back toward him and he watched it stop ten yards away. As he pushed open the passenger door, he pulled his handgun.

Painfully, he jumped down into the water flowing in the ditch, then ran quickly around to the back of his truck, scanning the roadside for any other cover. He knelt behind the driver's side back of the truck and peered around. The two men were getting out.

"Stay right there!" Alex yelled. "Charleston Sheriff's Department!"

No response as both men ran across behind their truck and into the woods alongside the road. Alex moved quickly to the other side, but the men had already disappeared into the woods. He scrambled back across the ditch up onto the shoulder, keeping the truck as cover. He reached for his cell phone but realized it was still in the cab. He tried the driver's door again, but the crunched metal had left it too damaged to open.

Listening for any sign of the men, he moved to the back and looked over the truck bed. The woods were dense and dark, no nearby lights to illuminate the area. He heard footsteps and limbs breaking.

He yelled again. "Charleston Sheriff's Department! Come out now with your hands up!" He knew the demand was useless but was trying to buy time and think through a line of defense.

The first gunshot exploded from the woods and the round pinged off the far side of his truck. The second shot hit the rear window of the cab and shattered into a thousand pieces. Alex ducked to avoid the flying glass and keep his head down from another possible shot.

He turned as lights from another car approached from the north and sped past, apparently not interested in engaging with a crashed vehicle and sheriff's deputy taking cover with his gun out.

Movement down the road behind him caught his attention, and he fell instinctively to the ground rolling to the side. Two more gunshots rang out and both rounds hit the ground near his head, sending dust and gravel flying. He rolled under the truck and took aim at where the shots had come from.

He saw the man approaching in a crouched position, his gun pointed out toward the truck.

Alex fired his own weapon three times in close succession. He heard the man scream and then stagger and fall to one knee, then crumble over onto the road.

He tried to catch his breath, the gunshots ringing in his ears, the smell of gunpowder heavy in the air under the truck. Listening for sounds of the other attacker, he managed to crawl back out and stand behind the cover of the truck again. Looking down the road, he saw the still body of the man who had just fallen.

The sound of water splashing from the other direction caused him to duck down and look back the other way. The second man was racing toward the side of his truck. He threw open the passenger door and jumped in. The truck was still running. Alex saw the brake lights come again as the man got behind the wheel and put the vehicle into gear. Gravel flew out in all directions as he slammed down on the accelerator.

Alex watched the truck swerve twice then gain purchase on the blacktop. He aimed his weapon at the back window and fired off four rounds in quick succession. The glass shattered and the truck swerved hard left, almost going into the far ditch before the driver recovered and sped away.

Alex stood there a moment watching the taillights racing away. He lowered the gun and leaned back against his own truck. He sucked in a deep breath trying to gather himself. He looked back the other way and saw the prone figure of the man he'd just shot. Headlights were approaching and he watched the car slow as the body and the wrecked truck came into the driver's view.

Alex started walking in that direction. He kept his gun at his side. The car slowed to a stop and the passenger's side window came down as it pulled onto the shoulder just past the body. He looked in and saw an older woman staring back wide-eyed.

"Officer, is everything okay?" she asked nervously.

He thought for a moment, looking back in the other direction, then said, "There's been an incident. It's under control now. Thank you for stopping, but I need to have you move along."

"Can I call someone?" she asked.

"No, thank you," Alex replied, suddenly thinking of Hanna. "No, but thank you."

Hesitantly, the woman said, "Well, if you're sure."

"Yes, you need to get moving along... and have a good night."

He watched her nod and then pull back onto the road and drive away. He looked back at the man lying on his left side next to the road. He aimed his gun at the body and started walking slowly toward it. He pulled the small flashlight he kept on this belt and aimed it with the gun. There was no movement and he saw the man's gun lying a few feet away in the grass.

He came up and pushed the man's back with his foot, still keeping the gun and the light pointed down, ready to fire. There was no response. He knelt and shined the light in the man's face.

Ingalls!

He looked back down the road behind him into the darkness. He knew the other man had to be Gallagher. He reached down and felt for a pulse on the man's neck. Nothing. He stood and walked back to his truck and found his cell on the seat. He dialed the duty officer at the Sheriff's Department.

This is Deputy Frank. There's been a shooting incident on Highway 17, about two miles south of the Dugganville turn-off. I have one man down, apparently deceased. Please alert local and state police to be on alert or a black pick-up truck headed south, body damage on the front and passenger's side. The driver may be Deputy William Gallagher. He should be considered armed and dangerous."

"What?" he heard the dispatcher say in surprise.

"He and former Deputy Ingalls just ran me off the road and tried to kill me."

There was a pause on the line, then the woman said, "I'll get the alert out right away."

Alex ended the call and looked back at the dead body of Ingalls. As he thought through the situation, it appeared that Gallagher and Ingalls knew they had to take him out to avoid being implicated in the drug deal and with Pepper Stokes hovering near death, there would be no one else that would be on to them.

He walked around his truck to see if there was any way he could back the vehicle out, but clearly, that was pointless.

He reached for his phone again and called Will Foster's number. The FBI agent took the call after a few rings.

"Alex?"

He ran through what had just happened with Gallagher and Ingalls.

"Whoa! So they were both dirty?" Foster said.

"Gallagher has nowhere to go now. We're all on to him. I've got the dispatcher sending out an APB on the truck."

"We're wrapping up here," Foster said. "DEA has what they need. Still no sign of the shooter."

Alex thought for a moment about Lando Tern. The man had to still be somewhere near Dugganville unless he had commandeered a vehicle or another boat. In the distance, he heard the low wail of a siren then saw emergency lights approaching from about a mile away, coming from the direction of the Dugganville turn-off. As the car approached, he recognized the colors of a State Police cruiser.

"I'll stay in touch," Alex said. "State cop is here. I need to deal with this shooting."

"Keep your head down, partner," Foster said.
"Yeah, right!"

CHAPTER FORTY-FIVE

"You're sure you're okay?" Hanna said, standing in Skipper Frank's living room as Alex relayed the attack he had just survived from his phone. Skipper and Ella were listening intently from the couch.

"I'm fine," she heard Alex reply. "Crime scene investigators are coming. I'll need to be here for a while longer. They still haven't found Tern, so please be alert," he warned.

"Skipper has his shotgun ready," she said, looking over at the old shrimper.

"I'll call you as soon as I can get away. If it's too much later, I won't wake you. I have a key to let myself in."

"Please be careful!" she replied.

"A little late for that."

She ended the call and sat back across from Skipper and Ella, relaying all that Alex had just shared about the assault out on Highway 17.

"Damn, there's dirty cops everywhere!" Skipped flared. "Good to hear Alex took one of the bastards out."

The explosion of shattering glass outside caused them all to flinch. The sound of a car's horn blaring in succession followed as an alarm had been set off.

Hanna looked over at Skipper Frank, who was standing and reaching for his shotgun.

"You all stay in here!" he demanded.

"Skipper, don't!" Ella pleaded, grabbing at his shirtsleeve. "Let's call the police."

"Not gonna let some sumbitch come round here!" He walked quickly to the front door and turned the bolt latch. He made sure the outdoor lights were on then opened the door, the big gun pointed out. "I'll be back! Y'all wait here!" He closed the door behind him.

Ella raced to the window and Hanna followed. She could see her Honda parked out by the road. The emergency lights were flashing, and the horn continued to blare. She went back to her bag and pulled the gun out. Thoughts of the mocking face of Lando Tern came to her and the image of him falling back off her deck as she fired shots at him.

She joined Ella at the window again. Skipper was approaching the car in a low crouch, his shotgun pointed out ahead."

"Dear God!" said Ella.

Hanna put her arm around her then yelled out, "Nooo!!!" as she saw a dark figure racing toward Skipper from the side. The man had a rifle and he hit Skipper on the back of the head with it. Hanna watched him fall immediately to his knees as he stumbled from the blow, then over onto his side.

Ella screamed out, "Skipper!"

Hanna moved on instinct to the front door and raced out through the screen porch. As she ran, she clipped off the safety on the gun. Her chest was pounding, and the horn blared in her ears. She pushed through the screen door and down the few steps to the front walk. The man was looming over the fallen figure of Skipper Frank, the barrel of the rifle now pointed at his head.

"Stop!" she yelled out, slowing now and raising her pistol. She saw the attacker turn and could see the face of Lando Tern in the light from the porch. A smile came across his face when he saw her.

"Hello, pretty lady," he said.

Hanna saw his gun start to turn in her direction and she didn't hesitate. Only ten steps away now, she fired six shots.

Lando Tern stumbled back. His rifle fell to the ground. He tripped on one of Skipper's legs and fell over onto the ground.

The gunshots echoed in Hanna's ear over the blare of the car horn. Her hands started shaking uncontrollably as she kept the gun pointed at Lando Tern. She started forward.

Tern rolled over and struggled to get to one knee. He looked up at her. Blood was dripping from the corner of his mouth. He smiled again and his teeth were covered red with his blood.

She pointed the gun at his face, now just a few feet away. "Get back down on the ground!" she ordered. From behind, she heard Ella rushing up.

"Skipper!" she yelled out, kneeling down beside her fallen husband.

Hanna was distracted for just a moment, and when she looked back at Tern, he was reaching for the rifle. Without thinking, she fired three more shots into the chest of Lando Tern. He grunted and fell back, his arms flying up as he tried to catch himself. She watched him tumble back onto the grass on his back, staring straight up through the trees. He lay still, his chest rising in gasping breaths.

Her legs went weak and she fell to her knees, choking for breath, the gun still pointed at their attacker. She felt a hand on her shoulder and turned to see Ella beside her.

"Skipper's hurt!" Ella yelled out. "We need to get help for Skipper!"

Alex rode in the passenger seat of the State Police cruiser as it turned onto the street along the river towards his father's house. The lights of two police cars and an ambulance flashed in the trees. The car screeched to a stop in front of the house next door and he started running up to the front yard of his old home. He saw a man still down in the grass face up, his arms laid out wide. He knew it was Lando Tern from Hanna's description of the shooting. A cop knelt beside the body, examining the man. He scanned the crowd of people for Hanna and saw her standing beside a gurney next to the ambulance.

She saw him running up and turned and rushed into his arms. He held her close and felt her shaking as her emotions caught up with her and she started to sob.

He held her close. "It's okay. It's okay. He's gone." He looked over her shoulder. His father was sitting up on the gurney. A paramedic was treating a wound on the back of his head. He could hear the old man scolding the technician to leave him alone.

"I'm fine, dammit!" Skipper yelled out again. "Leave me the hell alone."

Alex walked with Hanna in his arm over to his father, who was trying to get up off the gurney. He felt a tremendous sense of relief come over him that everyone was safe. Ella was trying to push her husband back down on the gurney.

"Let them help you!" Ella scolded.

Alex came up to his father. "You need to learn to duck, old man," he said. Before Skipper could reply, he took his father in his arms and pulled him close. "I'm glad you're okay," he whispered. "Thanks for watching out for Hanna."

Skipper pushed back. "That lady can take care of herself!"

Alex's cell phone rang. He pulled it out and took the call. It was an emergency room doctor calling from the hospital.

"I'm here with Sheriff Stokes," the doctor said. "He wanted me to call you. We've stabilized him, and we're taking him up to surgery in a moment. He wanted you to know he's okay."

"Can I talk to him?" Alex asked.

"No, I'm afraid not," the doctor replied. "We need to get him into surgery."

"Tell him to hang in there," Alex said, relief washing over him that he hadn't lost another friend to the carnage caused by Xavier Lacroix and Lando Tern.

He turned back to Hanna. In the lights from the house and the emergency vehicles, he could see the stress and exhaustion on her face. A wave of guilt swept over him as he thought about the chaos and danger he had brought into her life again. He held out his arms and she came to him again, her face on his shoulder as they hugged each other close.

"I just killed a man," she said sadly.

"You did what you had to do."

"He was going to hurt Skipper. I think he was going to kill him," she said, desperation in her voice.

"Hanna, you did the right thing. He can't hurt anyone else now." He felt her squeeze him tighter. "You did the right thing."

CHAPTER FORTY-SIX

Special Agent Will Foster stood beside the skipper of the Coast Guard patrol boat as they sped out through the low swells of Charleston Harbor toward the mouth of the Atlantic Ocean. The looming shape of Ft. Sumter could just be seen ahead in the morning mist as the sun came up over the far horizon. The clouds were lit with a fiery red glow and gulls scattered from their overnight spots on the water as the boat sped past.

Xander Lacroix's boat had been tracked down at a marina on the bay further in along the harbor from downtown Charleston. Air and land observation teams had been set up overnight. A message came in at 6 a. m. that the boat was leaving its slip and heading for open water. A Coast Guard helicopter and land radar units were tracking the course of the boat, which was currently a mile out into the ocean on a southwest course toward the Bahamas. A second Coast Guard patrol boat was on its way up from the south and was coordinating with the skipper of the launch Foster was on to take over the Lacroix vessel together. The helicopter would remain at a distance on standby until the patrol boats were close enough to overtake Lacroix.

Fellow agent Sharron Fairfield was also onboard. Both of them had on tactical gear and bullet-proof vests, as did the Coast

Guard crew. All were heavily armed. At current speeds, the two Coast Guard vessels would overtake Lacroix within the hour.

Foster had received word from Alex Frank that Sheriff Pepper Stokes had come through surgery well and was resting comfortably. It was not clear what long-term damage may have been done, but the old sheriff seemed to be out of danger. He also learned that Lando Tern had been killed during an assault on the Frank house in Dugganville.

Foster had not been surprised to hear from Alex that Hanna had taken down the man as he was attacking Alex's father. In the past few years, he had developed a deep respect for Hanna Walsh, her strength of character, her intellect, and now her courage in confronting the crazed Lando Tern.

Alex poured another cup of coffee for Hanna as they sat out on the back porch of his father's house. The sun was coming up through the morning pines and breaking the chill of the night. Neither had slept well after a previous day and night of extreme emotion. He had held Hanna in his arms for much of the night, and she clung closely to him for comfort.

"You're sure Pepper's going to be okay?" Hanna asked, then took a sip from her coffee.

"Doctor seems to think so. I'm going to head over there a bit later this morning after he gets a little more rest."

"And Will and Sharron have Lacroix in their sights?" she asked.

"They think he's onboard and they're hoping Brenda Dellahousaye and Jordan Hayes are there as well and still alive."

"I can't believe your father wouldn't let the paramedics take him to the hospital last night to check out that head wound," Hanna said. "He must have a concussion, at the least, after the blow he took."

"He's the hardest-headed old bird I've ever known," Alex replied with a wry smile.

Hanna managed to smile as well, though Alex could still see the stress and anxiety in her face.

"Any word on the other rogue deputy... Gallagher?" she asked.

"No, we have his house and other known haunts under surveillance. There's no way he can stay around here now. Everyone's on to his alliance with the drug ring."

Ella came out the back door. She was dressed in her usual green plaid robe reaching nearly to the ground. Her feet were bare, and she balanced a coffee mug in one hand and held a big donut in the other.

"How's the Skipper," Alex asked.

"Still snorin' like a freight train."

"Good," Alex said. "He needs to get as much rest as he can.

"He had three or four shots of bourbon before he hit the sack last night," Ella said, shaking her head as she sat at the picnic table with him. "Said he needed a little something to calm himself. Yeah right! Had to practically tie him down to keep him from runnin' down to *Gilly's* to drink with the boys. Ella reached over and took Hanna's hand. "Thank you, sweetie. I know I told you last night, but thank you. You saved the old coot's life."

Alex watched as Hanna flinched at the reference to how close Lando Tern had come to killing her new father-in-law. She said, "I'm just glad Tern is out of commission."

Will Foster could see Xander Lacroix's boat clearly now up ahead about a mile. A big wake pushed out on both sides, the curling waves shining in the early morning sun. The Coast Guard skipper leaned over.

"They're picking up speed. They must know we're coming in after them."

"What's the plan of attack?" Foster asked over the roar of the big outboards on the back of the launch.

"We'll have the chopper come in fast, ID themselves and demand the boat come to a stop with all passengers up on deck. We'll move in with the other boat. If they refuse, we have the 50-caliber machine gun mounted up on the bow. If we light that thing up, it will convince them we mean business."

"We may have a hostage situation if the Dellahousaye woman and the old senator are aboard."

"We're prepared for that eventuality," the Coast Guard skipper replied.

"Let's just hope Lacroix is actually onboard," Foster said, looking out ahead again as they were noticeably closing the gap on the big cruiser.

Hanna watched Skipper Frank shuffle barefoot into the kitchen in his red boxer shorts and a white t-shirt with the Atlanta Braves logo printed on the chest. He was hatless for a change, and his scraggly gray hair pushed out in all directions. His face was puffy and flushed from the night's sleep and the booze. A small bandage was taped over the back of his head.

She was sitting at the kitchen table with a fresh cup of coffee, reading through the messages on her phone. Alex had left to go out to the hospital to see Pepper Stokes. He had taken her Honda even though one of the back windows was smashed out by Lando Tern. Alex's truck had been towed back to a body shop near Dugganville for repairs. Ella had left her to go take a shower.

"Mornin', Hanna," Skipper said in a hoarse voice. "Where's the damn coffee?"

She got up and went to the counter for the pitcher. "Here, let me pour you a cup." She pulled a mug down from the cupboard, poured the coffee and handed it to him. They both sat down at the small table, Skipper grunting in discomfort as he plopped down.

"How you feeling?" she asked, knowing full well he certainly felt terrible.

He took a long sip from his coffee, then another. With tired eyes and hands visibly shaking, he said, "I'll be alright. Just glad you parked enough rounds into that asshole last night to take him off the board."

Hanna didn't respond. She could feel a rush of dread sweep over her again as she tried to push aside images of Lando Tern's last gasp efforts to hurt them all. She could still hear the gunshot blasts echoing in her ear. She could smell the gun smoke and feel the hard grip of the pistol in her hand. She could still see Tern falling and laying there on the lawn, the big rifle beside him, his eyes lifeless but still mocking.

"You okay, honey?" Skipper asked.

She nodded. "Long night."

"Hey, I was thinkin'," he said. "Love to have you and Alex head out on the salt with me this afternoon on my shrimp run. Never had you out there."

She thought about the invitation for a moment. A little fresh air and beautiful scenery were exactly what she needed. "Love to!"

Will Foster watched the big orange and white Coast Guard helicopter sweep in fast to overtake Lacroix's vessel. The boat he was on, and the other patrol boat, were approaching from opposite angles. A crewman was up on both bows behind the big 50-caliber mounted machine guns ready to fire if necessary. The rest of the crew were positioned on the decks of the speeding patrol boats.

Foster heard the booming loudspeaker from the helicopter as it came in and took position above Lacroix's boat plowing through the calm seas. "U.S. Coast Guard! Stop your vessel now!"

Foster strained to see ahead. There were no visible passengers on the rear deck of Lacroix's big cruiser. He did see the shape of a man at the wheel of the ship inside the cabin, apparently paying no attention to the big chopper flying above or the two heavily armed patrol boats coming in fast.

The pilot on the chopper repeated the warning, and still, the boat pressed on. The patrol boats came alongside Lacroix's boat and took up the same course on each side about 100 yards out. Foster turned as the skipper on his boat barked into the radio to the crewman up front.

The sound of the 50-caliber erupting was deafening. Foster watched as the rapid-fire rounds from the gun peppered the water in front of Lacroix's cruiser. The other patrol boat did the same from the other side. Still, the boat didn't slow.

Then, they all ducked when a man came out from the cabin with what looked like an Uzi submachine gun and started firing back at the boat Foster was on. The skipper had his crew take evasive action and they swerved hard to the left away from the cruiser. Foster looked back as the other patrol boat took dead aim at the cruiser's cabin. The windows exploded in flying shards of glass and the man with the Uzi went down.

The big boat began to slow. Foster could see the name now on the stern, *Dangerous. No shit!* he thought to himself. He watched as the boat pulled up completely and rocked in the swells from its own wake. Both patrol boats took position off each side, all guns trained on the cabin. The giant helicopter hovered above, the sound blasting the morning air.

Foster heard the helicopter loudspeaker again. *"U.S. Coast Guard. All passengers on deck now, hands raised."*

Nothing happened for at least a minute. The captains of each patrol boat and the pilot of the helicopter were all talking on the radio as they waited. Then, Foster saw a woman pushed through the back door of the cabin. It was Brenda Dellahousaye. She was followed by another man dressed all in black, holding a pistol to her head. Over the radio, he heard a voice from Lacroix's boat say, "Everyone needs to back off! We will kill our hostages one at a time until we are allowed to proceed. We are not bluffing!"

The Coast Guard officers were conferring on their own radio channel. Foster leaned in and shouted. "They must have Senator Hayes inside, too."

The Coast Guard leaders agreed on a course of action and the loudspeaker barked again. "You will not be allowed to leave under any circumstances! Surrender now!"

Foster watched the man on Lacroix's boat with the gun to Brenda Dellahousaye's head turn and listen to someone inside. He looked back at the woman and fired one round into her skull. She went down in a heap on the deck of the boat. The man ran back inside the cabin and the boat powered up and started forward again.

Foster heard Agent Fairfield yell out in surprise, "Ohmigod!"

Both skippers ordered the 50 calibers to open fire on the waterline of the boat. Dozens of rounds exploded into the white side of the hull, water erupting when they aimed lower. The boat still kept on gaining speed. The Coast Guard vessels and helicopter kept pace, the big guns still firing.

"Take out the cabin!" the skipper beside him yelled into the radio to his man up front on the big gun. The walls and windows of the cruiser exploded in a frenzy of destruction as the big shells came in. A radar tower on top of the cabin exploded and fell off the side of the boat.

Finally, the boat began to slow again, then turned in a slow arc to the left. Orders were issued to stop shooting. Foster tried to see if anyone was still at the wheel of what was left of the cabin on the cruiser, but he couldn't see anyone. The boat came slowly to a stop and smoke and flames were suddenly visible coming from below deck. A propane line for the stove had probably been hit. Foster could see a gas slick forming around the boat now coming from the boat's fuel tanks. He knew it was just a matter of time before the tanks exploded. The Coast Guard skipper was talking heatedly with his colleagues on the radio. The boats were ordered to back off to a safer distance and the helicopter did the same.

Foster looked up in surprise when he saw a man run from the flaming cabin and rush to the rail, climbing up and diving out into the water. He heard more shouting on the radios by the Coast Guard skippers. He watched the man trying to swim away from the boat. The flames from the fire onboard somehow ignited the gas on the surface of the ocean, and suddenly, the floating vessel was surrounded by a flaming inferno. The man in the water seemed to be engulfed in the flames, but then Foster saw him emerge and keep struggling to swim away. He was coming toward their boat.

The air in the cockpit of the patrol boat seemed to be sucked away as a huge explosion of fire blew out from below decks of Lacroix's boat. The entire boat seemed to lift before it exploded in a huge mushroom cloud of fire and debris.

Foster and Fairfield ducked instinctively as debris rained down around their boat. The Coast Guard skipper beside them was yelling out orders. Foster looked up and the floating carcass of what was left of Lacroix's boat was still in flames. There was no sign of life anywhere and no one else visible in the water except the man still swimming toward them, a sea of flames on the water behind him.

The boat maneuvered to pick up the man and Foster rushed out to the rail. Two crew members leaned over and grabbed the man's hands, then pulled him up on deck. Foster was completely stunned to see the wet and terrified face of ex-Senator Jordan Hayes. The man was coughing and gasping for air.

There was another small explosion on Lacroix's boat, and they all looked over as the wreckage seemed to split in two from front to back, and then each flaming mass slowly slipped below the surface of the water. Flames from the fires on the gas-soaked water continued to burn. Foster scanned the water and the burning debris for any other survivors, but there were none.

Foster made his way over to Hayes, who was being attended to by a medical officer. "Hello, Senator," he said.

The man looked up in surprise. "Agent Foster! Where the hell have you been?"

"I was going to ask you the same," Foster replied. "Was that Brenda Dellahousaye on deck who they shot?" he asked.

Hayes looked back in surprise. "What... I don't know. I was down below. They shot her?"

"Yes, I'm afraid so. I doubt she would have survived the explosion," Foster said. "How did you get away?"

Foster watched Hayes close his eyes tight and shake his head slowly. "There were bullets coming in all around us in the cabin down below. The man who had been guarding me was hit and knocked down. I started running and made it to the rear deck. Thank God, I got off when I did."

"Was Lacroix onboard with you?" Foster asked.

Hayes shook his head. "I never saw the man after they took us from the house to the boat."

CHAPTER FORTY-SEVEN

Alex walked out of the hospital into the heat of the morning. He'd just left his boss and friend, Pepper Stokes. The man was weak and still listed as "critical", but the doctor had assured Alex he was most likely out of danger. The old sheriff had been pleased to hear the drug bust had gone down successfully and that Lando Tern was dead. He was not surprised to hear of his two deputies, Gallagher and Ingalls, role in the scheme. He had a couple of suggestions for Alex to follow-up on to try to find Gallagher.

He'd also just ended a call with Will Foster, who brought him up to date on the takedown of Lacroix's boat out on the Atlantic, the death of Brenda Dellahousaye and the recovery of the wily old senator, Jordan Hayes. He was not pleased to hear that Lacroix was apparently not onboard.

It was fifteen minutes back to Dugganville. Alex got in Hanna's Honda and started back. He tried to think where Xander Lacroix would go. He would have to be on the run. His involvement in the drug deal, the abduction of the Dellahousaye woman and Hayes was not in question. It would all lead to a quick trip back to federal prison.

Alex pulled out into traffic on Highway 17 again, thinking back on how close he had come to dying on this road the night before. His thoughts returned to Gallagher. He pushed the button for the front car windows and the fresh breeze swept through the car. One of the rear windows had been broken out by Tern. He couldn't help but think with a smile, despite all the chaos brewing around him, *Hanna's needed a new car for a long time anyway!*

The big private jet lifted off from a small airport north of Charleston. Xander Lacroix sat back in the plush leather seat and took a deep breath of relief. He was away and out of the reach of the Feds, who were surely scouring the state for him. He lifted a crystal glass filled with ice and bourbon and drained the whisky. He filled the glass again from the bottle on the shelf beside him.

The plane banked over to the left and he could see the coastline of the Atlantic coming up. He would be landing at a private airstrip on Eleuthera in an hour or so, then staying at an old friend's estate on the island until he could determine a longer course of action.

He had been in constant communication with his man on his boat, which was also headed for the islands, until they had been commandeered by the Feds. He had listened to much of the attack and knew all aboard were likely killed when the big boat exploded. He felt no emotion about the loss of his men. They were expendable. He also felt no remorse for the death of Brenda Dellahousaye and Jordan Hayes. *The world is a better place with both of them gone*, he thought as he took another sip from his bourbon.

He looked across the aisle at his girlfriend, who was looking out the window on the other side of the plane. Her short skirt revealed long legs stretched out into the aisle.

At least I'll have company on the island, he thought to himself and took another drink, smiling as he looked back out at the shimmering ocean below.

Alex pulled onto the main street of Dugganville. The familiar storefronts passed by, a few faces he recognized on the sidewalks. He had planned to go back and check on Hanna and the Skipper before going back to work, but he decided to stop at the park first. Something was still nagging at him about the old fire tower.

He pulled into the small parking area beside the tower. There were no other cars. He looked across the grassy area around the tower. Boyne Combes' body had of course been taken away the previous night. He got out and closed the door to Hanna's car behind him. He walked across the freshly mowed grass to the base of the tower. He turned and surveyed the spots where both Boyne and Ally Combes had met their deaths.

He needed to clear his mind and map out where he needed to go, what he needed to do next. The events of the past days had left him frazzled and numb. He also hadn't slept.

He walked to the base of the stairs leading up to the observation deck on the fire tower and started up. He stopped twice to catch his breath and then finally made his way up the final flight and onto the deck, leaning on the rail, breathing heavily. He looked out across the scene before him leading all the way out to the Atlantic. The broad stretch of green treetops was cut by the meandering river leading out to the bay where the drug deal had been taken down and the ocean beyond.

He looked down and saw the spot where Boyne and Ally both lay dead within the past few days. He closed his eyes in sadness at the loss of two young people in the prime of their life, one lost to drug addiction and dangerous men, the other, her husband Boyne Combes, falling victim to bad judgment and involving himself with those same men to try to save his business.

He looked up in surprise when he heard the sound of the slide of an automatic weapon snapping back into place. He turned to his left and saw Gallagher standing against the rail, his

9mm handgun aimed directly at his chest. He also saw the man's blood-soaked shirt and some sort of bandage wrapped around the man's neck, it too, soaked in blood. The man was clearly struggling to stay up, leaning heavily against the rail with his hip, both hands holding the gun.

Gallagher tried to speak, but the words wouldn't come. He tried to swallow and spit out a big gob of blood over the rail.

Alex tried to keep his composure. He knew he was moments from death. This man was clearly desperate. He tried to buy some time and said, "You're all through, Gallagher. There's nowhere for you to run. Everyone knows what you've been up to."

"Shut up!" Gallagher shouted back and then spit again, the blood landing now near his boots on the deck.

Alex looked into his eyes beyond the gun barrel. They were clouded and distant, almost as if he couldn't even see him. "What are you doing up here?"

Gallagher swallowed hard, then said, "I'm gonna die, asshole. Couldn't think of a better place. Now I get to take you with me." He tried to hold his aim steady, but his hands were shaking, and he was having trouble keeping his arms up.

"Tell me what happened to Boyne and Ally," Alex demanded.

Gallagher seemed confused at first but then managed a thin smile, blood dripping from the side of his mouth. He spoke slowly, stopping at times to spit and catch his breath. "The woman was a mess. She was strung out on cocaine. Tern had destroyed her. She turned to me when I started working with her husband on the drug deals. We had a *thing*."

Gallagher stopped again and his knees nearly buckled. Alex was almost ready to rush him, only a few steps away, but the gun came back up pointed directly at his head.

"She liked to do it up here on the tower. Like I said, we had a *thing*."

"How did she die, Gallagher?" Alex pressed.

The man looked down, keeping the gun pointed out at Alex. "That night, we were up here. We were inside there," he said, looking back into the glass observation room. "All of a sudden she started screaming. She was crazed on coke or something. She rushed out of the room and fell over the rail."

He started coughing and doubled over, the pain clear on his face. He took one hand off the gun and held it to the bandages on his bleeding neck. He kept the gun up with the other hand.

Alex waited on a hair-trigger to rush the man. He knew it would be his only chance.

Gallagher pulled himself back up on the rail, looking back almost blindly at Alex, his body weaving.

"And what about Boyne?" Alex asked, taking another step closer.

"We knew he'd ratted us out. I found him down here crying over his wife. I did what I had to do."

"Put a bullet in his head," Alex said.

"Exactly," Gallagher croaked, struggling to get the word out. "And now... it's your turn. You've been a pain in my ass from the beginning."

Alex watched the man's face, knowing at any second the finger on the trigger would pull back and the round would blow a hole in him. Gallagher would then surely finish the job.

The man coughed again and reached for his neck as the pain flared.

Alex knew this was his only chance.

He dropped to his left, then leapt out across the space between them. He hit Gallagher full force in the stomach with his shoulder as the gun went off. The round pinged off the metal rail behind him. Gallagher fell back and Alex landed on him and came up quickly, throwing a punch into the man's bandaged neck.

Gallagher screamed out and then, with surprising strength, pushed Alex off to the side.

Alex saw the gun and his hand and caught it as it swung in his direction. He slammed Gallagher's hand down hard on the deck once, then three more times. The weapon came free and clattered across the wood deck.

Alex got up on one knee and saw Gallagher trying to stand. Both men locked in a fierce struggle of arms and bodies as they came to their feet. Alex went for the man's vulnerable throat again and squeezed as hard as he could on the wound.

Gallagher's scream echoed out across the treetops.

Alex pushed him up against the rail, his hand still in a vice grip on his neck. He came up hard with his knee and caught Gallagher in the groin, which forced another blood-spitting scream.

Somehow, Gallagher managed to gather enough strength to throw a roundhouse punch from Alex's left. It caught him on the temple and stunned him for a moment.

He staggered back a step and watched as Gallagher pushed away from the rail and came at him again. He reached out and caught him with both hands grabbing his bloody uniform shirt.

Alex spun hard and threw Gallagher with all his remaining strength into the corner of the railing. He watched as the man tumbled over the rail and then disappeared from view. He could hear Gallagher's scream as he fell toward the ground below.

He reached the rail in time to see the man still falling, his arms flailing as if he could find something to catch himself in mid-air. He landed on his head and right shoulder and crumbled in a lifeless heap, his neck surely broken at impact.

Alex fell back against the wall of the observation room, his breath coming in ragged spurts. He sunk down and sat on the old wood deck, his hands at his side to steady himself. He looked over and saw Gallagher's gun lying nearby.

He closed his eyes and tried to catch his breath, to let the rush of adrenaline coursing through his body begin to subside.

Finally, he was able to stand again. He walked back to the rail and looked down. Gallagher's body was there, close to where both Boyne and Ally Combes had met their final moments.

He closed his eyes and felt a breath of wind on his face. He heard the sounds of birds in the nearby trees, a car honking downtown, children playing nearby. He opened his eyes and looked out again toward the ocean, a deep sense of relief overwhelming him that he was indeed alive.

Chapter Forty-eight

Jordan Hayes checked his hair in the reflection from a window next to the intercom box at the condominium in downtown Charleston. It was a reflexive action from years of focus on his dress and appearance. *Presence is everything in Washington,* he always said.

He found the button for Ophelia Dellahousaye and pressed it twice. The girl didn't come on the intercom to check who it was, she just buzzed to let him in. He had called ahead to let the twins know he was coming over. Ida and Ophelia were staying in town for their mother's funeral, though her body was not recovered from the flaming wreckage of Xander Lacroix's boat offshore.

Hayes walked across the lobby to the elevator. He thought back to the frightening moments that he and Brenda Dellahousaye had been aboard Lacroix's boat on their way to certain death offshore. The Coast Guard and the FBI had somehow found the boat and intercepted it. The gun battle that ensued had caused the boat to explode in a fiery end that had killed everyone aboard... except him.

Somehow, he had been able to jump overboard during the chaos and swim through the flames to the Coast Guard ship. He had only minor burns when he was checked. It was later he learned that Brenda had been executed on the deck of the ship by one of Lacroix's men. He was below and thankfully hadn't seen it. He was sure now that he would have met a similar fate.

The elevator door opened and he pressed the floor for Ophelia's condo. He felt he needed to see the girls, though his people had strongly advised him against it. Fortunately, there seemed to be no press around and this could be a private meeting.

Ophelia's door was open when he came down the hall. He walked in and saw one of the twins sitting on a couch with a cell phone to her ear. He thought it was Ida, whose dark brown hair was a bit longer and styled differently, but he was never sure. The other twin came out of the kitchen and now he was certain this one was Ophelia, the *wild* one as her mother and father had always referred to her. She was wearing a dark gray t-shirt with a marijuana leaf printed on the front. She had also dyed her hair a deep red with streaks of blue.

"Hello, Senator," Ophelia said, coming up to him and giving him a hug.

He looked over the girl's shoulder. The other twin, Ida, wasn't getting up and from her expression, she obviously wasn't as pleased to see him. Ophelia held on longer than he had expected, and he finally had to push himself away. They both walked into the living room with an expanse of big windows looking out over the skyline of Charleston.

"Hello, Ida," he said.

She didn't respond, placing her cell phone down on the coffee table, eying him with clear disdain.

"I came to pay my respects and offer my condolences," he said in his most practiced and senatorial ease. "Your mother was a dear friend…"

"Cut the bullshit, Jordan!" Ida said, standing in defiance.

"Excuse me?" Hayes said, truly surprised at the outburst.

"Ida, really…" her sister said.

Ida stared back for a moment. "You were only friends with our parents because they paid you to use your influence.

"Ida!" Ophelia broke in.

Ida looked over at her sister. "I can't believe you're falling for this nonsense. The FBI was very clear with both of us why this monster Lacroix was after all of us. Our dear mother set herself up to be killed with her foolish attempt to win back our father's business. And the *senator* here was playing both sides, taking money from our mother *and* Lacroix.

Ophelia shook her head as if she couldn't bring herself to believe any of this.

She sat down on the couch and reached for a half-smoked joint in an ashtray.

Hayes said, "Ida, I'm sorry you feel that way, but..."

She would let him finish. "No! I want you to leave now!"

Hayes stared back in disbelief. He truly felt an obligation to check in on the girls and extend his sympathies. But, of course the girl was right. His relationship with the Dellahousayes, going all the way back to the patriarch, Asa, the girl's grandfather, had always been about business and influence.

He steeled himself and regained his composure as Ophelia lit the joint and took a long pull, blowing the smoke up toward the ceiling and leaning back on the couch in resignation. "Ladies, I'm truly sorry for your loss. Brenda was a fine woman, just a little misguided in the end."

"Misguided!" Ida shouted back. "She was greedy and obsessed and she almost got all of us killed."

Hayes had heard enough. "Okay, dear... "

"Don't call me *dear*!"

He started backing away, indeed sorry he hadn't listened to the advice of his team. As he was letting himself out, he heard Ida scolding her sister.

"Would you put that damn thing out!"

He closed the door and started back down the hall, thinking about the Dellahousaye twins and what lay ahead for them. Both had considerable trust funds from their father and would certainly inherit more from their deceased mother. One was on her way to medical school. The other was likely on her way to a long and troubled life of drugs and excess.

As Jordan Hayes walked out into the sunlight from the Dellahousaye's building, he was surprised to see Special Agent Will Foster standing at the curb leaning against his government-issued blue sedan.

"Hello, Mr. Hayes," Foster said, as his female partner, Sharron Fairfield, got out on the other side of the car.

Hayes tried to remain calm and smiled uneasily. "Agent Foster, what a surprise."

The two agents came up and stood before him. Foster said, "We just needed a little time to build our case."

"Your case?" Hayes said, his gut lurching.

"The list of charges is too long to even begin," the woman said.

"Charges?"

"Yes," Foster said. "We're taking you into custody, Mr. Hayes."

"Custody!"

"You can call your lawyer on our way over to the Bureau office," Fairfield said.

She reached for his arm and turned him, pulling his wrists together behind him. He felt the cold steel of the handcuffs and listened as Foster read him his Miranda Rights.

His driver came up from his car parked down the street. "Senator, is there anything I can do?"

As he was lowered into the back seat of the car, he thought to himself, *these people have no idea who they're dealing with.* In his gut, though, he feared a bullet in the head

265

on the back of Xander Lacroix's boat might have been a far better end than the years ahead in a federal penitentiary.

CHAPTER FORTY-NINE

Hanna sat in a folding chair next to Ella on the deck of the *Maggie Mae* as the old shrimp trawler made its way out of the bay and into the blue Atlantic. The afternoon skies were clear with only high swirls of wispy clouds above. A flock of gulls followed closely off the stern, screeching for a handout.

Both women had glasses of cool sweet iced-tea in their hands. Hanna could smell the salt of the ocean and the stink of shrimp and diesel from the boat, but in her mind, it was the most glorious day.

Alex and his father were up in the wheelhouse. They had just lowered the outriggers for balance heading out into the big water and in preparation for lowering the nets off to each side of the *Maggie Mae*.

She looked at her husband and her father-in-law, Skipper Frank, and said a silent blessing that they were all here, together, and safe from the calamities of the past days.

Alex turned and looked back at the women and smiled when he saw his wife looking at him. He came out, dressed in old khaki shorts and a gray t-shirt wet with sweat from the work getting the boat ready for the shrimp run.

"Really, ladies, don't get up!" he shouted out, smiling over the din of the boat's diesel engine. "We got this. How's the tea?"

Hanna stood and put her glass next to the rail. She pulled him into her arms and held him close.

"What's this for?" he asked in surprise.

"Oh, just shut-up. Can't a girl hug her guy?"

He kissed her on the cheek then stepped away. "Got to get the nets down."

Hanna sat back with Ella and the two of them watched Alex winch down the big outriggers letting the nets run deep for the first run of shrimp. Hanna knew he'd been doing this work since he was a young boy and he obviously knew what he was doing.

Skipper Frank leaned his head out of the wheelhouse and barked out a few orders, but Alex had it all under control.

Ella leaned over. "I wish he'd take his shirt off." She pushed Hanna's arm and smiled with a lecherous grin.

"Ella Moore Frank!" Hanna said. "You are a naughty one!"

"You better believe it, dear!"

Hanna stood and walked to the rail, looking out across the vast ocean and the beach growing more distant to the west. Another shrimp boat was far down to the south working in the other direction. Two kids on jet skis came in close and the Skipper came out screaming at them to get away with hand gestures that were more than clear.

Hanna had to laugh at the old goat. He was truly an original.

An hour later, Skipper slowed the *Maggie Mae*. Alex came out with the deckhand, Anthony, and both men worked the winches to lift the outriggers and nets back over the rear deck of the boat. Hanna went to the side and watched the first net come up dripping in the afternoon sun. It seemed like a billion shrimp were squirming inside and she let out an excited cheer.

Alex expertly worked the net in over the deck, then loosened the bag lines along the bottom. The shrimp spilled out in a shimmering pile and spread across the deck. Anthony did the same with the net on the starboard side of the trawler, and soon, the catch doubled.

Hanna waded in and felt the shrimp flopping around her bare feet. She held her hands and let out a scream of joy. "Nice work, boys!"

Later, the shrimp had been sorted and stored below deck. The *Maggie Mae* was turned back toward shore, running at slow speed under Anthony's watch. Skipper and Alex joined their wives in chairs beside them on the deck, still slick from shrimp. They had cold beers in their hands and shared them with the women.

Skipper Frank held up his beer in a toast. "To the best damn shrimp crew on the Atlantic."

"Yeah, *we* were a lot of help!" Hanna said and they all touched their bottles for the toast, laughing.

"I'd like to make a toast," Alex said, holding his beer up. "To the two most beautiful women any shrimp boat has ever seen."

"I'll drink to that!" Ella yelled out.

The beer was cold and wet, and Hanna savored the taste and the moment they were all sharing. She was able, just for a time, to push aside all they had recently been through. *This is what life should truly be about,* she thought. *We're here with the ones we love, together on this beautiful ocean.*

Hanna felt Alex take her other hand in his, and she looked at his smiling face, shaded with an old ball cap, red from the day in the sun, joyful in the thrill of the catch. *Yes, I am truly blessed,* she thought.

She realized they were coming back in close to the shore of Pawleys Island. She looked down the long stretch of beach and homes up in the low dunes. She could see her own house coming up and the circle of Adirondack chairs around the fire pit in front.

As they grew nearer, she noticed a lone woman walking south along the shoreline wearing a long white dress. Even from this far out, the woman's fiery red hair shined bright in the afternoon sun.

Hanna watched as the woman stopped and turned to look out over the water, watching the old shrimp boat drift by offshore, then lifted her arm to wave.

She waved back and then looked over and saw that Alex was watching, too, smiling back at Amanda Paltierre Atwell on the beach.

Yes, I am truly blessed!

THE END

A Note From Michael Lindley

Thank you for reading *THE FIRE TOWER*!

You got this far, so I'm guessing you enjoyed meeting Hanna Walsh and Alex Frank and you may even have completed the entire six-book series.

If you haven't read the other books in the Amazon #1 bestselling *"Hanna and Alex Low Country Mystery and Suspense"* Series, or my earlier novels, the following pages have quick descriptions and links to their Amazon pages.

Hanna and Alex's often tenuous relationship faces many challenges as they take on the dark forces of crime and corruption in the Low Country of South Carolina. I also have two books in the *"Charlevoix Summers"* series and the first book in the *"Coulter Family Saga"* series.

All the books are available to purchase at the Amazon links that follow for both eBooks and paperbacks. They are also available as a free download for those of you *Kindle Unlimited* subscribers. Thank you again!

First up is *The EmmaLee Affairs... (next page)*

Other Novels by Amazon #1 Bestselling Author Michael Lindley

"The Charlevoix Summer Series" Book #1

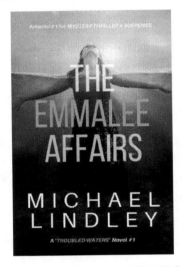

THE EMMALEE AFFAIRS

Amazon #1 for Historical Mystery Thriller & Suspense

One grand ship. Two love affairs decades apart. A quiet summer resort town torn apart by tragic loss, betrayal and murder in this *Amazon #1* romantic suspense tale.

Amazon Five Star reviews for *The EmmaLee Affairs*
"Engaging, captivating, beautiful writing."
"Wonderful! Loved every minute of every page!"
"A sweet reminder of loves lost and new beginnings."
"I wish I could give this book ten stars!"

GET YOUR COPY ON AMAZON AT THIS LINK:
https://www.amazon.com/EmmaLee-Affairs-Troubled-Suspense-Thriller-ebook/dp/B07QZ6W57G/

Read the opening chapters of The EmmaLee Affairs free at the "Look Inside" link.

"The Charlevoix Summer Series" Book #2

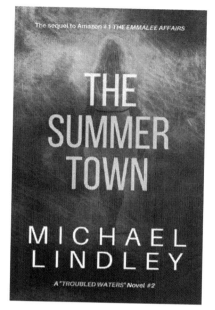

THE SUMMER TOWN

The sequel to Amazon #1 *THE EMMALEE AFFAIRS*

A captivating story of a shocking crime, bitter betrayal and enduring love, bridging time and a vast cultural divide..

Amazon Five Star reviews for *The Summer Town*

"... another stellar novel."

"... even more compelling than EMMALEE."

"... a great success."

"... a delightful read."

"... after falling in love with THE EMMALEE AFFAIRS, this was a must read!"

GET YOUR COPY ON AMAZON AT THIS LINK:

https://www.amazon.com/gp/product/B07646944J/

The "Coulter Family Saga" Series Book #1

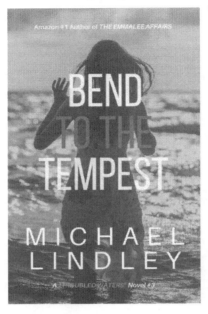

BEND TO THE TEMPEST

From Amazon #1 bestselling author Michael Lindley; an emotional story of love, betrayal and bitter compromise set in 1920's Atlanta and a remote village on the northern Gulf Coast of Florida.

Amazon Five Star reviews for BEND TO THE TEMPEST
"… wonderful character development"
"… one of my favorite authors"
"… hated to reach THE END"
"… WOW - totally impressed."
"… great characters and I love the author's style."

GET YOUR COPY ON AMAZON AT THIS LINK:
https://www.amazon.com/gp/product/B07QXG2SC1/

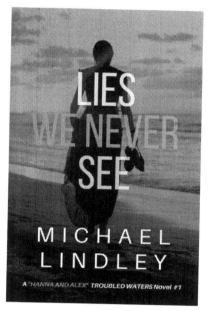

LIES WE NEVER SEE Book #1 in the "Hanna and Alex" Series

The Amazon #1 bestseller for Mystery and Suspense.

The Low Country of South Carolina is the setting for this twisting tale of tragedy, betrayal and new hope in this *"unputdownable"* first book in the Amazon #1 bestselling *"Hanna and Alex"* suspense thriller series.

Amazon Five Star Reviews for *LIES WE NEVER SEE*
"Great book! Could not put it down!
"Can't wait to get to the other books in the series!"
"I loved reading every word of it!"
"Love, love, love this book! I read it in one night!"
"This series is one of the best I've read."
"Loved this book! Never suspected the ending."

LIES WE NEVER SEE unfolds across the beautiful and historic Pawleys Island and Charleston in the Low Country of South Carolina.

GET YOUR COPY ON AMAZON AT THIS LINK:
https://www.amazon.com/gp/product/B079W7SKCG/

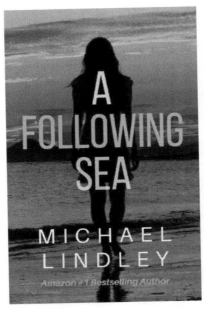

A FOLLOWING SEA Book #2 in the "Hanna and Alex" Series

A captivating and twisting tale of crime and suspense set in the Low Country of South Carolina and the continuing and often tenuous love affair of free legal clinic attorney Hanna Walsh and Charleston detective Alex Frank.

Amazon Five Star Reviews for *A FOLLOWING SEA*
"Once I started, I couldn't put it down."
"A very good mystery and thriller. A must read."
"I am a fan and will be eagerly anticipating the author's next book."
"I thoroughly enjoyed Michael Lindley's latest novel and highly recommend it."
"I have read all his books and loved them all!"

Free legal clinic attorney Hanna Walsh was starting to believe she might have a future with Charleston Police Detective Alex Frank until his ex-wife returns intent on making up for past sins.

GET YOUR COPY ON AMAZON AT THIS LINK:
https://www.amazon.com/dp/179160837X

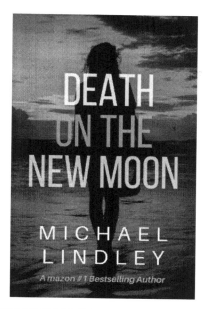

DEATH ON THE NEW MOON Book #3 in "Hanna and Alex" Series.

#1 for Crime and Psychological Thrillers; an engaging and surprising tale of love, betrayal and murder in the Low Country of South Carolina and the always precarious love affair of Hanna Walsh and Alex Frank.

Amazon Five Star Reviews for Death On The New Moon
"... a page-turning thriller."
"I love this author and everything I've read."
"This is a sit at the edge of your seat thriller."
"... a 10 Star thriller."

In **Death On The New Moon**, Hanna and Alex seem to have found a promising new start for their lives together when Alex encounters a tragic loss and near-deadly run-in with a dangerous crime syndicate. As Hanna tries to help him through his recovery and search for a dangerous killer, the surprise return of a lover from her past sends all hope of her future with Alex into a tailspin.

GET YOUR COPY ON AMAZON AT THIS LINK:
https://www.amazon.com/dp/B07SC3P9LP

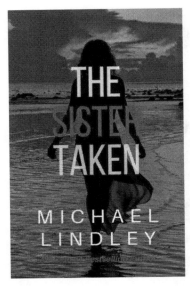

THE SISTER TAKEN Book #4 in the "Hanna and Alex" Series.

AN AMAZON CHARTS BESTSELLER.

A missing twin. A wayward sister. A "jaw-dropping" twist.

Michael Lindley's latest dark and twisting tale of corruption, betrayal and murder set in the Low Country of South Carolina and the precarious relationship of attorney, Hanna Walsh, and now former Charleston Police Detective, Alex Frank.

Amazon Five Star reviews for *THE SISTER TAKEN*
"... engrossing, thrilling, mind-blowing!"
"... a real page-turner with many twists and turns."
"... you can't wait to get to the end, but then wish it hadn't ended."
"... I STILL cannot believe how it all unfolded!"
"Totally loved this book!"

In ***THE SISTER TAKEN,*** Hanna and Alex again find themselves in the *troubled waters* of love and commitment. Alex returns to South Carolina with the promise of a new start but with strings attached that Hanna may never be able to live with.

GET YOUR COPY ON AMAZON AT THIS LINK:
https://www.amazon.com/dp/B083XTGVR2

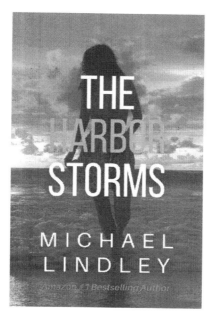

THE HARBOR STORMS Book #5 in the "Hanna and Alex" Series

AN AMAZON CHARTS BESTSELLER.

Hanna and Alex face their most dangerous challenge yet when the murder of a past friend and associate leads them to a plot that threatens to be one of the most devastating terrorist attacks in US history.

Here's what readers are saying about the *"Hanna and Alex"* series and *The Harbor Storms*.

"Love this series!!!"

"This series is one of the best I've read!"

"So good. Loved this series!"

If you love mystery and suspense with twisting plots, compelling characters and settings that will sweep you away, find out why readers are raving about the *"Hanna and Alex"* series.

GET YOUR COPY ON AMAZON AT THIS LINK:

https://www.amazon.com/gp/product/B0983QDL7G

Follow Michael Lindley on Facebook at Michael Lindley Novels. If you would like to join his mailing list to receive his "Behind the Stories" updates and news of new releases and special offers, send a note to mailto:michael@michaellindleynovels.com

About the Author

Michael Lindley is an *Amazon #1* author for *Historical Fiction/Mystery Thriller & Suspense* with his debut novel **THE EMMALEE AFFAIRS** as well as #1 for Historical and *Psychological Thrillers* for **LIES WE NEVER SEE** and **DEATH ON THE NEW MOON** with the more recent "Low Country" mystery and suspense series focused on the present-day storyline of Hanna Walsh and Alex Frank in Charleston and Pawleys Island, South Carolina.

The settings for his novels include a remote resort town in Northern Michigan in the 1940's and 50's, Atlanta and Grayton Beach, Florida in the turbulent 1920's, and most recently, 1860's and present-day Charleston and Pawleys Island, South Carolina.

Michael writes full-time now following a career in Marketing and Advertising and divides his time between Northern Michigan and Florida. He and his wife, Karen, are also on an annual quest to visit the country's spectacular national parks.

"You will often find that writers are compelled to write what they love to read.

I've always been drawn to stories that are built around an idyllic time and place as much as the characters who grace these locations. As the heroes and villains come to life in my favorite stories, facing life's challenges of love and betrayal and great danger, I also enjoy coming to deeply understand the setting for the story and how it shapes the characters and the conflicts they face.

I've also been drawn to books built around a mix of past and present, allowing me to know a place and the people who live there in both a compelling historical context, as well as in present-day.

Michael Lindley's "Hanna and Alex" Low Country Suspense Thriller series recently reached #1 on the Amazon bestseller charts.

60323576R00161